FIT FOR PURPOSE

FIT FOR PURPOSE

Angela Burdick

First published in Great Britain in 2025 by
The Book Guild Ltd
Unit E2 Airfield Business Park,
Harrison Road, Market Harborough,
Leicestershire. LE16 7UL
Tel: 0116 2792299
www.bookguild.co.uk
Email: info@bookguild.co.uk
X: @bookguild

Copyright © 2025 Angela Burdick

The right of Angela Burdick to be identified as the author of this
work has been asserted by them in accordance with the
Copyright, Design and Patents Act 1988.

All rights reserved. No part of this publication may be
reproduced, transmitted, or stored in a retrieval system, in any form or by any means,
without permission in writing from the publisher, nor be otherwise circulated in
any form of binding or cover other than that in which it is published and without
a similar condition being imposed on the subsequent purchaser.

This work is entirely fictitious and bears no resemblance to any persons living or dead.

The manufacturer's authorised representative in the EU for
product safety is Authorised Rep Compliance Ltd,
71 Lower Baggot Street, Dublin D02 P593 Ireland
(www.arccompliance.com)

Typeset in 11pt Minion Pro

Printed and bound in Great Britain by 4edge Limited

ISBN 978 1835741 467

British Library Cataloguing in Publication Data.
A catalogue record for this book is available from the British Library.

This book is dedicated to those people in our NHS who battle against the odds for all of us, from the moment we first open our eyes until we finally close them.
Thank you.

ONE

I tumble down, my nose stinging, my throat burning, my lungs protesting, my feet caught in slippery sludge as the river sucks me into another world. Water is swallowing me whole. I stop struggling. That was the easy bit.

Something grasps me. Dredged through silt, I feel the squelch and pull of it, filth choking my mouth and nose. I'm drenched in a deeply disturbing, subterranean stench as squalid and rotting and as old as the planet. Warm hands grip my head, wrenching me up. Yanked out on to muddy, solid mother earth, I lie shivering and squirming, cold air shocking me. A voice asks if I can hear him. 'That was close,' he says. I mumble incoherently in answer. 'Good man. Well done.' He is pressing on my chest and a hand wipes away the slime blocking my mouth and nose. I vomit.

'That's fine,' says the voice close to my ear, 'well done.' I can't see who's speaking because my eyes are plugged with mud.

'It's okay now, thanks guys, I'll take over.' Someone wipes my eyes free of gunk. His breath is on my face, his comforting hand on my shoulder. 'What's your name?'

Spluttering and coughing, I try to answer, but no coherent words emerge.

'Take your time, buddy.' He turns me, and, with arms encircling me, abruptly clutches my chest several times, until my throat nearly explodes with water and crud coming out through my mouth and nose. 'Here,' he places a mask over my face, 'breathe now. Nearly there. Take a really good, deep breath. That's it. You're doing really well. Janice…' his raised voice drifts away from me, 'bring it here.' I hear a metallic rustle. 'This is Janice. She's wonder woman here to help you.' He's with me again.

Janice squeezes my arm. 'Hello there. What is your name?' she asks.

'I can't remember.' I manage to expel the words through a revolting taste in my mouth.

'Don't worry. Give yourself a minute while we warm you up and then perhaps you'll remember.' They wrap me in foil, and I'm lifted onto a stretcher and hauled oven-ready into the ambulance.

'How's that? Feeling a bit better?' Janice asks and I nod.

'My name is Tom. Can you open your eyes again for me?' says the first guy. To Janice he asks if the cops are on their way. She replies that they should be because she's given them another shout. I open my eyes. Everything is blurred.

I try to look at him while he continues to wipe away the remaining slime from my face, punctuated by me taking deep breaths on a proffered oxygen mask. He examines me closely for a few seconds, then he pours blissfully clean, cool water into my eyes. It cruises down my face. He makes reassuring noises while taking my pulse and listens to my chest with a stethoscope. He keys something into an iPad before asking me if I've fallen or been pushed into the river. 'I can't remember what happened,' I say, 'but thanks for taking the trouble to fish me out and clean me up. A disgusting task.'

'That's my job. You're not so bad!' he laughs, 'I've seen worse. We haven't finished with you yet. We still need your name please.'

'Dickhead might be appropriate,' I splutter.

'And address,' it's Janice again, slightly breathless, 'though if you don't have one, don't worry, we don't subscribe to the idea of not helping the homeless.'

'I honestly can't remember my name or where I live. It completely escapes me.'

'Well that could present us with a bit of a problem,' she says firmly, 'do you have a mobile with you – that might give us a clue.' I shake my head. 'Would you mind if we went through your pockets to see if you're carrying any ID?'

'Be my guest. I apologise again for the mess I'm in. Pretty disgusting. You're very patient,' I continue, embarrassed by my own need, 'let me do it. I feel awful that you should have to go through my filthy clothes.' A search of my pockets just elicits wet tissues.

'It doesn't matter what you have done,' she says curtly, 'or if you got stuck in the river trying to escape someone attacking you, we'll still need your name to admit you to the hospital.'

'Well then, I'll make it easier for everyone. I feel fine now. Don't take me there.' I try to move to get up, but Tom guides me firmly back down again.

'Steady! No need to be snippy. Heading off is not a good idea. We don't know how badly injured you are,' he explains, 'and this Serious Incident has already been logged. We can't close it without a full report. We all know that the powers-that-be like to keep tags on where all their citizens are, what we're up to and who's correctly completed their records.' This last comment was definitely splenetic. 'In any case, I'd like to check you out properly for your own good, buddy. Now that we have you in the bus we have a Duty of Care towards you. So we *can* treat you in the ambulance even without a name. We are obliged to do that when we arrive at the scene of a Serious Incident. But we cannot take you to A and E without a name for Admissions. And we're not allowed to discharge you without completing our records for the Serious Incident – which will be entered into your hospital notes. No name, no records, no admission. And no admission, no discharge. So we are back where we started. The cops will need to have a chat with you too, mate.' He chuckles to himself. Perhaps with relief at a job well done. He's saved a life, not something I've done every day. Or ever.

'Hey,' interrupts Janice, 'keep your eye on the ball, Tom. You're offside. He's a good man, but he doesn't know everything.' With a pantomime roll of her eyes she is laughing. 'We *can* have him *admitted* to A and E in Terminal Five without a name. Rules changed last week. Did you not know?'

'Ah! You know I've been on holiday, pal. Some folk keep their colleagues in the loop.'

'Try opening your emails.'

'You could have flagged up that one, partner.'

'Okay. But let's get him sorted first. I'll keep you up to speed later.'

I want to sound sympathetic, show solidarity, *be* with them in the struggles of our dear old health system. You know, pathetically try to balance things a bit by virtue signalling. While they strap me in, I tell them that in the past I've picketed a special unit for people with acquired brain injury that was threatened with closure. And that my girlfriend is an advocate for mental health patients. Janice comments suspiciously that she thinks it's interesting I can remember that but not my name. But I seem to have made some of the right noises because she talks about the stresses of working under duress, with insufficient staff. While Tom straps me in and begins the usual medical checks, she starts to expand on what she's already alluded to regarding admission protocol. 'Under the old rules, Tom's right; the hospital management team tried to exclude unconscious drunks and junkies. But that excluded unconscious RTA and other accident victims, deluded psychiatric patients and people with memory problems. As a result, management relented and changed the rules. So we *can* admit you to A and E in Terminal Five. Now we're good to go,' she says as Tom finishes his examination. 'Let's run. Bye for now.' Her bleeper goes off as she steps down, the door is closed and then Tom sits opposite me. The engine starts and we head off, siren screaming a tad ostentatiously, and blue lights flashing.

She's a great driver, speedy and confident, much like Megan who, let's face it, is better than I am at the wheel. Well, at most things, if I'm honest.

I'd first clocked Megs, a psychiatric social worker, following a press conference about five or six years ago at a local pub after a press gig. She'd been a witness and I was with the press group chatting when I caught her eye as she tried to order a drink. The barman wasn't exactly ignoring her but she'd been waiting longer than me when he asked me for my order. It seemed courteous to include her so she joined us at a table beside a window. It was a Friday, and after some snacks and several more drinks, and discussion about the case as well as other things, we found ourselves offered a lock-in. You know the idea – everyone except the regulars leave and the manager locks up leaving a few left in the pub. Not every night, and only when he can be bothered. Conveniently, there is a snug either end of the long main bar, and it's there that we, a few members of the press, are ushered into at closing time. The other snug is reserved for off-duty cops from the local police station who are also rumoured to work unsocial hours. Of course, neither reports on the other.

I cannot remember what we found so engaging to discuss but there were no embarrassing silences. And it's been like that ever since. After a couple more drinks, she offered me a lift back to mine, which turned out to be conveniently only half a mile from hers. I took this as an invitation, as you do. Getting my drift, as soon as we reached my place she leaned across to open the passenger door, saying, 'I do not go to first base unless you wear glasses.'

'Do reading specs count?'

'No, you clown. Work it out. And you must have sisters!'

'Sisters? Tick,' I said.

A few weeks later I was at the inquest of one of her service users. Because she was distressed by the coroner's conclusion, I took her for a drink to calm down. By the end of the session we walked to my place, is all I'm saying.

We kept meeting up, sometimes arranged, sometimes just finding each other at a loose end after a night out. It was always good.

A few months ago she rocked up late one evening at mine, almost incoherently elaborating about problems at the HELP! Hub. Her team set up this unit several years ago to provide daytime activities for patients with severe and chronic mental health disorders. The hub is under threat because funding's contingent on what she describes as a spurious aspiration. I know what they do, of course, but she insists on raving about it anyway.

'Imagine,' she said, 'you've lost your job after a breakdown, or you've never worked in the first place because you have chronic, serious problems, then you find sanctuary in a place of safety – somewhere you're given a feeling of worth, a secure, sympathetic space to go to during the day. It is free from prejudice about your mental state, a hub where your friends, your tribe, you could say, understand you. There are plenty of distracting activities to calm you and keep your mind occupied. And trained staff to check you're getting the help you need, thriving as well as possible and to make sure you have what you're entitled to claim.'

'Really? That powerful, is it?' I query, 'sounds like Paradise. Can I go?'

'Fuck off.' She's eloquent as ever. 'Why are you taking the piss? Helping to initiate this hub is the best thing I have ever done. We've all sorts of activities on offer: poetry, music, art, crossword puzzles, quizzes, outings to footie, the theatre, tea and coffee for a token charge, a place to chat and laugh, a cheap but nourishing lunch cooked by volunteers in tandem with service users. You know all this!' and she paused for a mini-second to catch her breath and looked intensely at me before continuing with her litany, 'and trips to cinemas, picnics in the park, a running team, expeditions to the galleries. All of that. Sometimes, when we're short-staffed, prisoners on day release come in to help with lunch. All these day-release chaps are long-termers. Committed murder, some of them. But they are surprisingly helpful. Stop smiling. Tough cookies that they are, they still make friends with our people. I'm serious. Knives in the kitchen have never been a problem. So trust is the name of the game. It works. When there's serious trouble, say someone loses it, has a bit of a meltdown? Then the whole team – staff, service users, prisoners and volunteers – sit down and discuss what to do.'

'Very democratic. What's the penalty? A yellow card?'

'Usually they're banned for a week.' She's not amused. 'Then they make an apology. All returns to normal.'

'And you think there'll be no problems with this. Psychopaths, murderers, and knives. Pretty interesting combination for a drama I'd say.'

'You're so fucking cynical.' She leaned across, checked my drink and emptied the bottle into her glass. 'It works. It's amazing to see. It's built on trust. Most people respond to that. Usually they'll find someone among the group that they connect with and befriend. Perhaps the prisoners sympathise with how gross it must be to be imprisoned in your head.' She drained her drink and lay back on the sofa. I put a cushion behind her head.

'And you don't recognise this is a recipe for disaster?'

'Fuck off. You don't know what you're talking about.'

'I was only asking. Just checking. Just saying.'

'Jeez, well, you would, wouldn't you? Let me tell you, John, there's no better comfort to our service users than their own peer group. They do not judge them, and exchange tips about how to get by in a world where they're often misunderstood and rejected. Some of these patients, those that aren't in sheltered housing, stay in hospital overnight. That'll give you some idea how seriously ill they are.'

'Has something happened to make you even madder?'

'I told you. To keep our funding, our new remit is to replace all these activities with training people to write their CVs. The purpose? To prepare them for work.'

'No, you didn't mention that. Is that why you're incandescent?'

'Some clown wants to transform our hub into a job centre.'

'I get the callousness of asking peeps who are already vulnerable and a bit soggy around the edges, to fail once again,' I opened another bottle, 'and again.'

'They've been supplied with a ton of laptops. The cost of that! We could've used that money more creatively. Effectively, we have to betray our service users.'

I tell her she's catastrophising. 'Listen,' I continue, 'you're not doing the betraying, it's the system.' This does not receive a good response.

She shouts: 'Set up a scheme to help people with severe and chronic mental health problems get employment? Then they lose their benefits – it's like asking them to go to sea without a fucking lifeboat. You think that's doable?'

'Sounds promising. Maybe they'd feel better if they worked. Good for their mental health.'

'Sure. If it was doable. Some have a lifetime of mental health problems. And others have developed them through trauma. If they could be transformed back to normal, our normal or their normal, whatever that once was, and be accepted, fine. But don't you think they would do that if they could? There's already legislation in place to direct companies towards employing a percentage of physically disabled people. How often do you think they adhere to this rule? Never.'

'Should we send the boys around to administer a little CEO knee-capping? They'd know what it was like to be disabled then.'

'Not funny. Sometimes I think you're deliberately obtuse. Just to cause a verbal dust-up. And I thought you'd be sympathetic. Especially knowing how keen you are to rubbish bureaucracy. That's what the government is using to close down our hubs. Asking for the impossible to justify their decision.'

'Typical,' I comment and top up her glass, 'you've convinced me. I get it. I'm not proud of my response to the craziness of the new conditions or your heartfelt reaction.'

'Thanks. About time,' but I can see she isn't convinced I'm on the level. 'If our people do get a job, how will their colleagues, without any specialist training to understand their problems, cope with our guys? No company's seriously going to train their staff to negotiate with colleagues who may inadvertently be provocative. Just ordinary day-to-day banter, say. Some desperately ill patients may respond inappropriately. Not all – some will be fine. But others may take it personally, or find it impossible and leave their post. Or they'll not get a job in the first place. So they're set up for failure. How's that going to help anyone?'

Her colour is rising – so I top up her glass further. And mine. She took a deep breath, and I noticed she was swaying slightly. And so we got plastered, as you do, and I did my very best to comfort her. But it was never going to be enough. I couldn't do anything about the funding question, nor make her feel that her people might be better off in work in the unlikely event they found sympathetic employers.

She's creative and enhances her surroundings with her capacity to turn a very unpromising situation around, so it surprised me that she gave up – that really isn't like her. I do see that the HELP! Hub has been given an impossible task. It's deeply, deeply sad to see her so distressed. She sometimes drinks a tad too much, but she's funny with it, inventive and generous, and when she's totally out of it and repeating herself, she kind of compensates by being outrageous and off the wall. But this isn't happening tonight. She's profoundly unhappy.

I look at her as she knocks back the wine, then lies back relaxed now the drink has got to her. Life with her would never be dull. She could make a palace out of a garage and lives in a couple of small rooms where she's found inventive ways to make the space attractive and totally hers. She's travelled a bit, lived and worked in Paris for four years, and she's had a couple of husbands who drifted away on the tide. But she doesn't want another one, and that's one of her appeals for me if I'm really honest.

'Would you mind if I go through your pockets to see if we can find any ID or anything else that might jog your memory?' Tom disturbs me, looking anxious.

'I already tried that,' I tell him, but agree, and he searches through trouser and jacket pockets and finds a tobacco tin containing a bunch of three keys. 'Sorry to be snippy.'

'Looks like you enjoy a smoke. And have somewhere to live,' he dangles the keys, 'so someone will probably notice you're missing and alert the police so they can claim you. Seriously, did you try to drown yourself?' Tom asks gently as he replaces the keys in the tin and into my pocket.

'I can't remember. As a pathologically indecisive person, I think it unlikely.'

'You can remember that?' He laughs.

'No, I don't remember it, I can *feel* it. *Feel* that making so significant and irrevocable a decision as drowning myself would be difficult for me.'

'Ah! Very new age. Do you think you were attacked, that someone pushed you into the river? Did you have a fight with someone?' I shake my head in reply to all his questions. 'Do you think you fell in, lost your footing?' That *sounds* like me, I thought, if you are talking metaphorically, but I tell him no, that's not something I remember happening. 'Did you pass out or something? Were you drunk, for instance?' The ambulance swerves but I'm safely strapped in.

'You have me there,' I say. 'It's a mystery to me. I don't remember drinking or falling. And before you ask, apart from being in an ambulance, I have no idea where I am.'

'That would have been my next question. Well done,' and he looks around, 'and your mobile. Where is that, I wonder?'

'Don't know.' His eyes work their way slowly over my face.

'Someone called the emergency services,' he's still intently watching me, 'if it wasn't you, and that seems unlikely as you were incapacitated, and you appear not to have a phone, then who was it? When people call us out, they usually stay with a victim until we arrive. Out of curiosity or simply a human need to know an outcome. Or to star in a dramatic story to show themselves as heroic.' He looks down. 'Leaving a critical scene of a drowning man is an offence, possibly suggesting whoever called us may have pushed you in and scarpered.' He solemnly shakes his head. 'What about the motive? Are you involved in drugs?'

'Not my scene,' I reply.

'Concussion can leave someone with amnesia, like, losing their memory of the time just before a trauma and the actual event that caused it. I wonder if they knocked you out. Let me see.' He examines my head, satisfied there is no apparent abrasion, then he busies himself on his iPad. 'I can't see any obvious injury but we'll have to wait until you're in hospital to confirm I'm right. The cops have details of the location. They'll examine the crime scene while we take care of you. But where to take you?' The ambulance swerves again, Janice blasts a different shout from the siren. 'If you are suicidal and jumped in, then you need the crisis team in Psych A and E, if you fell in the water after a dizzy turn you'll need to go to Emergency Medical, if you've broken something, it will be Trauma. And if you have been pushed in, the cops will want to question you.' He checks me out and finds nothing broken. 'I'll need to fill in forms for each of these eventualities. What *are* we going to do with you?'

He speaks into his top pocket. '*Step on the gas, Jan,*' he sings, '*we ain't goin' home no more, no more,*' and then he's grinning a big cheesy one as she speeds up, the ambulance swaying nimbly around whatever is in its way. These guys must have *some* fun, though perhaps he's relieved to know that he'll soon rid himself of me and get on with more serious cases or at least less filthy and more deserving ones. '*Take the high road to Terminal Five,*' he sings, and I hear the siren raise its voice, the engine rev a bit more and we speed along with blue lights flashing big time and he asks me to smile and put up my hands. 'Good.' He pats my arm and brings it down beside my body. 'Do you know what date it is?'

'Friday.'

'I was thinking more about the date. But Friday's fine for now. Can you smile for me?'

'I've nothing to smile about right now.'

'Well, of course, I get that. Okay then, think of me as your latest date; give me a grimace full of lust and desire then, will you?' And I laugh for him. He's putting a mask onto my face once more. 'Take a few breaths,' he says and takes it off again, 'we'll arrive in a mo. Do you think you can remember your name now, buddy?'

'How about John? It seems as good a name as any,' I reply.

'There, that wasn't so difficult, was it? Your surname?'

'Can't remember.'

'Okay. That's fine for now. We're getting somewhere, though the search engine might just crash if we feed "John" into it. At least we've made a start. As you have a front door key, someone could report you missing, and then to be sure we'll be able to match you up with the rest of your name,' he taps me reassuringly on the shoulder, 'I don't know whether you've really forgotten your name or are just playing a bit of a game. I do detect a slight American or Canadian accent, so perhaps you are not from around these parts? Did you know that in the US they request your credit card details before the paramedics will pick you up? So be glad you are here. Now. Just to reassure you, things are not so bad here. Yet! Emergency treatment is still free. Reason is, in some emergency cases, it's more costly to send injured patients back to their country of origin than to treat them.'

'Gee! You don't say!' I stare into his face. 'I guess I should be glad to be with you now.'

'You a Yank?' he asks.

'I sure don't remember that,' I say in a fake accent.

'I'm sorry. I didn't mean to be offensive. You only have to pay if you are a foreign national staying in hospital for elective treatment.'

I tell him with a crisp English inflection that I'm only joking and have been to Canada, but never been in the US in my life and neither would I want to, thank you very much. I apologise for being frivolous and offensive, indeed I thank him very much for saving my life and for all his care since and so far.

'Well, memory's coming back then. That's reassuring.'

'And what about you?' I ask. 'What do you do on your time off? If you have any.' He smiles, seemingly at a memory, as he explains that his passion is his fiddle. Plays with a small Hungarian folk group, just around in pubs and small clubs. He tells me where they are and I promise to check them out because I enjoy listening to live music when having a pint. When I ask why Hungarian, he tells me that his grandfather, who escaped during the 1956 uprising, taught him to play the violin from the age of five. In his grandfather's memory he plays the Hungarian folk tunes and thinks of him. We discuss how desperately hard it is for refugees to leave their families and start a new life where they know nobody.

He tells me his job doesn't allow him much time to play his fiddle, though he still tries to check in once a week for a session. The siren has stopped and soon they gently lift me out and take me through double doors. 'Do you drive a Volvo?' Tom asks.

'Honestly? Are you kidding? You think I look like I own one?' I reply. 'Why do you ask?'

'We could fast-track you in the outside lane if you're a Volvo driver,' he says, and I laugh as he continues to push me into the reception area. There's a sign over the door which tells me I'm in the Emergency Department of NHS Trust Terminal Five, just in case I think it's the Ritz. Scarlet flashing neon capitals headline that the ACCIDENT AND EMERGENCY DEPARTMENT IS SPONSORED BY VOLVO. So he wasn't joking. I see a row of small lights along a corridor and it feels as if I'm losing control of my destination, and it's both a little exciting and chilling and oddly comforting all at the same time. We stop and he begins to say goodbye and good luck, and then stops for a moment and smiles and tells me he expects to see me at the next session if I get discharged. I raise a thumb, nod agreement and thank him before I register the significance of what he's just said. I think it's time to close my eyes for a bit.

TWO

Just before my touch base with Neptune, while enjoying a pint after work in The Flounder and Lemon, I sat watching the sun leave across the Thames. The settling dusk activates, in unison, the lights in the iconic buildings opposite. Watching the show relaxed me enough to think I've got away with it. That's bollocks of course. I slip to the bar to order a third colourful cocktail to match the scene across the water, and too late, I see Megan jostling her way through the rush-hour crush. She thwacks a chair with a newspaper before parking herself beside me ready for attack. *Oops*, I think.

'Thought I'd find you here. Why?' She glares. 'Why did you miss it? For fuck's sake what's wrong with you?' She's feeling friendly.

'I did the difficult bit; staying with him while he died. At least he can't know I missed his funeral.'

She glances up and down at my pressed suit, pink shirt and black tie. 'Let me get this right; you dress up like a tart but then decide not to show at the last minute? So what happened?' I pick up the cocktail menu and read through the goodies on offer but she's not fooled by my distraction techniques. 'Okay, dickhead, I get your priorities, staying with Ben while he was dying was great, really difficult, and really kind. But you needed to go to the funeral for *you*.' She turns her head, looking around for Joe.

'I don't know why you are kicking up, you didn't especially even like him,' I retort. She taps Joe's arm when he arrives with my cocktail.

'Coffee for me,' she tells him. 'Decaf, please. Look at this guy, Joe, dressed for a funeral he didn't attend.' Joe laughs, telling her I look grand and so I begin to relax again, and that's exactly when Megan inadvertently takes my breath away. And with words so simple she probably didn't even know she revealed her betrayal. 'Here,' she fishes in her bag, takes out a pair of unfamiliar sunglasses, 'you left these at mine. I thought you might need them at the funeral.'

'Thanks, how typically thoughtful of you.' I stare at them, mesmerised.

'Well, they're yours,' she says, 'aren't they?' I say nothing, but a nasty blob of rage is forming as I shove them into my top pocket and bend to kiss her on the forehead.

We're both quiet for a moment. Perhaps she realised a tad too late. I look at the Thames and sip my drink. A metallic cold sweat sweeps over me, my head throbs, a sharp tap hits my solar plexus and my heart nearly explodes from its fierce pounding. Whatever way I look at it, there's only one thing to do. I decide, for the first time in my life, to take control and take action. And so, after my spending a decade of pathological indecisiveness, as Megan would describe it, the charge in this incident has primed something.

'I'll tell you why I didn't go to the funeral. I hate the thought of some religious nut who never met him pontificating about who Ben was and his place in the "next world". It makes me sick listening to that sort of clichéd stuff.'

'It's just ritual, John. You're well aware of that. You don't convince me this stopped you. Millions of people find it essential and a comfort to have a formal ceremony. It gives a shape to something they don't know how to otherwise handle. It takes away the responsibility of the bereaved to work out how to organise a funeral and cope in the confusion caused by grief – I should have thought that removing responsibility would appeal to you,' she said venomously. 'There are dozens of reasons why it helps. Some people need the spiritual comfort.'

I want to object that first of all there wouldn't have been too many bereaved at the funeral of a drifter. And remind her that organised religion isn't the only way to find spirituality, but I'm too much of a coward, feel too angry with her and depressed to argue. She waves to Joe and orders a drink in their own sign language. She goes silent on me. I think, how fudgy is our relationship, only kicking into any sort of honesty when we argue. I'm lost for a moment, searching for the right provocation that will take me past the winner's flag. Huh, I know exactly what to say. Later. Mute button switched on right now. The indecisive man's cowardly default position. God, I love myself.

When Ben became ill, his life slowly collapsed, until one day, one hand clutching mine, the other attached to a liquid lifeline, he just seemed to slip through the night and was gone by dawn. The casualness of death just kills me. Immediately after he died, even though I'm only just hitting middle age, and however shallow that motive sounds, and yes, that's another deeply disturbing attribute of mine, it shunted me into thinking about having someone to see me off too. And right at this moment I'm facing the lucky front-runner. But now there's no going back and I can't think how to dance myself out of the way of shooting myself in the foot.

She asks me what's really wrong, trying to get me to return her gaze, but I look away. 'Ben.' I know she wants to try to find a way in by being provocative, to force me to reply. I don't really want to speak to her. I feel petulance rising and sparks of irritation towards her and myself because Meg's usual level of intensity is too much for me now and forever. And yet, the sight of her sitting there looking vulnerable makes me realise I still want her. Maybe we could slip back to hers and I could be comforted. I think now those moments are all that there is. This thought is now smothering everything else and if she knew, she might surmise how selfish I am under the circumstances of my current decision. It would just be using and confusing her. Me too. I watch her struggle with knowing what to say and she asks me, her social worker-cap showing, where I was and how I felt during the time the funeral of my beloved Ben was taking place without me. Without my support for Ben, without her support for me.

'Please *stop*. If I hear the word "support" one more time I'll go crazy,' I tell her. 'Me next. That's what I felt, if you really want to know. That's what I keep thinking. And there's nothing anyone can do about it. And I know I'm doomed. We all are.'

She murmurs under her breath how ridiculous I sound. Then suddenly, anxiously, she asks if I'm ill. I tell her no, and while she's distracted for a second as Joe brings her wine, I indicate to him I'd like another of his special cocktails of the day, and then I drop in the info that I've resigned from *The Daily Misery*. She pushes her wine to one side and slowly and deliberately rearranges her cup containing only coffee dregs, turning the cup handle to suit her, her face remaining impassive. She's silent, fiddling with the edge of the table, drawing lines with her fingers up and down the grooves, up and down in an absent-minded way and not looking at me but looking down. I remember what it's like to feel my way slowly around the bountiful roundness of her jolly, plump breasts just peeping back at me and I really want to fuck her. A farewell fuck. Will this feeling ever go away?

* * *

There's a hand on my shoulder and then a voice says, 'Hello, John, how are we doing? I'm Dr Doctor. Can you give me your full name please?'

'Come again?'

'Dr Doctor. I'm Dr Doctor.' I squint at a smooth, somewhat immobile, over-protein-fed face. Or is it Botox? 'I need your surname please, John.'

'John John?' I say, but he is not amused. 'I have no idea,' I say. 'I keep telling everyone I don't know and so far that hasn't changed.' My head is banging.

'How are you feeling, John?'

'I'm feeling how you'd feel if you'd just been fished out of filthy water.'

'No need to be confrontational, John. Any records?' I hear the doctor turn away as he speaks.

'The paramedics said they tried to radio back but there was a delay. In any case they only had his first name, so no patient records,' a young man dressed in pink scrubs tells him.

'Well, we'll have to make some temp notes… so go fetch, please.'

Dr Doctor seems to be breathing hard as he listens to my heart. 'I'll be back in a minute, John.' He's looking a little disgusted. The young pink-clad man returns and clips an iPad to the end of my gurney and with a little smile he's gone too.

A nurse comes in and begins to wipe more of the mud from my face and hands. He doesn't say much so I ask him his name. He replies that he isn't here full-time, which doesn't seem to me to be the right answer. Someone nearby is cursing and vomiting. There's the sound of someone telling him off or maybe it's just himself, and then it's all quiet again for a few minutes before the urgent retching starts again. Now I'm trembling. Someone comes through the curtain and removes a sick bowl.

'Just checked. Local cops say no one has reported a missing John.' And he bends towards me, his strong breath on my face, his hand pressing on my shoulder. 'Ah, I see you're shivering. A bit cold and shocked I expect. You'll soon heat up in here. Can you just open your eyes for me for a minute?' I squint at the nurse. 'Maybe the shock of the trauma has given you a little problem with your memory. They suggest we ask for your National Insurance number or DOB so they can trace you that way.

We'll start with the easy one. When did you last celebrate your birthday?' He gives a little friendly chuckle.

'I can't remember.'

'Right. What age were you on your last birthday?'

'Twenty-five,' I say pointlessly. Is lying a passive way of staying in control?

'That's a good start. It would help me if you could have another little think,' he says. 'I'll be back in a minute.' I hear him talking to his companion a few yards away.

'He can't remember who he is.' He gives a short ironic laugh. 'Makes a change from Jesus Christ.'

For a while I listen to the sounds of the ill around me. Someone is speaking softly in another cubicle, reassuring a patient that they're okay. A fire alarm goes off, and I await my urgent removal from the ward, but nobody moves. Slightly alarming, I'd say. My neighbour's frail voice says he 'wants to go.' His nurse's accent sounds Eastern European, and her manner is immensely patient as she repeatedly asks him where he wants to go, and he repeats again that he wants to go. She tries to tell him he can't go anywhere until he's better. This impasse is only resolved when I hear her tell him not to worry, it could happen to anyone and she'll change the sheets and give him fresh pyjamas. Perhaps if she tells the story in the nurses' hub her buddies will explain the colloquialism.

A voice I haven't heard before points out that the fire alarm is still going. 'Don't worry,' someone says, 'it's only the fire alarm. Keeps doing that.' I wonder at the courage of peeps facing the sordid world of the dying under so much pressure. How have I managed to rock up in the demesne of the sick and sad, when I'm sure there's nothing wrong with me? I need to get out of here, and must plan how to do this, if only I didn't feel so ghastly. Wasting their time is making me feel really guilty. Though, I have to admit, I think among all these peeps there are some interesting and truly heroic and hidden everyday stories. It's not for nothing that the publishing world's hunger for medical confessions is trending.

'Better get Cross in here to check him out.' I'm still trussed in a silver foil coating. At this level I'm uncomfortably aware of passing people staring at me in an open-ended cubicle. I close my eyes again like a child when they don't want to be seen. A few minutes later I feel myself being wheeled around and deposited in another cubicle. Soft hands remove my armour, and place a gown over me, and then another blanket, and this peep asks me if I'm still cold. Someone is moaning. I open my eyes to find I'm staring at the young doctor asking how I am.

'I'm not so cold now. Thanks.'

'Good. Good. You just tell us if you get cold again. Although it's warm out, the water was probably chilly, so you may have become a bit hypothermic while immersed. This isn't always as destructive as you may think in the situation you found yourself. Cold water can ameliorate some of the damage that lack of oxygen would otherwise cause. And how are you feeling, John?'

'None too great.'

'Well, that isn't surprising. We'll try to help you. Let me introduce myself. I'm Dr Cross. Do you know you're in a hospital?' She regards me with a worryingly beatific smile.

'I'm guessing that from the noises and maybe your stethoscope's a bit of a giveaway.' My mouth tastes ghastly, sour and rotten.

'Fine. Fine. Well you seem to be okay, then. At least you have regained consciousness. Can you tell me what happened to you?'

'No. Do you think I could have some water to drink, please?'

'You don't know how you came to be in the river?' She bends towards me with a glass and watches while I drink. My mouth is still foul.

'No. Well, yes, I know I was hauled out of a river, but not how I got in. And ironically, now I'm in here, I'm told I can't get out. Don't get too close to me. I stink.'

'Yes, yes, good,' she says absent-mindedly and leans back and I notice a strand of her hair has loosened. 'Well, you're possibly a victim of a crime by the sound of it. Have the police interviewed you yet? No?' she responds when I shake my head. 'Well, all in good time. First, we need to find out what damage you have sustained. I wonder if you suffered any recent medical event, John. Any fainting? Or like a feeling of weakness, any collapse at all, anything that might be worrying to you? Can you remember?' Her voice is firm and expressive now. Engaged, I would say.

'No. The paramedics have already asked me. Can't remember.' I'm worried I sound impatient. 'I'm sorry – if I knew I would tell you.'

'Okay then. So, you remember them asking you this just a short time ago? That's reassuring, but it does seem as if you still have a slight problem with your memory.' She sounds a little smug now. 'How about girlfriends, or a partner? Are you married? Any children?'

'I don't know if I'm married,' I said, 'I can't remember.'

'Someone will miss you, I expect, and be in touch. We have to hope that it's soon, so you can be reunited.'

'Now you ask, the name Megan springs to mind, though I've no idea if we were partners or not.'

'Well, that's good to have a name of someone who will be missing you. After the police interview you and when they put out a public appeal for information, she's bound to come forward in response. And are you employed? What is your job? You can't remember, right?' I acquiesce. 'Would you mind if I examine you?' I tell her to be my guest, and she listens to my chest again. She holds my head in her hands for a moment, examines it, and then with studied concentration goes through the now familiar rigmarole, murmuring, 'good, good,' and I watch her elegant, fine-boned, manicured hands, with so much power in them for one so young. Her eyes look wondrously clear as you would expect in someone of twenty-five or so, although I can tell by her skin that she's a smoker. Her hair's pulled back and up and she's wearing a delicate silver necklace with a pendant and tiny blue glass earrings to match. 'I just need to ask you a few more questions.' She asks me the name of the Prime Minister, what date it is and to repeat '12 West Street,' and apparently she's satisfied with my answers. Then we go through the stroke testing ritual. Finally she checks I can feel my feet. She's evidently satisfied with the results and spends the next few minutes writing in what she calls my 'temporary hospital records' on the iPad. Her bleep goes off. She looks at it briefly. She clips the pad back where she found it and tells me I'm fine, that she'll see me later.

'So ready for discharge? I'll need my clothes. I seem to have lost track of where they are.'

'Not quite ready to go yet. I expect your clothes have been collected by your next of kin.' I shake my head. 'Well, perhaps they went into the laundry system if they were not destroyed by being in the mud and water.' So it's goodbye to my seriously classy new outfit. Stylish pink shirt and all. Damn, I thought. 'More importantly, I believe the police will want to interview you, though of course you can go to the station yourself when you leave here and perhaps that will satisfy them. But this is a Serious Incident, you could have died. Someone telephoned the emergency services so that means someone saw how you entered the water. I'm going to order a head scan to see if you have a problem there, though I don't know how long it will take before they have a slot for you. By a process of elimination we may be able to determine what happened to you. For now, I'll leave you to rest.' And then she hesitates and turns back to me. 'Did you try to take your life, John?'

I tell her that I cannot remember, but that there would be no reason for me to try to kill myself as far as I know.

Then she leaves, and pulls screens around, allowing me to read her notes unobserved. *Temporary Hospital Records, No known Hospital Number, Admitted to Terminal Five,* today's date, *Male, "John Anon", DOB unknown, approx. 35–45* and underneath, *To be destroyed in one month from above date.* She's made some interesting observations. Apparently I don't seem to be on any existing drug regime, although blood tests will confirm this conclusion. I show no sign of psychosis. I am of unknown, possibly American identity, according to the paramedics, though apparently I have denied this. *If he was born in the US but has lived in the UK and adapted his accent for a while, a seizure, stroke or serious trauma can,* in her experience, *return him to his original accent. His refusal to give his name may be attached to a fear of being charged for medical services if he is not a UK national? Homeless. Lack of identity is going to produce problems when he needs to be discharged.* She remarks that I cannot remember if I am married. I have been dragged out of a local river? How long in water? I deny any suicidal thoughts. It isn't known whether I fell accidentally, deliberately or was pushed. There is an added complication that there is a question about the identity of the individual who called the emergency service so this would indicate it was likely that I was attacked. Local police have been alerted. The patient is currently not considered well enough to be interviewed. Though she's found no external evidence of a head injury she will action a scan. I seem rational, and am not a danger to anyone else that she can detect. So that's reassuring! From her notes it seems that the decision to section me and admit me to the psychiatric ward is predicated on whether or not I'm a danger to myself, and this is a tricky one until a criminal act is eliminated; no one saw whether I fell into the river or slipped in deliberately. As the doctor has only had a short, cursory interview with her patient so far, to be on the safe side, she's requesting more follow-up tests and keeping me on A and E Terminal Five until the results are through. Then I may be transferred to psych. Dr Cross doesn't know if my confusion is a result of a traumatic incident, immersion in the water or some other underlying, unrelated cause. She'll consult with a psych colleague about whether I should be admitted as a voluntary mental health patient, be sectioned, or discharged. The final words of the report read: *In view of the fact that the patient is unknown and of uncertain age or employment, with debilitated memory and without apparent NOK, the patient is NOT FOR 222, NFFP. As his present status is without hospital records, we could usefully send him to the Soft Day Area. Otherwise, I suggest Dr Doctor discharge him into Community Watch. Will recommend after final consultation with colleague.* I replace the iPad in the clip. What's Community Watch? I vaguely remember hearing about it but as my memory is totally fucked, I can't think what it represents or even is. And what on earth does NOT FOR 222 mean? And NFFP? And the Soft Day Area? Sounds cosy.

THREE

When I'd finished my cocktail, I tell a subdued Megan that they've been making people redundant so I need to shift out of here before the paper takes off for Liquidation Avenue with everyone on board. Newsprint hasn't been able to compete with the internet. Too slow, too expensive. Good thing for the planet really. The lockdown didn't help. The chilling thing is, they haven't bothered keeping all staff in the loop. He may not think he was observed but the chief number-cruncher was seen peeking at the sits-vac column over a pint. That told me enough. I'm abandoning the sinking ship before the other rats. We are all small, lost creatures crawling around the forest floor searching for nuts and berries, eager not to be crushed. I let her know that I'm sorry if it sounds as if I've hiked down to Self-Pity City but I am leaving town. That's the way it is.

'Christ!' she exclaims and now she looks up, takes a sip of her wine, all pretence of indifference lost. 'What's that about? Leaving work and leaving town? You have always hated change, John. Are you sure it isn't just a knee-jerk reaction to the shock of Ben finally losing his life?' She's trying to catch my eye, and puts her hand on my arm, and I feel a spark of guilt about yet again being so short of what I think she needs me to be. 'You're not in trouble, are you? You've been there forever. They won't push you out first. You'll forfeit any chance of redundancy pay if you resign. And your pension? Fuck it. You're only forty! You haven't thought it through. My God, you'll miss the newsroom action; you're a complete news junkie.'

'Newsprint won't exist much longer! Which is a tragedy because printed paper has been around for eons and all the electronic stuff constantly changes and will continue to do so. Gradually the record of our history will be lost in time as technology perpetually advances. Paper evidence survives. It is unchanging, and it's frustrating that nobody opens this out enough. I can't alter that. I know exactly what I am doing. I've never been surer about anything. Even should the rag survive in some form or other, I don't ever again want to be writing other people's stories whose ending we can almost always predict. Every bloody day. And it is always bad. You know, I want to take a risk. I only hung about for this long while Ben needed me.' I realise how cruel that must sound to her, my lover, my heart.

'Risk! You chancing your arm?' Do I detect tears sneaking into her eyes? 'So it'll be the SAS you'll be joining then?' She leans forward and puts her hand on my forehead. 'You're not well.' She's judging my temperature but her hand on my head just finishes me; little puddles form and threaten to fall. I back away.

'I've been a hack for the *Daily Disaster* for the last twenty years. I've adjusted to technology and ethics as they've changed. Like you, none of my colleagues understand why

I resist promotion. I like the small guys' job of investigation and am deeply suspicious of my ability to organise or take on a managerial role. Even a minor one. What's the point of all that extra effort and responsibility for a few more quid? Status doesn't interest me. And I don't see any pleasure in pushing bits of paper or people around. I think I'm good enough at what I do. All peeps in managerial positions end up *not* doing what they most love doing. CEO of physics department? No physics. Head of art college? Never teaches, never paints. Head honcho at the hospital? Doesn't practise medical stuff. Heads of departments never do what they're best at. Now I'm tired of soft options. My whole life has been one soft option. I need to recalibrate before it's too late.' I take a deep breath in.

'You're definitely not well.' She looks solicitously at me. But she's also riled up.

'Don't say that. I'm fine.'

'Are you drunk?'

'No. But I could be if you like.' I hold up my empty glass.

She asks me if I want to stay with her for a few days to sort my head out and then she gets up to go to the loo. I know she's leaving to give me time to calm down and think it through. Although it's tempting to take up her offer for a while, I notice that it's not unlimited hospitality on the table. Are we sometimes reasonably close even when we are not arguing? In a crisis, I think I'm her go-to person. I can't let her be mine though.

I mean, when things got worse for her last week, she came bounding in to me. Pretty angry. 'The mental health hub, HELP! is fucked,' she said. The worst had finally happened. They lost all their funding because the remit to help their service users find employment wasn't working. The one safe place, where they were completely accepted, now effectively rejects them by closing down. That must feel like a betrayal.

So she was already making changes too. Thinking of becoming a counsellor. Meggie continuously asks questions already, and she analyses every motive. Of course, it would be great to stay with her, because she's companionable, kind, funny, and reliable. And sexy. Though I questioned her wisdom of taking a mid-life change of direction from being an advocate, to training as a therapist. Every second person I meet is doing the same thing, I told her. She was not amused.

After breaking the bad news to me last week, she stayed over and I made a big production of bringing her breakfast, freshly squeezed orange juice, eggs Benedict and coffee. I listened while she called in sick and later we went for a walk on the canal bank. While we sauntered along chatting, I told her I didn't think she needed to *train* as a therapist, she's pretty good already. She dismissed that, saying I have no idea what I was talking about.

Because she's worried about how I'm handling bereavement, she's Mother Teresa today, and that's not cool because she's more fun when she's wild and mildly irresponsible. Now she's forced me into a position where I'll have to tell her something. Because heaven forbid that I tell her the truth.

'I'm still not with you.' She returns from the loo, refreshed her lipstick I note, and looks determined, looking for a fight. 'It's interesting that we are both making a life change at the same time. Something in the air, perhaps.'

'My favourite sister is going to take care of me,' I lie. She wasn't expecting this. Well, I wasn't either.

'I didn't know you had a sister, never mind a favourite one. You told me your sister died.'

'Well, I do. And yes, one of them died. Perhaps I didn't mention her because she's not usually in my orbit. She lives in Philadelphia. Leonora. Leonora was married.' I begin to elaborate on what her husband did, but run out of ideas, and instead pat the pocket of my jacket. 'Yesterday, I bought a ticket and tomorrow, I leave from Heathrow.' I can't help silently laughing, just watching Megan's face. What a shit I am. 'Leonora's got a couple of teenage kids, so there'll be plenty to occupy me and she'll take good care of me. She split with her husband a few months ago, so she could do with the company. And here's another thing, she's got a very large house and a sweet bit of land so I intend taking up gardening. I'll make a vegetable patch for her. You're always on at me to take more exercise and eat healthily, you should be pleased.'

'Don't be ridiculous, John. Fuck off. You're having me on. You'll pass out if you try to lift a garden fork.'

'Thanks, Meggie. You always have such faith in me. And so the wanderer will be returning home at last.' I sound horribly pompous. 'That can't be bad.'

'You can't just up sticks like that, especially so soon after a major bereavement? What with leaving the mates you've worked with for years. It's unnerving and emotionally punishing to say goodbye to pals who really know you.'

'None of them really matter. Apart from you.' I interrupt her flow and she smiles at last. 'You've been great to me. But I need to go home. You must see that. I can't remain an expat forever. Besides, I'm going to check it out first and if I find it truly awful, I'll be back by return of post. Unopened!' I giggle.

'You've lived in this country since you were twenty, for gawd's sake. That's all your adult life. You'll die in America. You'll hate to be away from Europe. How do you think you will cope?'

'I went home for a visit for both my folks' funerals. That's twice in ten years.'

'And you *loathed* it,' she interrupted with terrible emphasis. 'I remember your vitriolic comments about the place when you returned. You said it needed a complete heart transplant.'

'You know, if you leave the country of your birth, you really do have to return to your roots at some stage. For me, that's now, while I still have my sister there.' I get up to fetch another drink. 'What do you want?' I nod towards the bar.

'Shut up and sit down,' she replies. 'You should have gone to Ben's funeral. That's what this is all about. It was fine. You would have been okay. Why didn't you go?'

'I couldn't. I just couldn't do it. If you start lecturing me and not drinking anything yourself, I'll be off.'

'John. Sit down. Chill. Take it easy. Stop catastrophising.'

'Enough. Let me get you a fresh cup of coffee or something stronger to celebrate, perhaps a brandy?' She nods at the last suggestion. 'I'll order it. Back in a minute. I need a piss.' I go to the bar, order and pay for her brandy and then take off for the John where I can take a breather and a pee. My heart is pounding. I comb my hair and take a peek at what looks like myself. Nothing much different, a bit pale, but maybe it's the lighting. One bulb is flashing, not quite turning on and there's an odd feel about the place I cannot quite get a handle on. On the thin shelf under the mirror is a tobacco tin, and as someone flushes the toilet I pick it up to return it to them. 'Yours, mate?' but old Frank just shakes his head.

'How you doing?' he asks, as he washes his hands.

'Fine,' I say. 'They buried poor Ben today.'

'Sorry to hear that. Terrible for you. Good funeral?' I tip my head indecisively so he's no wiser. 'See you.' And he's off. I shake the tin. Open it. Just a small butt-end inside. I close it and turn it over. Just the stuff I used to smoke in my teens. Someone obviously came in here for a sneaky one and I'm thinking how I could just take up smoking again. I loved the ritual rolling, the anticipation, the first draw and then I think what bloody nonsense and prizing open the lid, I tip the butt-end into the waste bin, place my keys inside, snap it shut and put it into my pocket.

I slip through the side door to the back of the pub and get some notes from a cash dispenser. I sit on a bench nearby for a moment. I fish in my pocket, retrieve the specs she gave me and examine them. They are certainly not mine. They stink of someone else. I feel sick; I get up and lean over to throw up, but it doesn't happen. I hurl the stranger's shades into the gutter. Who had been staying with her last week then? How could she betray me? I really don't want to know. I just want out. While a large, curious and probably hopeful blackbird observes me, I attack, crushing the frames and glass to smithereens and leaping up and down, stamping on them long after they're destroyed. I catch my breath for a moment before entering the ring to face the music.

'This is no time to start a new life. How will you support yourself? Finding an interesting job in a new country is pretty impossible. Especially now.' She's had time to get fired up and present me with a menu for the prosecution. Joe sets her drink down on the table.

'Thanks, Megan. I'm going to stay with my family. It's not a new life; it's part of the old one. If I live with my sister while I'm feeling my way around, I can take freelance work while I make decisions about what next. I'll be taking up where I left off years ago. You can come visit me. Good weather and great hospitality.'

'Don't be ridiculous. You haven't lived with them for decades. And I'm not likely to enjoy it any more than you. Fuck it, John. You have no idea what they're really like. And they don't know you. You've never seriously had to share your life with anyone for any length of time so whatever makes you think you'll adapt to your sister and her family? And teenagers!' Her voice is rising, in that awful high-pitched way she sometimes uses to vent. It's too much. The whole place is listening now, and I really can't allow this kind of exhibition to take place in public.

I stand up. 'Bye for now,' I bow and push a wad of notes discreetly into her jacket pocket, then squeezing her warm and soft hand I say, 'have a holiday or buy a round of drinks for everyone in here on my birthday. August 15th, remember? See you soon.' Her jaw slacks open and I watch fascinated while she searches for words that she can't seem to find but are scurrying all over her face and then she takes the cash from her pocket as I back away to leave. She tries to throw the notes after me, but they flutter up into the air, landing like demented, hungry pigeons.

'You'll be fine,' I shout, still slowly shuffling away and leering a sort of schadenfreude grin. 'Really fine.' And then because that isn't enough, and I realise that as usual I have made a terrible error of judgement about her that it's now too late to remedy and in any case what on earth can I do to make it up to her, I stop. 'I'll be fine too.' I throw up my hands and as I back off again I notice a woman I don't know nearly overturn her table, then scrabbling around, she collects the notes from the floor, turning her head between us, unsure whether to return them to me or give them to Megan. I make my way unsteadily towards the door before Megs can begin another attack. Old Frank is laughing and shouting that it's warming up in here and to please leave the door ajar for air. I turn for a last glimpse of my old stomping ground, and then as I make a final dash for the exit some joker slams on 'The Shores of Amerikay', so, with my back to them, and arms in the air, I wave farewell to its strains.

* * *

'Hello there, John.' Another voice has entered my private domain and I turn to see a vision. 'I hear you've had a nasty accident. Is that so? What trouble have you been getting into, young man?'

'Hi,' I say, 'lots of trouble it seems.'

'My name is Sheila.' I could see that from her lanyard. Sheila Tucked. 'I need your age for the records. Can you tell me how old you are?'

'Twenty-five.'

'Now, now, John Anon. You might feel like twenty-five or you might indeed wish you were twenty-five, but we both know you are older than that.' There's a grin in her voice. 'Okay, we'll leave that detail for now. I'm going to take your temperature and pulse,' not again, I think, but don't resist as she takes my wrist in her cool hand, 'and you know, don't you, that you are in Terminal Five? After you've had another little rest, we'll need to do some more tests.'

For two days I've lain in bed, intermittently distracted by Nurse Tucked – I am too shy to call her Sheila at such short acquaintance, though the things she does for me are very personal indeed. For some reason my legs are so weak, I'm unable to walk. I'm bemused by the novelty of being taken care of; a reasonably comfortable exchange for incarceration for now. But I have to find a way out of here before I go crazy. Another nurse known as Nurse Laura Remarc comes on night duty, and she is surely a great source of reassurance and comfort too.

But there is a serious problem. My head aches like I'd never experienced before. When Dr Cross passes by she says I'm now an urgent case and sends me off for someone to take skull shots. Returning from the scan, I'm put behind a screen to await further blood tests. The man who comes to take the bloods mumbles a bit and though he doesn't make eye contact, I notice his eyes have a sort of unnatural shine. He's very efficient with the syringe and doesn't speak much except to order me to roll up my sleeve. He smiles and chuckles to himself a lot.

Later, Nurse Tucked helps me as I try to walk around the ward. This seems like good news; I'm suffering seriously from cabin fever. During our little trip, I lean on her arm, both of us chatting apparently companionably about nothing really, until I feel able to walk on my own. She asks me more about what I think happened to me and though I repeat again what I've told everyone, I can see she's not convinced. I feel her contempt. I can see exactly why; after all, if she's in doubt about me, and has to do so much personal care, this must seem like an indulgence on my part. I'm feeling pretty guilty now. The only way to resolve this is to escape.

I wake to find Dr Doctor staring down at me while he attaches a drip to the cannula on the back of my hand that must have somehow been connected to me in A and E. He is breathing heavily. 'Let me introduce myself again, in case you don't remember me,' he says. 'Dr Doctor.'

'Hi,' I say. 'Of course I remember you. How could I forget a name like yours? How did you come by it?'

'Well, it's a funny story, and a long one. So for now,' he bends over and points to the cannula in my right hand, 'let's see how we can help you.' He holds my left hand in his warm one, a seriously strange, distracting feeling. Before I recognise what's happening, he releases the contents of a syringe into the portal on the top of my right hand. 'This will give you added nutrients while we rehydrate you so that you will begin to feel a lot more conscious and less sleepy. Wonderful stuff!' He laughs as he withdraws the syringe and reconnects the drip. 'We need a little chat.' He pulls up a chair beside the bed. I notice the curtains are closed. This is obviously confidential.

I tell him that I'm feeling fine, and ready to go home. Whatever rules they have about discharge are ridiculous. If I hadn't come here, they wouldn't have known I had no hospital records. I just want to get back to square one. And I thank him and the hospital employees for all they have done for me.

'It doesn't work like that, John. Whether you agree or not, we feel you have a problem. And therefore we have a Duty of Care for you. We're temporarily admitting you to St Sepulchre's Ward.' He looks out of the window. 'You must agree that your memory has deteriorated, yes, yes? It's now NFFP, Not Fit for Purpose is it?' He shifts slightly in his chair and I notice his leg rapidly jigging up and down as he briefly glances back at me. 'And besides, if, as it seems, you cannot prove you are a UK national and therefore have no health insurance, we need to look into how we can manage you financially.' Why is he racking things up? He looks away again. Hesitates. 'As we are a teaching hospital, there is a way for you to help us and be relieved of your predicament, yes indeed,' he glances at me again, 'to avoid having to reimburse us retrospectively for your treatment, I have a simple solution. And a benefit to us. We would be happy to have you on our ward as yours is an interesting case. Yes, yes. Research!' His tone suggests this comment is some sort of praise. 'We can help you, if you help us. Some people are happy to do this, as they like to contribute to our good work. For our medical students, it is important to have complicated cases such as your own – complicated and interesting – you straddle somewhere between medical, psychiatric and criminal.' I wince. 'Well, of course, I'm not saying you *are* criminal but the circumstantial evidence tips in favour of your involvement with some sort of gang feud. If someone pushed you in, is it because you're part of a drug cartel? We need to eliminate that possibility before giving you a definitive diagnosis. The police wanted to speak with you, but we have held them off, explaining that you're too unwell to be interviewed. You'll be pleased to know that, I expect. But we need some answers, yes, yes, indeed.'

'That's a big leap,' I say. 'I'm not sure if I was attacked. I can't remember. It's monstrous to suggest that I'm involved in running drugs.'

'That still doesn't gives us a reason to discharge you, John. We're still left with a conundrum; you're not Fit for Purpose. We have eliminated any physical reason for your collapse into the water, so if you weren't attacked, we must assume you tried to take your own life. In that case you need to be detained for your own safety. We *can* section you,' he shakes his head, 'though we're keen to avoid that route. We prefer patients to submit to treatment voluntarily. Keep in control of their own destiny. A better outcome usually. You would prefer that, yes? Can we count on your cooperation? We'll pay you a small fee.' Now I'm confused. He seems to be implying that if they treat me, then they'll pay me. This equation does not compute. And most confusingly, I'm beginning to feel unaccountably content and mildly euphoric, despite this rubbish conversation.

'And in the meantime, just to be sure you can complete the tests, and we don't lose track of you, I'm placing a small implant into your arm.' And before I can quite take in what he's just said, he takes my arm, rolls up the pyjama sleeve and taps a metal gun-like thing onto my upper arm. It stings but not unduly, and certainly not in proportion to its implications. I pull away in shock and humiliation, stunned by his swift, furtive movement.

'You can't do that,' I exclaim, rubbing my arm.

'I'm afraid I just have. And I can.'

'But surely not without my permission.'

'We have a Duty of Care for you, John. What I have just done is inserted a small microchip to make sure you don't lose yourself anymore.'

'That's nonsense.'

'You've lost your name already, so you don't know who you are.'

'Does anybody know who they are?' I retort. 'Perhaps being anonymous is the only truly honest way to live with any integrity.'

'That's an existential question, John, not a medical one. It's more than our job's worth to lose any more of you. Goodness knows how we can be accountable if you absconded and went missing. We'd look ignominious, and lacking in care if we sent out an alert without a name. How on earth would we explain that to the police? At least the tag gives you some security,' and he stood up, and I swear he bowed his head before taking his leave.

After he goes, Nurse Tucked leads me to a new bed in St Sepulchre's where she tells me to settle down for the night. What on earth have I let myself in for? I've been tagged with a microchip like a criminal. Short of digging it out of my arm, I'm stuck with it. Coward that I am, mining my arm for implanted electronics is not an option I relish. Perhaps I can find a way of short-circuiting it? Would a shower destroy it while it's still newly installed – with the skin surface presumably still open to access? I'm not going to take this intrusion into my freedom lying down.

Someone at the end of the ward is coughing so energetically that I begin to worry that he's in serious trouble. As there don't seem to be any staff around, I get out of bed and wander down the ward until I'm close to the coughing someone and hand him a glass of water. 'I'd rather have beer,' he says. That's how I first get to know Liam.

We chat quietly for a while about how long he'd been on the ward and he tells me he's also signed up for a 'nice little earner,' as he put it, tapping his nose, 'you know,' he nods. I'm none the wiser.

'Do you have an electronic tag?' I ask.

'Sure.' He laughs. 'Have you been on the Resurrection Ward?' he asks and I tell him no. 'Are you violent and dangerous?' Again, I say no. 'I am,' he says. But he seems companionable enough, smiling and obviously wanting to chat, offering to obtain ciggies if I want them and telling me where to smoke without detection.

'What do you think of Dr Doctor?' I ask. 'I think he has a very strange manner, you know, talks in a monotone, doesn't make eye contact, that sort of thing. A bit imperious and too handy with the syringe.'

'No need to worry about his eccentric body language,' Liam replies, 'as for the syringe, think yourself lucky. Most of the guinea pigs would love one and many would pay a lot for that.'

'Guinea pig? What do you mean?' He shakes his head and tells me I'll find out sooner or later but that it's nothing to worry about. 'I don't like being so out of control,' I tell him. 'The doc made an odd proposal,' I begin, and Liam raises an eyebrow. 'No, not that! And here's the thing. His name? I mean, it's odd, is all,' I reply.

'Oh that. Yes. Dr Doctor. Well he has a history. Listen,'

he says, 'if that's what's troubling you I can explain. It's nothing sinister. Dr Doctor is an immigrant. He hails from Eastern Europe. At least his parents did, fleeing fascists. The family name was Doctorow but they took the "ow" off, as a doctor does,' he laughs, 'because they thought that name would be more acceptable in this country. They didn't realise that their only son would become a doctor. Some of the old patients on the ward don't know when to stop and keep calling after him, doctor, doctor, doctor, doctor.' I think he's making this up.

'So he's an immigrant, not a UK national?' I ask.

'Sure.'

'How do you know about his personal history?' He waves his hands and laughs at me. He begins to tell me about the scams he's running – something to do with offering objects and services for patients that the NHS doesn't provide. But I'm beginning to feel faint, although in a good mood, so I excuse myself and tell him to please elaborate tomorrow.

'Busy man. Get you!' he replies. 'I'll count you in if you stay around long enough,' he shouts after me as I drag my trusty drip, like a quiet little dog, back to bed.

FOUR

After I'd left Megan sitting confused in the pub, I hit the trail out of London. Some of what happened next isn't entirely clear to me but I do remember boarding a train, taking a window seat in a carriage sour from the heat. Meggie's right, I thought. Of course I'll miss the daily drama of the newsroom. I pick up a newspaper left by another passenger. Today's lead story steps right into my burning obsession with the retreat of trust in the face of the relentless march of bureaucracy that's eviscerating our most valuable institutions. On the front page is the story of a small boy in trouble in the sea off Devon. Onlookers summoned lifeboat assistance. A prospective rescuer is trumped by the strength of the waves and riptide, forcing him back to shore. The nearest lifeboat is deemed unseaworthy and so the crew are refused permission to launch it. Another lifeboat is six miles away and by now the little lad is exhausted. The main focus of the next paragraph is indignation about the delay in launching the nearest lifeboat, because of "concerns" over its seaworthiness. However, as a team, this lifeboat crew decide to overrule caution and rule book. Out they go, and indeed have saved the child, who, no surprise, wants to be a lifeguard when he grows up. The article emphasises the reprimand the crew now face for ignoring health and safety rules – accompanied by a cute photograph of the lad huddled in one of the crew's vast life jackets and sitting smiling beside one of the men who saved him. The happy little boy is back with his family, the unseaworthy lifeboat has been seized, and crew are to be disciplined. Bureaucracy rules okay. I toss the newspaper back onto a seat.

This reminds me of another recent incident. I found Ben vomiting uncontrollably, rang the emergency number he'd been given if he got worse. They told me to bring him in. Megan lent me her car to take him to hospital. I left him in the emergency outpatient clinic while I went to park the car properly away from the emergency drop-off point. No parking space available. I drove away in search of a legal space.

When I returned he wasn't in the waiting area. I tried to discover if he was still in the hospital, whether he'd been taken off for tests, been admitted to a ward or even discharged. They said, 'We can't tell you, you're not next of kin. Patient confidentiality.'

'Never mind that,' I said, 'I dropped him off. I'm not requesting medical details. I just want to know, is the man I left with you still here? And if he is to be discharged, I'll take him home.' They refused all information. I went home in the end and he called me the next day from the hospital bed from which he never returned. I still feel bad about that. My mind's foggy with grief. And the irony is, I later discovered he'd nominated me, but neglected to tell me, that I was his next of kin. It was there in his hospital notes.

I watch the changing landscape for well over two hours from the train window. After a while the track divides just at the point that we pass a derelict industrial site abutting the railway track. It consists of half-deconstructed elements of concrete and metal turning rusty, an old discarded source of income now lost and alone. I catch sight of a tall chimney, and then what looks like an observation tower but it's gone from sight before I can identify what it is and then I'm just left staring at soft, rolling hills.

I get off at a small, unattended station, turn the tobacco box over in my hands to hear the reassuring clunk of keys and contemplate whether or not to toss it into a trash can, but hang on to it for now, and begin to walk along a path beside the track, welcoming the chilling down day after a stuffy, warm afternoon. I come to a gate, unhook a latch that gives a comforting, old-fashioned click, and find myself in a meadow-like park, most of it ungroomed and bursting with wild flowers. Along the perimeter is a loose stone path and someone is walking in front of me. I'm conscious of the crunch my own footsteps make too, so I take to the grass, feeling a bit of a furtive fellow, but sense something troubling about the way the man in front moves. He turns and glances back at me, before continuing on in the same direction. I wonder what he is doing. I see two more men further ahead, one turns and waves back towards the first man. He runs to catch up with the two youngsters, one with a bike and another swinging something like a bat in one hand. I instinctively think I should avoid them, but don't want to leave the meadow and before long they've turned into the depth of the woods at the meadow's edge.

I pass a huge chestnut tree. The leaves on one side are a subtle but a discernibly different green to the other half. The trunk seems to be split, or I am looking at two trees fused together? Walking around it I can see that there are two distinct trunks coiled around each other. It occurs to me that it isn't a Siamese twin of a tree, but that it began as two separate trunks that have bonded together to become one as they grew. Looking at the other trees, there is no doubt that this sort of double one has thrived to become the largest in the park despite both of its trunks having to fight for survival. I think about how they must have grown so close, vying with each other for sunlight and water, neither surrendering, but locked together in a battle which has become an embrace.

I remember the sweaty schoolboy pleasure derived from conker battles. Megan, who acts as my inside council mole, told me that some county councils are demanding the execution of these glorious great giants, nervous that the council could be sued if someone trips on them or a child is injured playing conkers. My paper ran an article last winter on our local council's perceived notion of the dangers of litigation if people slipped on fallen nuts. Well, you can imagine the headline.

I continue walking with my thoughts on the strange tree until I reach a small path that I follow until I reach a stream. I saunter along the bank for a while until I find I'm becoming tired, so when I reach a small slatted bench I take a rest. I empty everything out of my pockets, tear all the paper into tiny pieces and throw them into the river where they float until two ducks think I'm feeding them. I feel bad about that. After a while I see the ducks take a hike up to the other bank and settle down for the night. I half watch for a moment, lost in thought.

I sit ruminating about the last bleak day I spent with Ben. After a while I decide that this level of concentration on grief is fruitless and depressing and it's getting dark. I get up and slowly saunter up the towpath. Just then, a small group of geese float past, interrupting my reverie, making too much noise for my liking and tormenting me for titbits. There are a couple of goslings and I'm relieved that as far as I know I haven't dragged kids into the equation and let them down by my inadequacies. I wonder if anyone told Ben's son that he had died. I don't know if he attended the funeral. Meggie didn't mention him, so I guess not. Now I'll never know, never have the chance to tell the young man what his father was like at his best. *Excuse me*, Megs would say, *this isn't about you*.

The geese have given up and sailed off, I guess to tuck down for the night like the ducks, but there's a small moorhen nodding as it navigates its way through the reeds and up onto the higher bank. It's close to dusk, and the river has turned dark jade.

The moorhen has returned and is jerking its way in the opposite direction across the river. Rising fish are forging little circles on the surface. The light is rapidly fading and I notice a few small leaves floating on the top of the water. Something isn't right. I don't know why I cannot hear birdsong and this is very distressing as it's the perfect time to hear their last sweet sounds. I see a dark, sleek shape make its way across the river and disappear into yellow bog irises at the water's edge. I decide to make my way down the steep bank to see what the dark, sleek shape is. I begin to clamber down the soft, spongy edge in the hope of getting a clearer look but the bank is a bit soggy. There's a distant call of a blue-light siren.

* * *

Water has always fascinated me, I can watch it for hours; the way it plays with light, distorts layers beneath, how it refracts and enhances reflection, suggesting something denser and darker down below. I have less fear of water than is healthy for someone who is not a great swimmer. I think about my sister, no, not Leonora, she is pure fiction, like some of my news stories as the sub-ed might say.

My real sister, Florence, was born nine months after my parents' European honeymoon trip to Italy, and named for the city where she was conceived. This enviable young couple adored their tiny, fairy girl, sweet and tender, clever and smiling and then, five years later I followed, a yearned for sibling for beautiful, delicate Florence. My mother held me close to hear the reassuring quiet tick of her heart, her very breath stoking my sense of love and security, her touch so gentle and soft, her voice so warm, her breast so sweet, her body so sensuously enfolding me, her pretty feet stepping me confidently into a promising future. Our family lived in a traditional turn-of-the-last-century house, surrounded by a garden in which a little pond lay, filled with tiny living things, a mesmerising magnet for small girls. My pram would be out on the patch of grass, just below the beech tree so I could be lulled to sleep by the slow drift of its leaves on the breeze. On tippy-toes Florence peeked in to see me, as five-year-old big sisters do, poking and smiling, joyful and happy with delight that I, her baby brother, loved her so much, that I cooed and responded with laughter at the sight of her sweet smile.

Emboldened by the glow of her own power and warmed by the love of her little brother, she confidently set off to see what creepy crawlies dwelt in the garden pond in the leafy glade. Full of curiosity and wonder, she bent over the little pool of water searching for signs of life and its treasures. Was that a little boatman? Is that a tiny new frog? And is a dragonfly fairy gliding by? It hovers to amaze and delight her before darting away. What beautiful colours are all those little stones on the bottom! Are they jewels? Look how the water sparkles and tinkles at the flick of her hand across the top. She bent further across the water and glimpsed herself. There she was and then she was gone, taking my mother's heart with her.

FIVE

Nurse Laura Remarc arrives on the ward with a new patient. He just lay on the bed in his day clothes. When she tries to undress him, he resists. I try to be helpful and make friends by introducing myself and I ask him his name and why he's in here, but he can't seem to follow me and looks confused. He keeps saluting every time I finish a sentence. Nurse Remarc takes a photograph from his locker, places it on top, murmuring approving sounds. 'Don't fret too much, Wayne, I'll be back soon.' And away she goes. It's a photograph of a young soldier. The picture is a cheaply printed, faded copy and creased, but the face is of a young man in uniform standing next to his bride. After the nurse has gone I ask him who it is in the photograph, but he doesn't reply. Now I look more carefully I can see the soldier looks very, very young, perhaps not even out of his teens, and somewhat frightened too but nothing like as much as the man in the bed. 'Wayne,' he says. Just that word. 'Wayne.'

'How's it going, Wayne?' I ask rather stupidly. But he replies only with his name. 'I wish I knew mine,' I said. I see his patient info clipped to the end of his bed, but am too worried about being caught to actually examine it for clues.

I return to my bed and find that Liam has arrived with a memory stick for me to view, a freebie, he says, and, at his insistence, I follow him into a room off the visiting area that I haven't seen before. 'A viewing room for anyone interested in watching stuff downloaded from a computer,' he tells me.

'Here's John,' he announces to the row of five seated men, new to me. 'He's my partner,' he says, brushing away my protests. 'Sit here,' he continues, 'let's get started.' He turns off the lights, as the picture on the screen lights up the faces in the front row. I've seen plenty of stuff like this when I was a young man, and I can't say the environment here does anything for the libido. After about two minutes of heavy action on the screen he turns it off. 'So that's a sample of what we have here.' He holds up a handful of memory sticks. I excuse myself and prepare to leave. He seems disappointed. 'You've got a freebie, are you not going to subscribe to any more of my goodies, then?' He happily and rapidly hands out sticks to some of the others and trousers a chunk of change.

'Not really interested, old pal,' I reply. 'I've already seen more excessive porn than this and in any case it doesn't interest me.'

'Ah well, you don't know what you're missing. It gets better. And look,' he turns to the room, 'the other guys are happy enough. I'll still cut you in if you do the advertising for me, you know, I suspect that you're good with words. We need a bigger audience.'

'You seem to be doing just fine on your own,' I say, 'though it's generous of you to offer to include me. I can't really see great potential for huge profit, so why would you want to divide the proceeds?' He tells me he's sure that there's big money to be made supplying long-term patients with stuff they need. I tell him that there are commercial outlets in the hospital already supplying everything a patient wants or needs. Of course, he knows about the shops but the merchandise he's suggesting, he says with a lurid chuckle, isn't on their shelves. I'm getting bored with this now so saunter off back to my pad, celebrating the fact that I can walk independently again, and trying to work out how I can leave without demob papers. Don't want to go AWOL and have the cops looking for me. Just need something else apart from patient scrubs to wear on body and feet. A bit of cash would help too, so I may consider Liam's offer though I'm reluctant to encroach on his patch, as it sounds dubious. I'd wager there'll be a forfeit to pay and I cannot imagine what that would be.

Shuffling back through to my cell in the ward, I find Nurse Remarc taking Wayne's blood. 'There, there,' she says as he winces. 'You've done very well.' He still looks confused. 'Now I need you to get into these clean pyjamas and into bed,' but he doesn't move. She struggles for a bit trying to undress him and I offer to help. 'No, but thanks, John.' She smiles at me. 'I can't let you help under health and safety rules. So though it's thoughtful and kind of you, no.' She struggles to pull off his shirt for a bit longer, while I watch disturbed by his anguished curses, and his aggression. I'm anxious for her safety. With flailing arms he's pushing her and repeating, 'No, no, no!' as she fails to remove his shirt. 'No, No. Wayne says no,' he says, spit spraying. She pulls on her mask and tries to calm him, but the appearance of the mask seems to make him even more troubled than before. 'No, no, no, no, no,' he screams, terror in his eyes. 'Fuck off. Go away. *No. No. No.* You're not my missus.'

'Okay. Okay. Don't worry, Wayne. I don't have that honour. Take it easy.' She sits down for a moment to collect herself and we chat aimlessly for a while as she tidies the top of his bed. After a while, seemingly having recovered her calm, she continues her effort to change him into his pyjamas.

'Right. Wayne. Attention.' She's speaking now in clipped tones and in a deliberate and deeper voice. 'Wayne. It's orders. Duty, man, duty! You must take off your uniform and put on your pyjamas,' she barks, and then salutes him. I watch in amazement as he salutes back and slowly and methodically removes his clothes. Then he puts on his pyjamas and gives her a salute again, which she returns with a smile. What kind of lateral thinking capacity does Remarc possess to come up with that solution? When he finally settles down for the night, I hear him make soft weeping sounds under his covers. She comes back and talks quietly to him but though the sobs are less intense, he hasn't entirely stopped by the time she has to move on when the lights go out.

Sometime during the very early morning, I find myself in a room with three walls, and facing me is a gap where the fourth wall should be. Even curiosity isn't enough to counter my resistance to peer over the edge. I lean back to touch the wall behind me in a feeble effort at clutching it, as if I might begin to slip towards the missing wall, though in truth there was no camber towards its infinite darkness. No rational reason for me to slide towards the opening. I begin to shuffle to the perceived safety of a corner only to find when I arrive there that I am back where I started. Coiled in a tight foetal position, I suddenly begin to slither towards the missing wall again and, falling, I can just discern, above the sound of my thumping heart, the regular hum of some electronic device and the snorts and snoring from my companions in the ward as they came into aural focus. With relief at being still alive, I push my feet down towards the end of the bed.

A soft light shines either side of the doorway, but it's otherwise dark, apart from a small LED light in the centre of the ward. I am disturbed by the dream and try to analyse its implications. I get nowhere, and failing to settle down again, decide a little trip to the refreshment vending machine near the nurses' station might just, right then, distance me from whatever it was I cannot grasp that led to the distressing nightmare. Hobbling towards the nurses' station, a sound draws nearer, a murmur of modulated tones indicating a quite heated conversation, although somehow also muffled. Heavenly sounds of female voices! I stop before I pass the window where they would see me. Frustratingly, I'm unable to make out what they are saying. Since I've been admitted here, I've found myself missing the intimacy of female chat, so I am keen to hear what juicy gossip they're discussing. This somewhat unpleasant side of my character used to be satisfied by overhearing the customers of The Flounder and Lemon in full swing as the ballad of their lives unfolded. I'm missing this company, the daily flow of hostile gossip, raucous rumour and laughter. Especially that of Megan.

As I've said before, she's the one person who I once thought I could settle down with. On the only occasion I'd hinted at the possibility on a slightly romantic, late dinner date, hoping to keep warm one harsh winter night, she responded with a chirpy, 'You can't keep trying to wring more life out of an old dishcloth, John, dear.' At first I thought, somewhat ungallantly, that she was referring to herself being perhaps a little threadbare, though when I then said, 'Don't worry, you're in pretty good shape,' and how I loved the sight of her, the great Titian hair, the softest lips on the planet and the bounciest breasts, it didn't change her mind. So perhaps she was referring to me. Thinking about it now, I see she probably meant our relationship. She'd have a very stern reaction if she knew what I was trying to do to compensate myself for her absence now. She'd be right. Eavesdropping might be an appropriate way to learn about secret things a curious child or adolescent wants and needs to know about family dynamics say, or sex, but in an adult it's pathetic and lacking in integrity and qualifies me as a borderline creep. Okay, an altogether full-blown creep. This has not stopped me being a lifelong snoop, a characteristic that served me well, with somewhat suspect justification, as a journo. This is not my motivation now. It is more a form of therapy for my lost world of women, a way of understanding. I mean, I'm surrounded by women working here, of course, but that's not quite what I miss. It would be inappropriate for me to barge into their conversations.

Contemplating devious ways to satisfy my desire for their company, I realise that if I slink a little closer and crouch down onto the floor below the window level, I will be able to hear them. But I am desperate for a drink. I'll have to settle for the hideous stuff that goes for coffee here, though something stronger would be more welcome. The only way to reach the vending machine is by walking past the window of the nurses' station, pretend not to see them, collect my drink and return past again. Which is exactly what I boldly do, carrying my instant, somewhat bitter, coffee. They spot me. I stop to smile confidently at Nurse Remarc and Dr Cross, who is rocking something white, rolled up and cloth-like in her arms, and who immediately stops rocking and enquires how I am. She asks if I need anything, any support, to which of course, I say as softly and seductively as I can that I'm fine, thanks, and decline help with a shy smile and short wave of my free hand. God, I'm a creep, wasting their time in this comfortable envelope of their kindness.

Dr Cross looks as if she's in her mid-twenties, a tall, toned, supple, strong woman, with a sad frown interrupting her features. I notice she's still wearing the same aquamarine pendant and earrings, made of what looks like sea glass, and it's just perfectly judged against the tone of her glowing, clear skin. Perhaps it has romantic significance. I feel a pang of jealousy. I can see from the way she sits that she could make a ballet of her limbs, the like of which sight I unfortunately haven't been exposed to for what feels like forever. They are sitting together, a lamp illuminating a pile of iPads on the table.

The nurses' station is an edifice that consists of a box-like shape curving back from the wide corridor, with a built-in desk thing that acts as a wall between them and us, and has usually open windows with transparent plastic protection, onto the corridor. It should be quite simple to double back, once safely past their hang-out, carefully slide down below the level where they can see me, all the while hoping that no one will pass nor that they can smell my coffee. With a slightly guilty feeling I stealthily double back. From this vantage point I am able to hear their conversation if I concentrate hard.

'Do you think he's okay?' It sounds like Nurse Remarc.

'Well, if you are concerned you can check him before you go off shift,' replies Dr Cross.

'I was thinking more that he's an odd one. I don't trust him. How can he forget his name? He seems a bit of a freak to me. I don't really believe a word he says. He shouldn't waste any more of our time. What do *you* think, Frances?' Huh! I think you're spoiling your chances with me, Nurse Remarc.

'I believe him. I think he's deeply affected by some trauma. He seems a gentle enough fellow. We have to be cautious about discharging him. He's a perfect candidate for St Sepulchre's. At least he'll get the help he needs, without being a full-blown burden on the health service.'

'Sod him! Anyway, back to where we were.' The nurse coughs. 'Oh, no, I'm fine. You know, you're the most highly valued of all the doctors on this ward. At least by the nurses. You always genuinely listen to our opinions. I cannot say that about any of the other fuckers. They pay lip service, but the old boys' network is still in place. The patients seem to relax when you're around too.'

'Well, thanks for saying that. You're a good friend, Laura. But it still keeps me in a desperate state of worry.

Doctors' little friend, Valium, keeps me going. God knows how I'd cope if I ever had got pregnant.'

'Here,' Remarc says.

'Thanks.' She laughs, but I can't see what it is she's talking about and long to put my head over the parapet. 'Maybe the nearest I ever get to holding my own little one. There, there. I can't see what to do to improve things. I have the constant feeling I'm not up to the job. Well, certainly not in the way I was trained to do it.'

'You're by far the most compassionate and effective doctor on the ward.'

'Thanks again, Laura, it's very good of you to say that, but your opinion isn't shared either by the consultant clinical manager nor the management team,' she gives a chuckle, 'and that's making me feel on edge most of the time. Here, take baby.' They both giggle. 'I mean, look at this pile here. Apart from all my normal work, I'm still having to do the stats on local hospitals. I know they're trying to close them down, so I feel compromised by being asked to prove that they are inefficient when they're actually lovely to work in and being community based, the patients and relatives prefer them. The study is nearly ready for publication, but I'm nervous to let it go because it seems dishonest to me. I don't agree with my own findings! Or rather, the parameters don't include patient results. It's just about funding.'

'Why don't you refuse to do it?'

'Not a choice. Besides, they'd still go ahead and find some other mug. And then there's this other stuff here; patient information for management, not the patients. There's just no chance of me completing all these records tonight even if I saw the point of them. It's going to take me the best part of three hours to finish, and I have no belief that anyone actually uses them for anything, which just compounds my frustration.'

'Most of us prefer to work at the coalface without all this bloody box-ticking to do. We're constantly faced with the cruel choice of either doing something for the patient or filling in a record to say whether we haven't or have. Most of us work an extra fucking shift without pay at the end of the week to catch up on admin work. I'm not sure I have the stamina for all this confounded slog. Some nurses just tick away without reading the question first.'

'Too much information. I wish you hadn't admitted that.'

'It's just admin. We'd never do anything if we took it all seriously. We're knackered, and you're knackered, Frances. That's the problem. Let me get you something.'

My coffee, which I've uncharacteristically managed not to spill, is just about the right temperature now to sip. I have to suppress an urge to take it to Dr Cross and put my arm around her lovely shoulders and comfort her.

'No, I'm fine. I have to finish this or they'll ask for my resignation. I've already had the yellow card. I can't just leave it.'

'Can't you just refuse to do the stats if you don't agree with the parameters?'

'I tried to question the lack of stats for patient outcomes and was told that wasn't my remit. That if I wasn't compliant, I'd be fired. I feel it's pretty weak of me not to find a way to stand up to them.'

'You're being ultra-hard on yourself. I don't believe the rest of The Firm doesn't value you. I've never overheard any criticism of you.'

'Well, I'm sorry if this sounds awful, but they'd hardly address it to you.'

'Sure. But we have ears.'

'Okay. But I know that I'm not up to scratch clinically. That is, I know what needs to be done, but I don't have the time to do the job properly.'

'The nurses have the same problem.'

'There you are then. As long as the walking paper clips are in charge, there's no hope of making the organisation function humanely and efficiently. And every reorganisational shake-up brings so many additional bureaucratic problems, taking away our precious time with patients, without providing extra time or money for what we need to do. That's where the problem lies.'

'If you leave, it won't help anything.'

'I know, and I feel bad about it, and haven't completely made up my mind. All NHS medically trained staff who go over to the private sector, take their training equity with them to benefit the private sector with no repercussions or reparation to the NHS. And that's against my principles. But,' and at this point I heard the doctor sob, 'I have no private life.' I hear a clutch of 'there, theres,' and the scratch of chairs being moved. She's now into full crying mode. 'I want the same things as everyone else, and I don't have time for them. I can't even keep up with my friends outside the hospital.'

'Oh dear, oh dear,' the nurse commiserates. 'I'm so sorry. Take this. I had no idea you were suffering so much.'

There's the sound of more sobbing. 'I was always a bit envious of you, to be honest. You seem to have everything, you know, a great job and you're lovely looking. And your youth,' she chides and chuckles, 'there's still time.'

'But I don't have time for *finding* a family life. All the male doctors have wives or partners who help them. Not true of the female ones. The hours for hospital doctors were set up decades ago and based on men, not women – however much things have changed, it's still just the same. The guys meet up for a drink after a shift so I guess the kids are ready for a kiss from Daddy when he arrives home and perhaps the chance for him to read a story to a freshly bathed and fed youngster who's pleased to see him. There'll be dinner ready on the table when he's done. Lucky buggers. I'm too knackered after work to have a conversation never mind engaging in a romp. We have equal opportunity and rights in all respects, except reality.'

Now the temptation to go and comfort her is becoming exceedingly difficult to resist. What I want to say to her is: *I'll take care of you. You can go to work, I'll stay home and make it welcome for when you return. There might be a bit of a problem about how efficient I am at domestic stuff but we can talk about that. Your white knight awaits you, Frances. I am he!*

'It stinks,' says Remarc. 'Most patients want reassurance, a kind word, a pat on the shoulder to make them feel better but we spend our time on admin, instead of doing that. When I worked in geriatrics it always felt absurd to try to pull them back to life with drugs and extreme procedures when most of them needed a hug and someone to listen to their fears,' she sighs, 'and to maybe say goodbye.' There's a catch in her voice. 'It's got steadily worse. Look, let me get something for you to drink and a snack while the ward is quiet. Bring your sugar level up.'

'Oh, go on then. If you're having one, I'll have a cappuccino please. And a chocolate bar. Kind of you. Thanks,' and she laughs. 'And I'm sorry to wail so, and bollocks to the lot of them.'

'That's more like you!' says the nurse and I hear the chair being pushed back as Nurse Remarc begins her nurturing mission.

I'm in a real panic now. I cannot get up and back to the ward without being seen. I put my coffee on the floor beside me as I hear her approach. I settle down flat and close my eyes. There follows a shout from Nurse Remarc, a flurry of feet as Dr Cross joins her. They discuss between them about why I've collapsed or what might have happened. A gentle hand holds my wrist while another feels for the jugular, which they should, if there is any justice in this world, have gone for, rather than checked for life. Would it be best to come clean, admit to my nasty little habit, to tell them I'd heard everything, or just pretend I'd collapsed or fallen asleep? They think I'm seriously ill and discuss calling the crash team urgently, and then Remarc asks Dr Cross whether she should try to revive me. I admit this is definitely an attractive idea. But if I successfully deceive them, I'd be adding more to their workload in a hands-on way and they'd have to write up yet another report and assessment and Dr Cross would be deprived of her much-needed refreshment break and more of her precious time. On the other hand, trying to convince them that nothing is amiss and I'd just fallen asleep in a place as unlikely as this uncomfortable position, would be a hard sell even for a habitual liar like Liam. I cannot immediately think of any story that would sound remotely plausible. Is there really anything I can honourably do apart from just die? I open my eyes.

SIX

Early the following morning, just as the light begins to slide across the green blind on the window into the corridor, I wake to find a young man standing beside my bed, disconcertingly watching me. 'Hi!' he says when he sees I've spotted him. 'I'm Mark, your primary helper. How are you today?' In hospital they really mean this question, but on the other hand I feel he's been spying on me, so I think for a while before realising it's probably not a major decision for me to reply that I'm fine. 'I've come to tell you that your first meeting as a Patient Representative is later. A seminar. Here,' he says, 'I have your notebook and the timetable.' He hands me a small briefcase. I think this is an excuse. I still think he's spying on me.

Spying seems a bit labour intensive; what's wrong with security cameras? That's what did for me last night of course. Dr Cross and Nurse Remarc had me on a security camera in the nurses' station throughout their entire discussion. They enjoyed my moment of embarrassment. Indeed, they'd watched me from the moment that I arrived, so when I opened my eyes to apologise and confess my idiotic reason for listening to their conversation, they were already laughing. Though I don't know if they realised I'd heard everything they said. I didn't check then because they were too caught up in my absurdity. Though I am not sure at what point they noticed me, I still believe Frances's tears were real.

They led me, fraudulently protesting, into their lair. They sat drinking coffee, me eating humble pie along with the hot chocolate they prescribed to help me relax. I encourage them to laugh at my pathetic antics, until I felt we're all cool enough with the situation for me to ask Dr Cross about what she'd recorded in my temporary patient notes, specifically if she thought I had mental health problems. 'We're all on the spectrum, or more accurately the gradient,' she says. 'In my opinion there's no such thing as an International Guarantee of Mental Fitness.' She chuckles. 'Just differences, some more socially harder to manage than others. This is not an area I can reveal too much about without incurring the wrath of the powers that be,' she confides, 'but, in my opinion, faith in the diagnostic and statistical manual of mental disorders, though a useful guide, is only that, a guide. My opinion's certainly not shared by everyone, indeed, very few openly concur. Though there have been precursors to my views. Very active ones in the past. Some big shots agree with me that there is currently really no certain way to make an accurate diagnosis. We're now working on a more comprehensive diagnostic tool, using scans and other tests. In any case, people's mental state fluctuates throughout a lifetime, and I dare say we've all been there, as they say. So please, John, do not worry about what I wrote in your temporary patient records. No one will suddenly whisk you away and lock you up.'

I tell her I think that I've already been whisked away and locked up on the pretext that I can't be discharged because I cannot remember my name. Not unreasonably she reminds me that not remembering my name is a symptom of my post-traumatic amnesia. I tell her that I can't help being suspicious about what's happening because I've heard the word *guinea pig* banded about. She suggests if I'm so curious and keen on answers, then I should apply to become a Patient Representative. She points out that very few patients want, or indeed are well enough to take on this role. I tell her I'm happy to do anything to help her, but ask what on earth does this commitment entail?

'You'll attend hospital management meetings,' she explains, 'they take place every week, though in an emergency, they'll sometimes call a crisis meeting. You'll be kept in touch with the latest hospital developments, and given minutes of each meeting. All in the spirit of accountability and freedom of information. I'd take notes yourself, if you want real accuracy,' she continues. 'I can see you are a person with an enquiring mind.' *If only you knew*, I think. 'And it would be a fine service to the community here.' When I agree, she tells me she'll put my name forward for the role, and inform management immediately to start the process. She expects them to confirm my appointment at her request and they will be in touch with me. All the while Frances is speaking, Remarc seems to be smirking, but thinking back now, it's probable that her demeanour's always a bit critical. I feel reassured about this when I remember that I didn't notice anything but kindness from her when I first arrived in a wretched state on the ward.

Now I'm confused about the appearance of this intruder called Mark. Is he a result of my own spying? I remember he told me he's my primary helper but now that Dr Cross has invited me to observe management team meetings, is this really why he's here? Why him? He told me he was on work experience, so what authority has he to be the messenger? On the other hand is Doctor Cross inviting me to be a Patient Representative a reasonable reaction to my spying on her? How did she action the request so quickly? Does Frances in turn want me under observation? Is he delegated to watch me? If that's so, I'm trying to filter her decision through my mind, but I'm feeling woozy and strange today, and obviously tired after last night's shenanigans, and my thoughts are confused, making it hard to believe her motives are pure. It's not something I wish to confide in Mark.

'Better in my head, you know, quite relaxed,' I lie as I take the briefcase and put it on the stand beside my bed. 'I'm not sure about physically. My legs are a bit weak. Walking's not great. Here's the thing, I'm finding it difficult to bend down and get up. You know, the strength is beginning to go.' But he's not taking notes so I guess he isn't too interested.

'That's from not moving them, not taking exercise. Like stuff you do when you are up and about, working or whatever you do. You know, going to the pub or making out with your mate. If you lie around all day what do you expect?'

'Oh, is that right? Just my muscles are not in tune, you think?'

'That sounds like the problem. You can always check with the medical team when you see them.' And he smiles at me. 'I see you've been given an SAS,' he says looking at my drip, suspiciously lasciviously. I hope it's not me he's after.

'What's that?' I ask, pointing at an addition to the cannula on my arm that I don't remember being inserted.

'SAS – it's a self-administered sedative pump. I'll have to disconnect it, I'm afraid. We don't want you stumbling about with it during the seminar,' and he begins to unhook me. 'I'm ready to take you down to the Meds R Us building now.'

'Eh?'

'It's the name of the company sponsoring the drug-testing wing of this hospital. You've signed up for drug testing, haven't you? With Dr Doctor? I've told you, I've been delegated to be your primary helper during the tests, to make sure you are doing fine, you know, not feeling unduly unwell, and doing the tests!' He laughs. 'Health and safety rules. And to encourage you to fill in all the forms. Not attempting to back out.' He explains, 'Some people get cold feet. But as you know, you won't get paid until they are over and certainly not if you don't complete them.'

'Sure. I remember Dr Doctor offered to help me if I cooperated. But he didn't explain exactly what I had to do, and I didn't sign up for anything that I remember.'

'Well, that's not surprising is it? They told me you'd lost your memory. Perhaps you don't remember signing the agreement when they tested your bloods, as they do with all of us,' he replies. 'If you can't afford to pay for treatment and can't prove you are a UK national, I don't see what choice you have.' I'm stunned. How come he is privy to all this new information? Are my patient notes open to all?

'I need to leave,' I say, 'there's no reason to detain me any longer. I can't have signed anything if I can't remember my name. I rest my case,' I say smugly. 'After I leave and have a couple of sessions in the gym, I'll get my strength back. I'm checking out before this goes any further. It all sounds far too invasive and risky.'

He says it is not his decision, which of course I know. My mind's scurrying around searching for a way out. I imagine he's young enough to be indiscreet, and that for a small consideration, he could well be naïve enough to show me the way to go home. I ask him where the exit is, thinking, who on earth would stop me leaving? I can self-discharge. He says he doesn't have this information and sits down on the chair beside my bed.

He doesn't make any move to stop me when I go towards the door to the ward, but Liam pushes his way in, holding me back and announcing that he's also graduated to this ward. He notices that I'm panicking, asks me why I'm in a hurry, asks me what's wrong and tells me to take it easy. I let him know how urgent it is for me to get out of here. 'I'll pay you,' I tell him. And then remember, with regret, my rash gesture to Megan. No money left. I'm stuck. Buggered. I'd be without work if I leave, and feel foolish that it's come to this but it's an insufficient reason to stay. I almost seem to have forgotten that being alive, even while I catch my breath, needs cold, hard cash. How have I let things get so out of my control? Liam grasps my arm in what seems like a vice-like grip. 'I don't have any cash with me,' I tell him, 'but I'll make sure to repay you when I'm out of here and find useful employment. I'm good for a loan.'

'Most of the other guinea pigs are in the same position, that is, they are homeless or unemployed or both. Or nuts like me. Mental health probs.' He laughs, pushing me back into the room. 'You're in good company. We can make this work for us. I have my ways, and as I've said, I'll cut you in. Meds R Us will open a bank account in your name, and after they've set up your payments, any minute now, you'll receive some dosh. When you've got sufficient funds I can spring you. I can transfer spondoolies into your bank for your future if you cooperate with me.' I can see a small problem with this, but let it go.

'How about a bit of upfront candy?' I ask him. He nods his head and says he'll think about how to sort this for me.

'You need to watch your step,' chips in Mark, 'if you're caught breaking the terms and conditions, they'll chuck you off the programme.'

'What programme?' I ask.

'Drug research programme.' He is chewing his fingernails and looking agitated. I notice that he's clacking his false teeth, and wonder how someone so young – he's maybe nineteen years old – has lost them. Then I realise. I'm not so out of touch I don't recognise his problem when I see it. I think of Ben. I don't welcome this reminder. Mark asks Liam for a smoke. When Liam refuses, Mark gets up and sits lurking on a chair by the door, shaking. Someone needs to give him a shot of something!

Liam continues to discuss his own package of events, something to do with supplying excellent value memory sticks, and the finest for those with the big readies. But there are some terms, though under *any* conditions, he tells me. He feels he has a Duty of Care to supply off the cards goodies. I'm not convinced. Although curious at what is actually going on here, I'm still more interested in how to get out. If I am on a programme to test prescription drugs, I want some guarantees. To know they'll improve my life, not suck it out of me. On balance, I'm thinking, in the absence of this assurance I'd prefer to exit here altogether and tell Liam that's my plan.

'I can retrieve a white coat from the laundry,' he says, 'if someone stops you, you're eloquent enough to talk your way out of here while wearing it.' I tell him I thought they'd abandoned the use of white coats years ago after finding most of them were contaminated because they were not washed enough. Then scrubs were introduced. 'Not on this ward, mate. It's a little-known fact that white coats are worn in the mental health and testing areas to distinguish the doctors from the patients. What's your size?'

Before I can reply, Dr Doctor appears at the door and swiftly, efficiently, strides into the room, followed by a posse of four white-coated peeps. They all conspicuously ignore Liam who scurries off to his lair.

'Hello, John, I'm glad you've met my ward assistant, Mark – who is also your very own delegated primary helper. Dismissed!' He claps his hands, laughs, and Mark skulks out of the room.

Dr Doctor sits on the bed, asks how I feel, and introduces his four acolytes. He takes us through the usual rigmarole of pulse and heart checking and then says he has an important task for me. As he has already explained, he reminds me, the hospital's research work needs willing volunteers, happy to contribute for a small fee. 'This ward is full of these good people who have answered our need to recruit volunteers for the prescription drug trials which are vital for everyone's welfare – ultimately, for the good of the world! *Good Pharma, Good Karma!* That's our mantra,' he exclaims. 'This medication may benefit our patient here, personally, and won't do him any harm,' he's speaking to his audience but taps my arm, 'and will enable us to continue our good work in the hospital as well as save mankind. A most altruistic patient!' he says to his row of silent, nodding acolytes and then focusses on me to observe my reaction. 'The medication will very likely eliminate many of your problems. Can we count you in? We really do need people.'

'There's nothing wrong with me,' I tell him, 'I can't see the benefit in this for me.'

'I think I'm the best judge of your health, John. I assure you, I primarily have your welfare in mind, which is why I've entered you for this task. For a start we need to understand why you have lost your memory, and I'm told you seem to have some muscle weakness. Need to check that too and the best way to fund your hospital stay is to enrol you in this wonderful study,' he says triumphantly, standing up and examining me by testing the strength of my arms and legs. Apparently satisfied, he nods and stands while I get back into the bed.

'I'm weak because I haven't been moving about because I'm stuck in here! I want to know what the medication is for. And also, will there be side effects?'

'We'll get you onto an exercise programme very soon. And about the medication, we will tell you what we think is necessary of course. Though we can't always predict side effects.'

'What about the Freedom of Information Act?' I say.

'We have a very knowledgeable gentleman here,' he turns to his team and chuckles, 'you can sign an FOIA if you like.' Then seeing that I'm not amused, he continues, 'We'll answer any questions you have. Just need to get you fit and well again so that you can move forward with your life.'

'Okay,' I agree. I surmise that if I appear to be cooperative, then it'll maximise my chances of checking out of here. If I alleviate their suspicions, catch them off guard and be ready to take advantage of the main chance of escape, I need to be operating without close scrutiny. If Liam can source a white coat, appearing to be affable is a good ploy.

'We'll tell you anything that is helpful. You know, we like to keep our patients who help us happy,' he glances at his watch. 'I'll have to let you go now,' he says, 'any more questions before I leave you in peace?'

'How many on the trial?' I can't think of anything else to ask.

'Twenty. These numbers are repeated in hundreds of groups in hospitals up and down the country so plenty of other patients cooperating well. This ward now contains all the guinea pigs we're using for the current trials in Terminal Five. You may have noticed a flurry of activity on the ward yesterday. That was the other cooperative patients either discharged healthy or on to other wards.'

'I have to say I didn't, perhaps I was too caught up in my own world,' I mumble as he takes my arm.

'We have to go down to sign you in at the testing wing now, and they'll give you something to eat there which is superior to the food on the ward. That's because during the seminar on the trial, our medical team will be attending and will expect decent food. So you'll also enjoy that benefit. It won't always be as good! I need to take blood and urine samples now, before we head off.' He picks up my robe and places it on the bed. 'You can put this on after I've taken samples. I just need you to roll up your sleeve.' He motions towards one of his acolytes to take my tests.

Finally after we're done, the various fluids sealed, and labelled, and everyone has rubbed their hands with hygiene gel, I'm led from the ward. Liam waves to me; he's in the queue too, and shouts, 'A grand day out!' as he passes. Mark has been summoned and accompanies me when we join a parade of patients making their way towards the reception area of the Meds R Us wing.

I know from reading, that thwarted ambition is the cause of much grief and depression, so my decision to just allow things to happen, not arrange or hanker after anything, seemed a constructive idea when I first took the trip down Unemployment Avenue. I thought the extra time to chill would give me an opportunity to check out examples of my pet preoccupation: the retreat of trust in the face of the relentless march of bureaucracy. Now I'm beginning to have some doubt about my state of mind. Is the price of allowing too many of life's decisions out of my own hands becoming a tad high? At last I think I'm desperate enough to take any possible opportunity to scarper. But first I want to ascertain what the hell is going on here. I grab my briefcase to check out the schedule for the seminar I'll be attending as Patient Rep.

SEVEN

I wake early and push the pillow over my head to obliterate the noise of electronic knick-knacks. The SAS isn't attached; I'm outside the state boundary of Euphoria County. Worry over! Mark arrives to give me a velvet cocktail.

Ladders are up, men in overalls tap away at a sign above our ward door. The drama today is a new neon sign in purple, *'St Sepulchre's Ward, sponsored by Meds R Us'* above the entrance where I'd signed in yesterday.

I'm just about to relish the breakfast tray Nurse Tucked brings, when Liam scrambles uninvited onto my bed, tapping his nose and chortling in his usual obnoxious way. 'I have a plan for you,' he says, 'for a small consideration, I'll help you take a fantastical route out of here. Don't think I won't miss you, buddy, but I can see you're desperate to leave. Want to know the plan?' He grabs the roll off my plate and tucks in. 'Thanks.'

'There's a price?'

'Modest.'

'You know I've no cash yet. So tell me how I'm supposed to get my hands on a big a chunk of change you're likely demanding?'

'Got a surprise for you,' he says, 'want to take a peek?' He opens a plastic bag so that I can just glimpse a rolled-up white coat. 'Yours for a small consideration.'

'Where did you get it? I hope it isn't a used one.'

'Have faith in your buddy. Of course, it's newly laundered. Fresh as a nun's bum. You have two choices: you can either wear this and simply high-tail out of here, or go in a more traditional way, you know, via a laundry basket.'

'No chance of me getting in a laundry basket. And the risks if I just leave in the coat?'

'You might be called on to treat someone as you saunter out. They're short-staffed. And there's something else,' but before he can tell me what he means by this, he has to close the bag as we are interrupted by a posse of minders come to fetch me for the meeting.

I grab my briefcase, nod goodbye to Liam, and Mark takes my arm, leading me down the corridor and into a room where about fifty people are waiting. I'm handed a file of papers titled *Programme for the Future* in a blood-red plastic case.

Dr Doctor rises from where he's seated on a dais, introduces himself and greets us, saying it's wonderful to see so many colleagues keen to make history. As the new consultant clinical manager, he informs us, his first mission is to save Terminal Five from government bailiffs. He's on a five-year rotation, so that's how long he has to achieve this vital goal. 'As you can see,' he holds up his copy of the agenda, 'we have a dauntingly large programme before us. Today, we will look at why your compliance is essential in order to reach our targets for constitutional obligations in order to remain in the game. We'll discuss our own responsibilities and that of the patients in this regard, and hope their representatives here will take valuable lessons and proliferate the information among their fellow patients on their wards and then, if and when they are discharged, carry them out into the greater world at large.' He's definitely fixing his eyes on me and I am beginning to feel faint. I'm unnerved by finding Liam, who I thought I'd left behind, and hadn't noticed arriving, sitting right there beside me, nudging and winking for reasons completely lost on me.

Dr Doctor points his red laser baton on to the board, and the following words light up: '*Targets: Rights And Responsiblities; An Exchange.*' 'I want to open up the discussion to everyone present. I especially hope our patients will feel free to give us feedback on the seminar. You'll find the relevant form for this purpose at the end of the file in your briefcase.' *You've set yourself quite a challenge here, Doc*, I think, as I scan the row of zonked-out guinea pigs.

He points the baton at the board again and the word, '*Re-engineering*,' lights up. 'You may know about a recent study that looked at the efficacy of different types of hospital, including the larger GP super-surgeries. Many of our decisions to continue re-engineering the NHS are based on these findings. We need to continue to eliminate the small hospitals. It is absolutely evident from this document that it is imperative that we have a clearance sale of local and cottage hospitals and all smaller units, transferring these funds to larger centres of excellence, our flagships, the central terminals, such as we have here.' His light taps the floor with his virtual baton.

I have no idea what prompted me to interrupt him, though it could have been a result of my early morning dose of pop. 'Why?' I stand up and glance around to see if anyone is looking at me. I seemed to command the entire room's attention. 'Why are you eliminating small hospitals? Eliminate seems a drastic thing to do. Is it a euphemism? Are you going to blow them up? Or flog them off? To the private sector?'

Dr Doctor shows no surprise at my interruption. 'Of course, I can answer that. Good question. I'm glad you asked me. We'll come to that later. There will be time for discussions when I have finished speaking.' He smiles in a somewhat condescending way. 'I will continue, but it is a quite absurd suggestion that we would blow them up! A quite absurd suggestion. Goodness, health and safety would certainly have something to say if we did! No, we can exploit the property and sell them off. Private sector are happy to purchase ready-mades.'

'Could you explain why you want to get shot of them?' I ask. Liam starts violently nudging me. I ignore him.

'We know that the smaller hospitals are not cost-effective. The stats up and down the country consistently show the same thing. The experts' consensus is that there is no justification for the expense that they command. As I said, I'll come to that later,' he glances down at his consultation paper, 'let us continue our discussion on the re-engineering plans.'

'Can you tell me why the smaller hospitals are so expensive?' I butt in again. 'Is it about capital expense, you know, I mean, is it because they use capital expenses on, for instance, a scanner that isn't used twenty-four-seven in a small hospital, but would be in a central terminal?' I'm beginning to feel a little out of my depth, and confused about the fact that I'm flashing down Sabotage Street without the slightest hesitation or concern for the damage it may do to my own welfare and any real knowledge of what I'm talking about. Look, I was too timid to ever put myself forward at work, and even consistently and constantly turned down proposed promotion, so what on earth has happened to make me so offensively pushy now? I try to sit down but cannot do so as my knees refuse to bend so that short of falling back on the chair, not a good look, I am obliged to reluctantly remain standing more or less immobilised. Right there. Centre stage. In a spotlight.

'Capital expense in smaller community hospitals? Oh, no.' He laughs. He had been tapping his file on the microphone while I was speaking, nearly drowning out what I had been saying, though curiously he stops for a moment before he begins to speak. 'Nothing like that. It's just that they keep the patients in far too long. We need to proceed with details of our re-engineering proposals for our own centre of excellence,' he says firmly. 'No more interruptions, please, or we'll get nowhere.' He presses a bell on his lectern.

'You've ducked the question,' I say, 'you haven't left room for discussion about flogging off smaller hospitals. And to whom? You indicated it is a fait accompli without discussion,' I continue, while he looks incredulously at me as the lights are turned up even more and indeed it feels as if I am caught in a sort of military-strength searchlight and any moment now a stealth bomber will begin its journey in my direction.

'Remind me of your name, young man,' he says.

'John.'

'And your surname?'

'You know I can't remember it,' I retort.

'So even though you are unable to remember your own name, you think you know more about this than I?' He chortles and looks around the room. 'Dear me, the patients know more than the doctors. Perhaps we should just consult you about everything.'

'Good plan. I thought you wanted consultation with feedback from us,' I say, 'all I want is just to know about patients in the community hospitals that you say are not cost-effective. The patients? Are more of them cured and discharged alive?' I ask, walking myself straight down into the wrecker's yard. He presses a bell on the side of his lectern. Am I securely in the crosshairs now? Is a drone on the way?

'Well,' he's looking heated, 'we're not looking at patient outcomes,' he laughs, 'that's not on the agenda or in the statistics.' He raises his hand to end the conversation. I notice two men come through the door and walk towards me. 'You're making a public nuisance of yourself,' Dr Doctor tut-tuts, 'pressured speech can be a symptom of a serious mental health problem,' he says in a loud voice to the room in general.

'You shouldn't say that. What about patient confidentiality?' I shout at him. 'Patient confidentiality!' I shout again, in case he didn't hear me the first time. Cue for two white coats to appear at the entrance. I've driven at full speed into a dead-end car park. Brakes squealing. No change. No card. Traffic warden approaching. Ah, no, a stealth bomber. No, it's a drone. Either way, I'm fucked. Ah, again I'm not quite accurate. It's two white-coated psychiatric paramedics, lanyards swaying. They take an arm each and drag me towards the exit.

EIGHT

A couple of hours later Dr Cross comes in to check me out. Since she caught me with my beard in the letterbox and I confessed to her my pathetic excuse for eavesdropping – she has been ultra-kind. I'm hoping her sympathy stems from understanding the hollow in my heart from lack of female company, and/or even better, an interest in me. Otherwise I don't really understand how she can forgive such a gross transgression as overhearing her at her most vulnerable self. I remember, after I opened my eyes, she pulled me up from my prostrate position and listened to me stammering the truth to her without responding with the slightest pejorative retort. I surprised even myself by being so lacking in imagination that I was unable to lie.

Now she asks if I've calmed down. And says that she has to assess my mental state. After a few questions relating to whether or not I ever listen to anyone else, tick, especially female, tick, tick, not funny, John, and if I felt anxious, tick, she says that, no, there's very little wrong with me. And that I'm probably not suffering from pressured speech, but I could be overcome with frustration and powerlessness and a feeling of not being heard. And yes, I am right, Dr Doctor had no right to shout out this diagnosis to the assembled company. 'Pressured speech can sometimes be a symptom of a mental health problem, but in your case I think it might just be that you were overenthusiastic and excited at the occasion and perhaps it was a response to intimidation. Under pressure we all do it sometimes,' she laughs, 'don't worry too much about whether or not you have a mental health problem. All of us are somewhere on the spectrum, as I mentioned to you before. I feel that on the whole you are usually quite measured in your responses, day to day, but you could do with building a bit of resilience to being thwarted. A bit more patience would serve you well, John. Everything you asked in the meeting made logical sense,' she says, 'except that your interruption and manner was inappropriate under the circumstances. I'm not going to recommend you for anger management,' she says, 'I think you have a passionate nature, and that you sometimes express this tactlessly. Nothing too serious.' She smiles as she signs something and I like her use of the word passionate. 'I find it's always more gentlemanly to let someone finish what they are saying before questioning it. Don't let this put you off being a Patient Representative. We need people to question political and significant decisions. You can go back to the meeting this afternoon. They'll be discussing the patients' rights and responsibilities,' she says, 'it's a pity you missed the list of NHS rights and responsibilities this morning. But it isn't a secret. You can obtain a copy from our patient services department. But for now, although I don't think you should be in hospital at all, I'm discharging you back to St Sepulchre's. You haven't had any visitors, have you, John?'

'No,' I say, 'nobody knows I'm here. I don't really have anyone.' I slide down to Self-Pity City, feeling like a little baby orphan who wants just to snuggle up and listen to lovely Dr Cross's reassuring heartbeat.

'Perhaps you should contact that friend of yours that you mentioned, Megan, was it? Was that her name?' She mirrors my nodding head.

'That was over long ago,' I say, 'she's history.'

'Not to herself. I'm surprised at your attitude and that's not the impression you gave me. It would be good to have a visitor though, wouldn't it? You must feel a bit isolated here. A long-stay ward is a difficult place for patients. I think that despite being surrounded by people, there's still the danger of feeling very cut off. It's good to see people who are old friends and faces from home.' She smiles encouragingly.

'I don't know where she is.' My voice is almost stammering. I'm shocked by the term "long-stay ward". She's just told me I shouldn't be here, so apart from Liam's scam to see me out in a white coat, that I can't follow through without cash or risk, my only hope is that she'll discharge me if I play my cards right. On the other hand, any chance I might have to acquaint myself better with her would be lost.

'Well,' she pats my bed, 'maybe it would be good to have a little think and see if you can remember how to contact her.' I know, with absolute certainty, that if Megan knew the conditions I've somehow managed to get myself into, she'd be in here giving me a very hard time before tenaciously demanding my release from the head honcho. 'Perhaps you can remember where Megan lives. You see, John, I have a little problem with you. You can remember Megan's name, but not your own. How is that, do you think?'

Now this is a tricky one. 'I don't have an answer.'

'It seems to me that if you thought long and hard, you might recall what Megan called you.'

'Many unrepeatable names,' and then I wonder how you go about thinking long and hard. 'I'll do my best,' I say.

'Good. As I said, it's not that I personally feel you should be here, but my hands are tied. I wonder if you realise how serious some of the side effects of long-term pharmacological testing will be on both your mental and physical well-being, John. Confidentially, I do recommend that if you can possibly remember who you are, then you'd be wise to apply for your medical records. And get out of here as smartly as you can,' she said with a small smile and she suddenly leaves me to contemplate my future.

Beds on an acute psychiatric ward are in even greater shortage than on almost any other ward, Mark tells me as he leads me away. So I am bounced back to St Sepulchre's quick like a bunny. I lie quietly, holding onto my naturally sourced place in the oblivion queue and am cruising down Comfort Street after the kind words of Dr Cross.

But en route I hit a hazard in the shape of Dr Doctor now squinting down at me, telling me that he "has concerns" about my suitability to remain on St Sepulchre's Ward, or indeed, with all my "issues" to be Fit for Purpose in his ward (which I take him to mean for his research programme). He's holding a piece of paper and indicating that I sign. Now this is highly suspicious. I want to leave, of course, but definitely not at his say-so. Only in my own time. I'm also beginning to think that the outside world might not be the safest place for me for many tedious reasons. But most importantly and strategically, I'm curious about manoeuvres here which would best be exposed, it seems to me, and the extent of which I have only just begun to comprehend. This stay is giving me a unique opportunity to study the machinations of how bureaucracy functions in this institution, which is, as you know, one of my dearly held preoccupations. Also, rare for me though it is, I have a slight feeling of responsibility and even more rarely, a sliver of decisiveness. So although I also have reservations about my safety if I remain here, on balance it is an entirely unique standpoint from which to experience my own obsession and write an exposé. Quitting now would waste that opportunity. And also, of course, there's the faint possibility that Dr Cross will be safer with me around or something. 'I thought we agreed that I couldn't be discharged without patient records,' I tell him, 'so what's the hurry to chuck me out?'

'Well, John, I could leave that to your imagination. You seem to have a well-developed capacity to make up stories.'

'That doesn't sound like me.'

'It does to me. That performance in the meeting? A quite astonishing calumny. We were forced to take cover from your dreadful outburst and delay an important discussion. Not good news for Terminal Five, is it? Without our plans being implemented, we run a serious risk of the terminal being closed. Yes, yes, and therefore letting down patients with urgent needs. I think you'll agree with me that it's not right, is it, to hold up our valuable work? I really do not know what you meant to achieve. Your outburst leads me to have serious and deep concerns about your level of paranoia and your mental state,' he sits on the end of the bed. 'I think it is time to let you go before you ransack the hospital's reputation. I'm sure the good you, the one you could access before the accident, would agree. Yes?'

'Ha, ha. Come on, Doc, you guys are way too big to be threatened by a little ant such as myself; an out of work, homeless, slightly unwell and mentally incapacitated individual.'

'I think you know exactly what you are doing, but perhaps are not entirely responsible for your actions today. So off you go. Just sign here first. We can't compromise our research by using someone who doesn't cooperate completely.'

'I can't sign if I don't know my name.' There followed a rather silly confrontation where he insisted that I must have signed something on my release from the psych ward – which I denied – and I was to use that same signature for his form. In desperation I tell him I felt that the drugs they were testing on me were responsible for my out-of-character outburst and that if I was released I would certainly sue them for putting me on the drugs without my signed agreement. After all, it would be impossible for me to sign anything without a name.

'We don't have you on any drugs,' he says.

'Nothing? You expect me to believe that? This cannula thing in my arm, attached to a drip bag, attached to the thing that I have to drag around, and with a syringe which I can depress whenever I like – what is this? My little pet?'

'Oh, the SAS? For your protection we are rehydrating you before allowing you to take part in testing, and also you were prescribed a mild sedative for use when you felt the need. For your own protection. It's considered very safe as the sedative doesn't have any counter-indications for use with other medications. And of course, you are self-administering whatever it is. So not a good case for litigation, is it?'

'So why do I feel so strange?'

'I have no idea, John. We don't know what trauma you suffered that was so serious you lost your memory.' He tells me that being deprived of oxygen while in the water probably caused my amnesia and only a series of scans over a period of time would possibly solve the question of whether the damage is reversible. I don't know why, but he decided to confide in me that American drug research institutions tested on healthy subjects, often illegal immigrants who were paid very little. But he pointed out that our current cohorts here are paid handsomely. I didn't have the bottle to point out that I've no name, no bank account, so have received no dosh yet. Perhaps to put himself in a good light, he tells me that in the past the US pharmacological research programmes also employed psychiatrically disturbed patients whose vulnerability was entirely discounted with disastrous reactions. It resulted in the death of several patients, until these institutions lost their licence. So there is a model of paying guinea pigs for their contribution in the US, he told me, by using unfit but seriously ill patients as well as healthy ones. In his opinion, it's different here. Individuals here are motivated by a desire to make a positive impact on the world by assisting in the production of safe medications for pharmacological companies. For those who are unemployed it is a sound, ethical way for them to contribute to the good of society while having the dignity of earning their own income and becoming less of a drain on the public purse. 'We pay a living wage, and they have their fifteen minutes of fame,' he finishes, 'so it's a win-win situation.'

'That sounds as if it qualifies me to stay here. As you already know, I'm unemployed,' I replied and got up to get coffee, offering to bring one over for him also.

'Thanks,' he nods, 'I will. And you are correct, John. You suffer from mild paranoia, very common in this day and age, almost normal, you could say, so I think you are mentally fit enough to take part,' and so without any more argument he makes a U-turn. Though I felt for just a millisecond that he smiles as he leaves me. As if he has somehow got the better of me and not the other way round. But that could be my paranoia, as he calls it. How am I ever going to be able to tell the difference?

After he left, I take a hike around looking for Liam. I haven't seen him since I was hauled out of the meeting. I want his reflections on that event, but when I find him he's sitting on his bed looking forlorn. He isn't pleased with me. 'You're my friend,' he says, 'I don't want to lose you and besides there's opportunities here, which you will miss out on if you leave.'

I tell him that although the doc nearly threw me out of the hospital for bad behaviour in the meeting, I don't want to leave him either and that I've talked my way back off the naughty step.

'I thought you wanted to leave. How come you changed your mind?' he asks. 'Why is everyone doing a U-turn?'

'I'm more comfortable waiting a bit to exit left,' I say, 'I'm curious about how this whole scenario plays out,' I tell him, 'and there's not much in the way of opportunity left for me in civilian life at the moment. I've seriously screwed things up there. Furthermore, I'll lose out on the payment for this research programme if I can't remember my name, as I don't have a bank account,' I tell him, 'so I need to remember who I am before leaving.'

He suggests he could help me by laundering my earnings through his account. Would they be party to transferring my funds to his account? I think not. Do I trust him? I decide not to worry about this right now. Besides, I have everything I need as long as I'm a resident here.

He tells me trust drug trials don't carry a high tariff, whereas highly invasive, risky procedures like endoscopy are far more lucrative. He wants to go for the big money but they questioned his suitability and altruistic motivation and have temporarily sanctioned his request until they ascertain his responses with the simpler tests. They also want to evaluate his commitment to the cause. After the current programme, if everything goes to plan, then he'll be assessed for suitability to join the waiting list of graduates to substantially more unpleasant but elevated tariff procedures. 'I have a high pain threshold,' he says, 'might as well capitalise on whatever gifts I have, and besides, there's always the SAS for a little relief.'

Mark is wearing a white coat when he arrives to take Liam and me down to the Soft Day Area. He removes the umbilical cord of my 'rehydration kit'. As we walk together along the corridor, he laughs about my performance in the strategy meeting, and says he is surprised to find me still here, telling me that he liked the way I challenged the doc and not to give up talking sense. He added that it would be great if I continued to question what was going on but warned me to be wary of being chucked out if I seemed too much of a threat to their plans. Actually he used the phrase, 'a pain in the neck'. I tell him that Dr Doctor and I had already sufficiently sorted out our differences so that I am to be kept on as the Patient Observer. He seems surprised I'd won the right to be reinstated. 'You don't know the half of it,' he says, 'they're looking to use more volunteers to work in even more departments. I heard a rumour they've substantially overspent last year's budget so that it's been cut back another twenty-five per cent for this year, making it impossible to run the show.' I promise him I will glean whatever information I can and feed it back to him if he wants me to, if he isn't kidding, but is really keen to know.

NINE

A dozen of us are seated around the perimeter of the Soft Day Area. According to Mark, this has been designated as a relaxation day-room for guinea pigs to hang out. He suggests that we introduce ourselves and try to bond with each other. Besides Liam, there's Graham, Rob, Adam, Kev, Dave, Scott, Ade, Ryan, Steve and Zak. Mark hands out lanyards to everyone. 'Wearing them will make it easy for all of you to remember who's who,' he tells us. The lanyards carry the legend '*Team Fides*' – to give us a sense of group identity, he insists. He hands us all a plastic folder and iPad for our feedback.

The room is very warm. We sit in comfortable, low, soft, jade-coloured, velvety easy chairs around a room that has a trompe l'oeil sky-blue ceiling, complete with small clouds. I think, why not use deck chairs to complete the picture? And make a mental note to suggest this in the feedback form. The walls are decorated convincingly to represent a garden, with flowering bushes of pink clematis entwined through tiny white roses climbing to the sky and there are flowers in front with miniature red peony bushes, and scattered among them, cornflowers and lavender. I must say the technique is astonishingly effective; convincingly like being imprisoned inside by the flowers and bushes outside. It is weird. One of the men staggers across and makes as if to pick a flower, but backs off when his head hits the wall. In one corner puffs of fragrance are dispensed from an ivory-coloured diffuser while bees appear gently buzzing, alighting on the flowers. I am confused by this until I realise that the bees are holograms. The effect is perfect and surreal. Mark reiterates that this Soft Day Area is for our exclusive use and we are to take advantage, using it whenever we feel the need to relax or are stressed. He points out a fountain and water dispenser and suggests we all help ourselves in an orderly fashion. The whole effect of light, soft buzzing, diffused scent and cosy chairs is soporific. We do as we are told.

A man in a white coat appears through what appears to be a glass conservatory door convincingly painted onto the wall opposite the entrance where we came in. He has a stethoscope around his neck and tells us that his name is Roger, and says we are destined to be part of medical history. This is because every new development in medical solutions requires some of what he describes as quietly heroic people who care about humanity and especially those who are vulnerable and sick. I wish he hadn't said that because it makes me trust him less, but I am here now and I certainly haven't had this experience before and the results could be interesting. Liam puts up his hand. 'What sort of experiments are you going to do? Do you mean on us?'

'I'm glad you asked that,' Roger smiles at him, 'it's a good question. I want you to all get to know each other. There are twelve of you left who were selected from the original twenty volunteers, so you're a pretty exclusive group. Privileged, you could say. We will start with refreshments,' and then he indicates a trolley filled with goodies that I hadn't noticed before. 'I'll take your photographs and transfer them to the lanyards so you'll all have accurate IDs, and effortlessly be able to get to know each other. Do any of you know any others here?' Liam again puts his hand up. He nods in my direction and says he knows me.

'Fine. A good start,' Roger says, 'I'd like you to interact with each other, spend time together doing whatever it is you like to do.'

'Where's the bar so we can get tanked up?' It's Liam, of course.

'Not quite what I had in mind. Can't have you all "tanked up", as you say,' Roger replies, 'but there'll be drinks at the appropriate moment. He methodically takes our pictures, prints our IDs and inserts them in the lanyards while we sit on the cosy velvet seats and finish our drinks. Eventually we are all labelled and good to go. I see my identity is still John Anon.

'We need to go through the protocol,' Roger says, 'the time element taking place today is sponsored by the hospital who only receive payment for the expertise of our research team after the results are published.'

'What about us?' Liam is quickly on his feet.

'I'll come to that in a minute. You will need to sign the terms and conditions agreement, where details of the remuneration protocol will be found. And also accept our disclaimer. Briefly, to answer Liam's query, yes, in line with information you already have, as long as the test programme continues you will be paid an ongoing sum directly into your bank account weekly. And a further sum when the results of our research are published. To protect your privacy we will of course use pseudonyms when publishing data about specific patient reactions. And if you don't already have a bank account, we'll open an account in your name for the duration of your stay.'

He tells us there are valuable benefits while staying here on our new journey, and he intends to take us around the whole area designated for our use. It has a number of excellent activities for us to enjoy, a gym and games room and other leisure pleasures. 'No expense has been spared,' he continues, 'as the prototype group of this new initiative, it is appropriate that you have the best of everything. You will understand that the success of this first trial will determine if further trials will be undertaken in the same way. So you carry quite a burden for success. I trust that you are all happy and honoured to take part, agreeing to become the trail-blazers in what will be a world record, a part of medical history wherever our pharmaceutical solutions are celebrated.'

'And we'll be earning big spondoolies for you guys, yes?' Liam says.

'Sure. You'll be helping the hospital into the black.'

He explains that drug trialling programmes usually take thousands of volunteers, costing very large sums. We are one of several groups in these settings, who together, as we are isolated, reduce the numbers needed for the trials, thereby eliminating unnecessary costs. From these limited but very secure numbers, extrapolations are made, and conclusions drawn. 'So you should understand how important it is to stay in the trial because in a small study every member counts, and if anyone leaves it will invalidate the whole thing.' Finally, he reiterates that after the hospital receive payment for the results of their research, we will all receive a very substantial bonus payout. This sum will be forfeited if anyone leaves as it invalidates the results. He points out that there are not endless opportunities for most unemployed people, without good work references, to earn good money while enjoying themselves. At this point two white-coated medics arrive and meds are distributed – a couple of pills and a small vial of water to wash them down.

Roger says we'll be given an outline of what to expect in the coming weeks and he leads us through to a well-equipped gym. He tells us that it's very important – indeed, part of the bargain with the pharma company – that people invested in the trial don't die. We have been chosen for relative fitness, you could say. He laughs. 'We expect you to spend an hour per day in here. Preferably in the morning. There's a place in your records to document exactly how long you spend in the gym, and what particular equipment you use, and for how long – no cheating now!' He chortles. 'Each piece of equipment will document the user and usage. We expect you to leave here fitter and healthier than when you arrived. I want you to take a minute to talk to our resident physio, Jim, who is here,' and he slants his arm towards a well-trimmed young man who nods, grins and says, 'Hi,' with a wave of his hand towards us. 'He will explain the workings of different equipment after assessing your level of fitness. Take good advantage of Jim in the gym,' he laughs, 'a great asset to you and to us.' Roger indicates for us to follow him.

We are in a well-equipped screening room lit by discreet lighting. A huge screen illuminates one wall, on another side, a troop of computer screens march along a long shelf, with chairs opposite each one. There's a slight buzz, and not just from the equipment. I can see that for most of us, sitting here scrolling through our fave programmes might be the easiest of options. 'Time on these screens is limited.' Roger is obviously responding to the sudden interest from his charges. 'And the chairs can be turned for watching on a big screen as a group. The screen will sense if there are less than four people watching and turn off. We want you all to bond, not to isolate, which is an easy thing to do if you don't get to know each other.' He smiles and looks around at the assembled gang of murmuring men. 'We want you to form a friendly tribe, to cooperate and take an interest in, and care for each other and develop a healthy, common purpose. That's how communities are formed in the outside world, or should be, but we are fast losing this capacity. We want you guys to try to alleviate the loneliness you might feel being cut off from your nearest and dearest. The best way to do this is by being a good team member and committing to this group of your fellow warriors in the fight against a common enemy – disease.' He handles his lanyard. 'I want you to look at this, *your* lanyard, *your* badge of honour, you might say; *Team Fides*. Take a moment to contemplate its significance. The meaning of fides is fidelity and trust. I'm sure you'll agree that it's an honour to carry this label. It is a pact that is based on reciprocity. We make that pledge to you also.'

Liam nudges me. 'Pretentious git,' he whispers, 'bloody Latin. Designed to intimidate us with his superior knowledge. We'll call ourselves The Drug Squad.' He laughs and I nod agreement and laugh with him – like a couple of naughty school kids at the back of the room.

Roger tells us we'll have regular blood and urine tests, and as they've already been completed this morning, that's all fine and we can take lunch now in the canteen. He hopes we'll try to become friends while we enjoy the meal together, before a quiet leisure break. He leads us through to the canteen. While we eat, Roger explains what to expect in the next few weeks.

Half the team are given meds to elicit trust and half given a placebo in what is called a blind test, meaning we will not be told who had received what. It seems to me that as trust is a highly subjective emotion, it'll be difficult to measure. I keep this thought to myself. Roger explains that every day at 10am we are to attend the Soft Day Area for our dose of medication, after which we are expected to take exercise, preferably in the gym. For the duration of the trial we are trusted to make a note of any unusual feelings we have in our feedback file, giving times and dates. There is a tick list with examples of feelings; we must fill this in three times a day until the programme finishes. Graham asks what side effects can be expected. Roger reassures him that so far as he knew, we should experience none. But if we do, then it is important to flag it up to him, and imperative that we make a note in our feedback file of any difficulties we encounter.

After collecting our lunch and drink (I choose a passable smoked salmon on rye and coffee, plus a glass of water) we assemble. There's room on the long table for all twelve guinea pigs, six down each side on benches, with Roger at the head. I notice Liam sitting diametrically opposite me on the other side and next to Roger. I have to introduce myself again to my neighbours. Graham on one side, and on the other, David, who speaks in a very quiet, nervous voice, swallowing his words somewhat, as he shakes hands. 'Pleased to meet you.' It's difficult to make friends to order, so I ask him what he does in civilian life. He looks confused by the question, and in reply, asks what I do. He looks even more baffled when I tell him I can't remember. At the other end of the table there is a murmur of voices and laughter generated by Liam, who's in a cheerful mood.

Roger says we've already been allocated our random group; half have received a shot of the trust drug, and the other half consist of the control group. This information feeds once more into my doubt about the advisability of agreeing to take part in research, and how powerful is the drug I was given this morning? As the day wears on, I do not feel completely myself.

Roger leads us, with Mark, along a short corridor, pointing out the toilets on the way, and into the Soft Day Area. In the brief time we were away, it seems to have been transformed. This is impossible, of course, but I don't remember the room being quite so extravagantly tall or so well-lit. I'm engulfed in a feeling of unreality as I glance around, buzzing hologram bees now in swarms and little butterflies attending to flowers. Curiously enough, the sight of them satisfying their natural proclivity, albeit only in virtual reality, you might say, is satisfyingly reassuring. This last thought could be construed as being mildly off the wall. This artificial sky seems even bluer with the clouds now apparently scudding by as the higher fronds of an upright, earnest-looking palm tree drift in the virtual wind or perhaps, in this case, the movement is precipitated by a small, silent fan. The walls are decorated with a huge variety of exotic plants growing in layers, on balcony-like structures. The fountain cascades at the centre of the far wall and seems seriously loftier than when we first saw it. Goldfinches fly around higher than we can reach, accompanied by a variety of birdsong. A couple of tiny wrens scurry happily around the third layer of foliage. A blackbird sits on the end of a branch tapping against a wall that is not far off my height. I look questioningly at my fellow guinea pigs but they seem unperturbed by the changes to the landscape and begin to seat themselves in a most relaxed manner in the velvet chairs around the perimeter. I'm drawn towards the fountain, mesmerised as I watch cascading water disappear into a plughole in a shell on the floor.

'Is this alien environment part of the experiment? By extracting us from anything we have ever experienced to see how we react?' I ask Roger.

'I can't see what you mean,' he says. 'Nothing wrong with this Soft Day Area, and to call it alien is ungrateful. We made every effort to see that you're comfortable in a pleasant place. No expense spared, as I said before. It may interest you to know that we subscribe to the notion that people thrive best in aesthetically pleasing environments. After all, the first housing estates contained a variety of wall paintings. For instance, the caves in Lascaux in France are perhaps the most well-known example of wall paintings going back many thousands of years. And many more sites have been discovered recently in all parts of the world. Animals were a common subject for these early painters, and so what do we have here? Nature in all her glory. Nobody else seems concerned by your worries,' he says, and it's true, everyone is seated comfortably, some chatting away, others just silently relaxing. I sit staring into the water as Roger wishes us luck, smiles and disappears through a glass door concealed behind the waterfall. He's gone before I can ask him where it leads, but not before I resolve to discover.

This is how it is working now; every morning after breakfast we line up for our meds. I must add here that I am nauseous most of the time and feeling physically weak. Liam is in Group A and myself in Group B. Are they really testing trust? None of us seems especially trusting about anything or anyone, but could that just be because we are either testing something completely different – which would probably account for the deterioration in my health, or am I suffering paranoia as suggested by Dr Doctor – which is mollified by the trust drug they are, after all, giving me? And is there a possibility that those in Group A are actually given, say, a truth drug? And do the monitor's assistants, a group of work-experience kids with addiction problems, sometimes reverse the doses of A and B, either for fun or because they are confused, having taken something stronger themselves? Or indeed our dose. We are undeniably an odd bunch; all of us have rocked up into A and E recently, and most are either unemployed or homeless, suffering mental health problems and often all the above. So perhaps we are not yet entirely typical of the population at large, though the way things are going it won't be long before we are.

I'm relaxing in the Soft Day Area when Liam trots over, saying he's formed some great contacts in the group, and will be dealing in films and things. He wants to discuss strategy with me. 'Not really a scam,' he says, 'more like another grand opportunity for a little pleasure to pass the time for all of us and a fundraiser for you and for me. Well, for a start we can organise a pop-up porn shop. I have the kit. And the viewing room allocated to us is bloody perfect.' When I don't show sufficient interest, he nudges me, telling me I still owe him. 'White coats come at a price, John. I've already had to shell out for the one you haven't bothered to use. I've stored it in a safe place. Ready for when you want it. We could have you sprung in a laundry basket,' he continues, 'bit smelly, but easier and historically successful. I'll wait until you've earned enough for the journey.' I tell him I've already said I'm not interested in the old laundry basket trick as I don't want to leave smothered in germs thank you very much. Besides, I can just walk out. When I'm ready.

Seeing I'm still not too keen doesn't put him off. After a gym session, he wants to meet up to discuss his plans again in the Soft Day Area, which I have to say I have a nasty feeling may be bugged.

A couple of days later at a lunchtime meeting of the whole group, Roger joins us. As tea and coffee is circulated, Roger asks questions about how the team is getting on. We nod and murmur, with a couple of yeses, and 'fine,' but this level of engagement doesn't seem to satisfy him. 'So, ready for discharge then?'

'No.' Graham, a tall man with a beard, looking slightly scruffy and with a tired-looking stoop, replies. 'I thought we were going to continue until the research is completed.'

'That's the plan. But I'm sensing a lack of commitment and engagement from the team, and you have all given less feedback than we agreed, so unless you can be more proactive, we'll discharge you and try out another set of guinea pigs. I haven't had anybody hand in a complete set of their feedback forms yet. So you are not being any help to us. We need them completed and handed in every day, please, if you are to continue to have our hospitality. Whether or not you feel like it. You're only useful for the research programme if you completely comply. So far, none of you have obliged as agreed under terms and conditions. If you don't, we will discharge and replace you.'

'Well, I haven't anywhere else to go,' says Zak.

'That's not the issue here. Perhaps you need to rethink your commitment. It's up to you. Your cooperation is not optional once you are signed up for the duration of the programme. If you do feel the need to cut out now, we will have to send everyone away and start the whole experiment from the beginning with a new group of volunteers. You will, I am sure, realise this is not cost-effective for us to abandon the tests now. We cannot do the research piecemeal. To give the research any validity we need all those who start, to remain until the end. If you really want to stay, then you must fill out feedback forms now and retrospectively, immediately, while you can remember. And daily from now on. Do not fall into arrears again. Six o'clock would be perfect. To remind you, the box in this room,' he pointed to what appeared to be a postbox, 'this is where you need to drop the completed forms.' He hands out printed forms, and clipboards to those who haven't brought their own, and for a while we all sit quietly trying to record the feelings and responses we had for the last couple of days since meds or placebos were administered.

The first bunch of questions were about how we felt, and apart from being tempted to put 'horny' after each one, I gave the nearest approximation of what I thought would be more appropriate. After the personal questions, there were questions about the monitor, the environment, what we felt about the Soft Day Area, how we felt overall, what we thought of our fellow team members, whether our mood changed during the day, if we thought the world was a safe place, if we felt suicidal, and what we thought about the various professional people we encountered and then about whether or not we would recommend this research programme. Another question was would we recommend this particular A and E department? If I was seriously injured I'd go to the nearest A and E, so while the question made me chuckle aloud, I had to restrain myself from answering facetiously. I'm surprised they didn't ask if we'd recommend Volvos. Well, if I'd been driving one I'd have had fast-track service. So a no-brainer.

TEN

The following day, after breakfast and the distribution of meds – or a placebo – in the Soft Day Area, Mark slips a lanyard over my head. The lanyard discloses that I'm a Patient Rep and Mark leads me into the seminar room where I'm invited to use the hygiene gel. I'm sweating and search for a tissue, find one in my pocket, and wipe my face and hands. Apart from Mark I'm otherwise stranded alone in a row of identical office chairs in a large room and in a hollow on the small shelf-like attachment to my chair is a glass of water. I pick it up and am considering its qualities, and hold it up to the light. Mesmerised by the shifting luminous brilliance of the substance, I feel that I have never really seen a glass of water before. I notice tiny, shiny fragments of some intangible provenance floating in it, causing my knee-jerk paranoid response to almost spoil the magic of the moment. While I am contemplating the extravagant beauty of water in a glass, wondering what it would be like to encounter something so clearly glorious for the very first time, I am aware that the room is filling with other peeps.

Looking around, I see some are wearing the artefacts that reveal them to be medics, and some peeps are in formal suits. But there's no sign of any of the guinea pigs, so I am aware that being their representative may require an assiduous concentration to detail that, in my present state of mind, I could be lacking. I begin to count the other peeps in the room, and as I do so, seek unsuccessfully to identify anyone I know.

My thoughts are interrupted by abrupt sounds, a harsh clearing of the throat, the scrape of a chair, a tapping of the mic, and someone suddenly lurches into, '…the policy for today; self-directed recovery, or patient-directed recovery,' the team leader, Duncan says, with a look of self-satisfaction, after introducing himself. He turns to direct his red LED pointer at these words on a large screen. 'The answer to the future is through AI. Self-directed recovery,' he repeats. 'Can anyone suggest what this might mean?' Mindful of the privilege I carry to represent our group, and like any good journo, I begin to take notes, as Dr Cross had suggested.

Before anyone replies to his question, Duncan explains that this new policy is one of the most powerful new tools in our armoury of recovery, involving the patient in a direct way with their own care. He tells us that The Trust is currently rolling out this new initiative whereby patients take responsibility for their own well-being. 'To give the patient maximum choices. It's not just that it's incumbent on patients for economic reasons relating to essential budget cuts, but self-directed recovery is deeply empowering for the patient. In a limited way, it was trialled in some GP surgeries during the pandemic.

Research has now proved SDR to have longer-lasting and greater effect than conventional medicine. Though medical mishaps are rare, they occasionally happen followed by inevitable litigation, and in patient-choice-of-treatment, this is avoided,' he tells us. 'A patient,' he emphasises, 'is able to judge how he or she feels, better than anyone else.' And he nods to the audience, some of whom echo a nod in agreement. 'We all know how informing patients of available therapy choices and allowing them a decision about their treatment, boosts the prognosis. Making those choices has proved efficacious and is currently seen, quite rightly, as good practice. We are developing strategies to take this one step further. Moving our practices into the twenty-first century at last. Empowering people saves funds, and on the way we will be educating the population. Whatever way we frame it, this is a win-win situation. By pulling back on the use of our precious staff and resources, and unnecessarily and expensive interventions, the creative practice of SDR frees up funds that the hospital can put to better use. The model for this has long been in use in substance abuse and proved to be easily the most effective and economic form of therapy. Do I need to remind you folk of the value of Alcoholics Anonymous? You will know that it has undeniably saved millions of lives since its inception before the Second World War. This is not the only example. Narcotics Anonymous followed and many other peer groups and self-help organisations will testify to their success in their own fields.

'However, I don't want to hide from you the fact that, as with any therapy, there are some drawbacks to which hospital staff must be alerted; some patients may take the opportunity to recommend inappropriate and expensive procedures. To avoid this, as much as technically possible, we will install foolproof, secure electronic safeguards. With cooperation from the Department of Health, we are in the process of developing, fine-tuning, testing and tracing, and installing the necessary electronic routes to be rolled out to all our patients. We will make full use of AI and our team will work on taking full advantage of rolling out the most effective algorithms. Our hospital is rapidly becoming a centre of excellence, and we want to be seen as a model throughout this country and beyond, for what we are, and can achieve. In this new initiative – for all your hard work, your effort, cooperation, contribution and expertise, you people should all be proud. Take a bow.

'But ancient rituals hold us back. We need to move forward, to take the lead. The ward round, for instance…' he looks around the room, '…is less than efficient in both time and energy. Yes, I know, old doctors learnt their precious trade in this way. But now? Is this archaic ritual really the best use of time? Is it just a nostalgic old anachronism, passed down from one generation to another? Could we more usefully direct patients to automatically monitor their own vital signs, check-out their readings and blood results on a personal electronic diagnostic tool? Could work-experience youngsters be usefully employed to explain to technophobic patients how to monitor themselves? You bet. And our medical students, could they best be trained by self-directed study as are other students, studying other subjects, in universities and colleges up and down the country? Are our medical and nursing students sufficiently able to learn this way? You bet they are.

'We have to ask ourselves these questions and the answer to all of them is a resounding yes. I want to keep you good medical folk in the loop about transformations in practice that you must usefully anticipate, and how you are expected to implement them. Just as patients will need to design their own care packages, you medical people need to help us formulate our policies and practices. Although I do not want to denigrate the value of ward rounds as sources of information and as teaching aids, they're not cost-effective. Archaic rituals hamper progress and perpetuate the medicalisation of health, the diametric opposite of how things will move forward into a more holistic pattern in the future where patients take care of themselves. We want to deliver twenty-first-century health!' Some of the audience look around at each other, eyebrows are raised, coughing and murmuring, before he continues, 'In the Third World, people die early of diseases we can cure, and of poverty and lack of nutrition. In the First World, the recent pandemic excepted, we most commonly die of lifestyle choices. Health will be just another of these choices.' He glances triumphantly around the room.

'Already, the move to close local hospitals, and to keep and expand only the large central establishments, and to discharge patients into their own homes and care homes for treatment, is well under way and working effectively. It is only a further small step towards self-directed recovery. SDR procedures are a natural extension of existing home blood-pressure monitors, medication vending machines, DIY blood analysis kits, test and trace kits, SAS – Self Administration System for complex pharmacological dispensing – fingerprint, DNA data, city-centre auto scanners and dopplers et cetera. And soon,' he looks around the room, smiling, his hands out in supplication or perhaps benediction, 'management and patients will form a force to determine the direction of their own hospital, so eliminating the need for most medical staff.' He sat down, evidently satisfied that – in my opinion – he had so confused everyone, myself included (nothing new there), that they remained stunned or catatonic. He may have interpreted their response differently, but if he did, he showed no sign. *You have to diagnose the temperature of the reaction in the room yourself, Doc,* I thought.

But as usual, I was wrong. Suddenly a low grumbling and louder murmuring began at one end of the second row. Two people began to shift and turn around and talk to those in the row behind. A rising sound of dissent began among the audience, noticeably among those sporting white coats and stethoscopes. Now the voices are growing belligerent and hands are being raised. 'Hang on,' Duncan can be heard, his voice forcefully elevated above the others, 'no need to panic, there's plenty of time for you chaps to raise issues that concern you.' He catches himself at the sound of a loud intake of breath from his audience. 'Er, and you ladies too.' And he pulls down his wand, which I am sure, from the expression on his face, he would prefer to use to make some of us vanish.

'It sounds as if your intention is to get rid of doctors and nurses?' The voice from the middle of the room is from a woman who stands confidently awaiting an answer.

'Certainly not,' Duncan says, indignantly. 'We have no intention of replacing *all* doctors and nurses, but there's currently a considerable shortfall in numbers recommended by the World Health Organisation for our country and we need to put this right; to find a way to spread those excellent trained medical people among the most urgent cases and to get the WHO to alter their idea of a satisfactory ratio in this matter. But also to make sure our medical staff are able to function at full speed without becoming ill through overwork. Our new initiative will free up the medical teams to work only on those patients who need them when all other procedures and self-directed recovery has failed.' His interrogator does not look entirely satisfied, but sits down without replying, glancing at her neighbour, her face a question mark. 'Don't worry,' Duncan reassures her, 'we will come to the details of valuable new roles for medical people later. In the meantime I have some very revealing and reassuring figures for you people. Especially for our dedicated medical staff here today,' he nods towards his interrogator, 'their sole ambition, I am sure, is the curing of the sick.

'First, do no harm. I am always mindful of the inspiring oath all you wonderful doctors have taken. We should all take it.' And he bows. 'We do not underestimate the terrific work of the nurses and other medical staff and technicians and everyone who contributes.' But there is now an escalating sound of dissidence in the room and he looks up smiling. 'Later, later. Plenty of time for questions when I have finished. And welcome questions, I will. Believe me, the new plans cannot work without everyone on board so it is absolutely vital that everyone's opinions are heard.'

How this relates to me or any of my fellow guinea pigs or indeed pharmacological testing, I do not know, but Mark indicates urgently that I take notes. I hadn't realised I'd been so engaged in listening that I'd stopped writing, and with memory not my best suit, and recalling my purpose for being here is as a Patient Representative, I set to work again. My shorthand, an old-fashioned concept, is finally useful. It seems ridiculous that I don't have the facility to record the proceedings. Surely, this is an oversight? How could they know I have my old training to hand? I may have to report back to whoever I am representing, though I'm not clear at this stage how exactly this is to be done. I really must check in with Dr Cross before any more time passes in this strange place. She may well have a handle on what the hell is going on. I hope. But maybe she doesn't. I hope she's okay.

Duncan points to the board with his red LED wand, showing columns of figures for recovery in similar patients through both conventional medicine and self-directed recovery. Then he suggests that while we digest what he has said we have a short break for refreshments, courtesy of Meds R Us – each taking with us a folder outlining the planned developments to read and analyse while we have coffee or something else. He wants us to reconvene again after refreshments so we can get back to the serious business of asking questions relating to the new plans and policies. 'Take your time to reflect over your coffee and formulate any concerns or questions or suggestions you may have,' he tells us. 'I want your valuable opinion and feedback. We cannot do this without your complete cooperation. We are powerless without your valuable input,' he says, glancing around the room. He looks at his watch. 'How about we reconvene at say, fourteen hundred hours? Thank you all for being here. I look forward to your responses.'

'I have a ward round,' someone says in a mildly hostile voice. 'I have serious work to do.' Duncan is beginning to walk towards the door.

'We all have. I hear you,' Duncan says. 'I do. Hear. You. Hang on. Not long now. Just bear with me, please. Examine the statistics. See for yourself.'

'Damn the stats. I have patients,' the same fellow says and he is joined by a few more men and women nodding in agreement. 'I'm going now on my archaic ward round to see if I can help people get better, reassure them, and instruct my junior doctors in the right way to help cure them,' he says with some venom.

They all walk speedily towards the exit, but not before Duncan remembers. 'Please do not forget to fill in the evaluation questionnaire you'll find at the end of your folder. Thank you.'

As the rest of us leave we are given handouts with the statistical information. Also a sample of a patient assessment form and questionnaire for SDR. I glance at the list of questions, opening with, *What do you think is wrong with you?* followed by, *When did you first imagine you had this problem?* Looks like an interesting start for the questionnaire. I could have fun with this.

Most of the rest of the audience of twenty-five or so white coats and suits make a distinctly angry noise as they leave. Mark pulls my arm to indicate another exit for us that opens into the Soft Day Area, thus quenching my curiosity about where the glass door in our special space leads.

We elect, Mark and I, to play some of the gentle music provided, and drink water from the fountain after which we lie around in the chairs rather than drinking coffee.

'Psychopath,' he says abruptly.

'Me?'

'No, the speaker. Psychopath. That's why he's successful. That's why he will get his way. Narcissistic psychopath. All successful people are trained psychopaths. Believe me.'

'I don't believe they train to be psychopaths.' I turn towards him and in the process find my left leg is not functioning properly and hurts considerably. 'Ouch!'

'You okay, man?'

'Sure. Nothing serious. Cramp, I think.' And I put my foot down and stretch my leg but it's still there. 'But what do you mean by training to be psychopaths? Sounds absurd.'

'Well, most successful people, the top richest in the world, leaders and all, are psychopaths,' he laughs. 'I'm going to train myself to become one. Quickest way to the top.'

'You think? A bit of a generalisation. Sounds nonsense to me. Quickest way to a hug from a straitjacket.'

Nobody else was using this space so we chat companionably without fear of being heard about his absurd though interesting idea. We also discuss the meeting and I say I think the concept of expecting patients to self-direct recovery is dodgy and Duncan can't prove it works, and Mark doesn't argue. He seems to have finished elaborating on his psychopath theory too, so I ask him how come he's involved in the programme here. He tells me he'd been okay before he got too wired by substance abuse one day and had to leave his job as an estate agent of a small student letting agency. One of the students had given him pop in exchange for a good reference. He tried and failed to kick the habit until he was chucked out of his job and accommodation.

The irony of a homeless estate agent wasn't lost on him, he says. Eventually he obtained funding for detox and rehab on condition that he agreed to work as a hospital assistant. He was already competent and experienced in administering injections and had cleaned plenty of piss, shit and vomit in his time as an addict and as a homeless person. So he didn't require much training except a bit of a catch-up in hospital ethics and after taking a few short courses online in biology and abuse effects, he qualified as a hospital assistant. This current work experience entitled him to more training if he stuck with it. Seems like the sensible option to take and he had already graduated in first aid and was looking forward to doing his NVQ in Sharps Disposal and Customer Safety and Conflict Resolution.

I ask him more about his theory – that those at the top are psychopaths and wondered what sort of training was involved for this trait. He tells me he thought he could hack access training for American military to discover the secret. For years, he says, US armies have been using the technique. I remembered I'd read that too, some time ago. When the military discovered most soldiers won't kill people they can see, they began psychopath training to compensate for their natural abhorrence at killing another person eye to eye. That's another reason why they have stepped up the use of drones. Just another computer game. We could download stuff about their training method. He promises that as soon as he can guarantee to be undisturbed while he checks out the programme, he'll pass on what he discovers.

When we return to the meeting, Duncan is counting heads. His audience has halved and he's making a big drama of looking downcast. Only one white coat is to be seen: Dr Cross. My little heart leaps into Superman mode. 'We'll give them a few more minutes.' Duncan looks at his watch. 'Busy chaps.'

He still looks uncomfortable, but he obviously finds the silence intimidating because, spotting Dr Cross in his audience he asks her what impressed her most about this morning's session. She tells him nothing impressed her as she hadn't attended. All the other consultants who had attended had ward rounds or surgeries. They had, therefore, delegated her to represent them with their questions. After a few more minutes of discomfort, Duncan thanks us for attending, then acknowledges his disappointment that the medical teams had not thought it important enough to attend this session and instead had elected to continue in their old ways. He will be sending out directives to them to attend future meetings. Obligatory. 'Boycotted! My goodness, what an old-fashioned lot they are proving themselves to be. Talk about sticking to archaic, ancient rituals! I suppose it's hard for them to break with tradition. But boycott? Now that's really going back a bit.'

'They haven't boycotted you.' Dr Cross speaks firmly. 'They were already committed to unchangeable patient appointments.'

'And you were where this morning?'

'In an unchangeable patient appointment. I had an urgent sectioning to do and an outpatient surgery. I'm here because they cannot be. They still want to have their say. As I'm the only doctor on The Firm available, I have been elected to represent their concerns and act as their spokesperson.'

'As you missed the earlier session I am not sure how

legal this is under the new protocols for meetings. I do not see how you can discuss something you did not hear or see. It would be hearsay, which is not admissible.'

Dr Cross is the only medic here and we're surrounded by suits, so will it be me who comes to her rescue? Now that would be cool. After all, I am the Patient Representative she herself nominated and I'm happy to extend that role, to be here for the medics too, if they'll have me. Dr Cross needs a hero? I am here.

ELEVEN

I try to catch her eye but she ignores me. I'm usually cautious about making contact with new people on the grounds that until you know someone, how can you know that you want to know them? But there are exceptions. Dr Cross's surprisingly generous response, when she discovered me spying on her girly confidential chat about working conditions with colleagues, might just have been professional restraint. Or something else. Have I mistaken her tolerant reaction as warmth, and maybe attraction? I wish people would just say what they think. I guess, if she'd lost her cool, it would have transgressed some professional expectations. But at least I'd know where I stood. I want to be her champion. How pathetic am I? This sounds like a teen crush.

I limp away from the meeting room for a piss, shrugging off any interest from anyone else, including my kind and cooperative, designated helper, Mark. I want to find space to be alone. To reflect on my incapacity to pick up signals and function like a normal human being and to sustain and maintain intimacy as other people seem to do successfully.

The disastrous ending to my relationship with Megan and the final hellish scene in the pub after Ben's funeral is just typical of me. Couldn't help myself; inside just exploding with grief and anger but keeping it under wraps. Why couldn't I just have it out with Meg? Tell her what hurt me? If I had, it might be that all that followed – my tossing money at her in such an insulting way, my dip in the river, and now my incarceration in this madhouse – would not have come about. Well, I would say that, wouldn't I? Does this sound as if I possibly blame her? I do. And you may well ask why, and the answer, according to Megs, is that I am too stupid to grow up enough to take responsibility – and she knows that all very well. I can restrain myself – well, I had avoided a scene at the moment I was forced to face what I perceived, but cannot prove, was her betrayal. At least I left it until I was heading off privately down Self-Destruct Street before entering into full drama mode. I have learned to control myself so that I show nothing. And I can leave a gap between a betrayal and rejection. So she'll never be able to connect my meltdown with what she put me through, how she hurt me. She should still be without any clue as to why I was pissed off. This could be interpreted as spiteful; to split up without letting someone know why or what they had done. How fucking English is that! Really, really low. I've been here in the UK too long. But the truth is, Megs knows all that about me and did nothing. So now, creeping in, is the possibility that she was relieved that I stomped off.

I know she had been married to what sound like shits, and deserves better; but she seemed to work on the same principle of freedom as I did, and I believe she still does. So in my defence, our lack of commitment worked well for us. We were great, best friends and lovers without chains. Fuck buddies. Civilised, I think you could say. Though I believe her brother said things about me she didn't reveal but hinted at his disapproval, and Ben, not in a serious position to criticise me I think, told me her brother had called me a fuckwit, whatever that is. Sounds a bit harsh. Ah, and judgemental too; Megs hates that.

Megan? What's she like? Funny, warm, intelligent, with strongly defined features that are beautiful in a handsome sort of way. I don't think she leans that way though. She always works hard, decorated her modest flat with panache, likes the best food and wine, is generous beyond belief, also a bit stoical about some of the things life's thrown at her. But she's capable of exploding into quite dramatic outbursts if provoked – which I find entertaining. Ben said he always thought I was a mug not to snatch her up. And I do regret it. I regret not telling her why I left and what had upset me, but expecting her to overrule what I indicated, and know why I was pissed off. How juvenile, I now see. She deserved better than to have yet another insensitive, selfish shit in her life. Oh there were some moments! Some laughter. Dear God, how I miss her.

There were some memorable times with Meggie. I remember most particularly one of my birthdays. I was reporting on a particularly savage murder case. Megs was giving evidence during the inquest on behalf of her social services team who had contact with the victim before the attack. During a break we went for a drink. She told me she was house-sitting nearby for a friend. When she realised I was only celebrating my birthday in a pub with workmates after the shift, she told me to rock up at hers after the inquest finished for the day. The friend's house had a huge garden. She had somehow obtained a parachute, no longer in service; pure white silk. She'd erected it at the bottom of this lovely walled garden, tying it to the trees and some sort of painted flag-pole and secured it with tent pegs. She told me to take a rest, while she had a shower and so on. Then led me by the hand, into her girl-cave where, laid out on white linen, was a feast of luscious summer goodies, fruits of the earth all prepared, I suspect, by a very smart deli. An ice bucket with champagne ready to pop, summer pudding drenched in cream with a little candle on top, and a music hub. I kissed her. She began to strip off the few clothes she had on while I watched and then she slowly unbuttoned my shirt, and kissed me before very slowly disrobing me completely. She handed me the bottle of champers and I thumbed the cork, which delightfully and symbolically rose with a resounding and satisfying pop. We drank a birthday toast. 'My challenge to you,' she whispered, biting my ear, 'is to keep time with the rhythm of the music I will play,' she was stroking me, 'we have a little over four minutes.' What a warning!

'I hope I can last that long!' I said as I closed in. She commands her smart speaker to play 'Summertime'. I needed no encouragement. We gigged to Ella and Louis. I told her how good it was for me, how beautiful she was and how she had made me feel too. I felt so sensuous in that moment, so grateful to her, and it's an understatement to say it was the best birthday ever. 'Just the first course,' she said. We got stuck in to the food, drooling over and devouring chunks of lobster, using tiny, pointy forks to fish out the tender, succulent morsels from the claws and dipping them in a lemon butter sauce that dripped down our chins. Our greedy hands tore at warm crusty bread to eat with olives, and watercress. Finally we ravished summer pudding, all the while she refused to put on her clothes so I too remained naked while we ate, and we laughed and laughed. I can't remember everything we played while we ate, but when we finished eating she ordered the speaker to play Beethoven's violin concerto. We took our time, 'No hurry,' she said, 'I want to work up an appetite.' Languorous does not describe it. I can never hear the concerto without remembering how we made slow, slow love! After we came, she wrapped me in her arms. I began to squeal. She held my head between her breasts to hush me, and I couldn't stop sobbing. I just sobbed and sobbed while she comforted me and whispered, 'It's okay.' Finally I fell asleep. We hadn't been lovers for long then so maybe, I thought at the time, it was just the commercial. But OMG, some advertising agency. *Mad Men* eat your heart out.

Just before Ben's death we had another romantic evening together. It transpired to be our final happy day. I was becoming more and more unbearable. Maudlin about Ben. Asking her unanswerable questions, I mean, like, how could I help him? 'You're already doing it by being there. Come on, sitting alone beside him in the terminal ward is going to depress you unless you move a bit,' and she persuaded me to come for a walk along the riverbank, where we found a sign I hadn't noticed before, declaring, *Parental Supervision Necessary*. 'Who's going to be the parent?' she asked and we just started laughing; something I hadn't done in ages. The ground was damp and slippery underfoot, and she linked arms with me and asked me what

I was really afraid of, and the warmth of her beside me as we sauntered along, and her total engagement calmed me down.

'Ben has made me concentrate on how terrifying I find contemplating death,' I tell her. 'The idea of total wipeout, not being able to see, feel, and know what happens next. I find it completely awful.'

'We all do. It's your ego, darling,' she said, 'everyone has those thoughts, you just can't live with it all the time. So stop thinking about it. After it happens you won't feel anything anyway. Not when you're gone. You might have a hard time getting there, but when it's over, it's over. It's not easy to imagine our own obliteration.' And although what she said didn't really add anything, it was so obvious, it didn't help me. It was good to feel I wasn't alone with those thoughts. 'So we need to live our lives now,' she declared.

'Like this?' I ask and pull her towards me and I kiss her. For a long time. We are in a dense part of the woods and it is silent except for the goodnight tweets from the birds. The light from the setting sun reflects onto the side of her face and bright sparkling gold springs from her hair as I get closer and somehow we are on the ground, frantically removing essential clothing, or rather non-essential clothing, and that was it. I put my raincoat underneath us. Best loving I can remember for a long time, well, since my birthday. 'You're my favourite bit of totty ever,' she says when she's done. Under these particular circumstances, not the worst thing I've been called, but close.

By the time we dressed and turned towards her flat, with the sun saying its last hurrah before the wind kicked up a bit, I began to appreciate how lucky I was to have her in my life. She put brakes on my worst excesses, kept my lowering head above water by joshing me, regular access to a good body – that sort of selfish stuff. Although it may sound banal, our eyes drank in the colour as we walked hand in hand in silence and I liked it that we experienced this together. It came to me suddenly that I could ask if I could move in with her for say, a trial period, to see how we got on. I had nothing to lose. And as soon as we entered her flat, with Ben dying just a mile away which seemed somehow wrong and right at the same time, honestly, I think if he had been in the next room I would still have done it. I grabbed her again, pulled her down onto the carpet; I greedy, she passionate, murmuring things I wanted to hear and I thought, *fuck it, I love you too.*

By the time we went to bed that evening, the urgency I felt towards not holding back, the courage I felt about taking a chance, started to melt away. Now, I am thinking, I should have just not thought about it, but acted. Instead, I resolved to wait and just maybe after Ben died, perhaps then I would discuss crashing together. I knew my feelings were exaggerated by the prospect of his death, and I didn't totally trust myself to make a good decision. Even if I did, would I stick with it? By suggesting it, I felt I'd somehow be more responsible for whether or not it worked, than she would. If she suggested it, right now, I thought, then I wouldn't hesitate to take a punt on life with Megs. All this rubbish was washing around in my mind when I could have chosen to simply fall asleep in her arms. You can tell I am an emotional coward. But what's new about that? Megan was especially gentle and loving when we finally hit the sack, so it made my resolution to sit tight and keep the status quo, even tougher. God, her skin is so softly beautiful. The thought of her hands caressing me is giving me goose bumps right now. Well, maybe a bit more than that, but I don't wish to be crude. So if you'll excuse me, it may be a bit late after all I've revealed to you, but if you don't mind, I'm going to close the bedroom door now.

The following morning we had our favourite Sunday breakfast of warm croissant and coffee, papers dropping off the table, relaxed and in my case at least, very humbly grateful for her loving. To say I now know, since I have been on the drug trials, that this was down to the release of oxytocin after lovemaking, somehow diminishes the occasion and I feel guilty even thinking it. I suppose I was in that wonderful sensitive state, full of gratitude and warm feelings which I didn't want to leave to enter the realm of dying that I was about to face in the upcoming visit to Ben in hospital. We spent most of the rest of the day, until it was time for me to leave, lolling around her flat trying to find energy enough to take another walk in the park. By two o'clock I would have to return to the vigil at poor dying Ben's bedside. Meggie again listened to how I felt about watching him die, torn between my own feelings of grief and fear and having to face this as Ben's closest pal, and my own terror about the end and compassion for him and helpless in the face of his pain and fear. All that stuff. I just knew my presence worked to reassure him he was loved and cared about, but then he was stronger than me; he wanted to put me out of *his* agony. Don't ask me how I knew; I could see it in his eyes. My presence put pressure on him to be stoic, more than my absence did. I knew Megs was trying all the time to make me feel better too. But it was impossible. She never said the obvious thing that it wasn't about me, it was about him. She tried to empathise with my fears and though she wasn't especially fond of Ben, she was quite moved by his plight. I told her how anything and everything I said to him felt entirely inadequate and it wasn't as if he and I had unresolved business to sort out, which would be a sort of helpful diversion. Just that he was dying and I had to be there. And I couldn't put him out of his misery. God, she is patient! And perhaps, what I can only describe in the cold light of day and at a distance, that is why I overreacted when I realised she might have betrayed me. Might! No, I didn't ask her. Perhaps, now thinking about it, they could have been her brother's sunglasses. The lethal thing was, I now see, I left it too late. What a lot to lose over something so trivial. Here come the gates to Self-Pity City again.

TWELVE

I return to the meeting. Duncan is wearing glasses and fixes on his notes set on a lectern. Dr Doctor has joined him and sits beside him on a dais. 'We have named our new programme after the Greek goddess Panacea. She is our inspiration for Panacea Health and Universal Cure, or PHUC,' Duncan announces, and looks up and around the room. 'I'm disappointed to see so few medics here. Their absence may also represent their numbers in the future when our plans reach fruition.' He gives a sinister chuckle, and I notice Dr Doctor raise his eyebrows. 'I'll ensure the meeting minutes are circulated to them all,' Duncan continues. 'I want you to consider the recent studies I have already touched on. The proof that, in the undeveloped world, the greatest cause of death is, put briefly, disease and poor nutrition – whereas in the developed world, the greatest number of deaths are caused by lifestyle choices. So, we indeed need an approach that helps people make healthier lifestyle choices. As you know, we are progressing with our personal diagnostic online tools available on your smartphones, laptops, IT hubs and so on. But we need to take this one step further. We need to use the appropriate technology that's now available. Algorithms will allow patients to browse for solutions to their problems in their very own homes.

'At the present time it is a choice about whether or not you see a doctor. This is not cost-effective; we need to curtail that choice. With self-directed recovery.' And so he continued droning on for a while. As I understand it, he was more or less telling us how the system will operate, though I didn't comprehend some of the terms he was using. Then he started on about the need to eliminate medical responsibility that engendered expensive litigation. 'Our radical, forward-thinking solution is to bring on board black-box thinking,' he says. 'You may know that this is how the airline industry has an ever increasingly, magnificent safety record – black-box thinking has been responsible for a truly awesome decrease in air accidents. If we follow them, it will substantially reduce litigation against individual medical staff, who will not be held accountable for mistakes and not be held up to the ridicule of persecution in court; but we will instead make every effort to help patients incorporate changes necessary to eliminate future errors. Whistle-blowers will be encouraged to let us know of medical blunders patients make, so we can put things right. Put simply, it also means that staff *and patients* will be able to put up their hands when something goes wrong instead of trying to cover it up. The system will automatically adjust every time to ensure the same error doesn't happen again. The service will pay damages when appropriate, of course, if our medical staff are implicated in *any* way. Under self-directed recovery the patient will be in charge of diagnosis and decisions about medical intervention, thereby reducing litigation to zero.'

Dr Cross arose from her seat. 'I wish to speak. I must represent my colleagues' fears.' She sounded slightly nervous, and I couldn't help thinking how much I would like to step in right now and help but I am too ignorant to be of any use and besides she hasn't actually said what she wishes to speak about. 'You are confusing two things here. You haven't elaborated sufficiently about patient or self-directed recovery, or the problems and questions arising, and suddenly you've moved on to black-box thinking about which I have no argument in principle as it will be advantageous to bring in a no-blame-but-let's-put-it-right-where-it-goes-wrong attitude in terms of medical people. But I cannot accept your rather flimsy and seriously flawed proposal for self-diagnosis, with built-in dangers relating to self-prescription, and your rather cursory explanation of the serious problems and adjustments needed with self-directed recovery. With zero litigation, where's the motive to keep up with errors in the system that need correcting? Can we go back to the patient please?'

'First and foremost, I always have the patient in sight,' Duncan says. 'And I'm glad that I have your imprimatur for BBT.' He bows slightly and I want to kick his teeth in. 'We can have questions at the end of the session, Doctor.' His tone drips with obsequiousness, and I'm sure he just stops himself calling her 'dear'. 'I am glad you have taken it on yourself to pose the questions put by your colleagues this morning – colleagues who seem to be less interested in attending this afternoon's session.' And again, his contempt is evident in his tone. 'We need everybody on board.

'Now let us consider how we can redirect the costs we have saved for radically advanced surgery. DIY surgery isn't currently available or feasible at the present time,' he continues with a chortle so it isn't clear whether or not he is trying to be funny, though I had a flash of memory about a film of some chap forced to cut off his own arm.

And so Duncan drones on and I can't concentrate on what he is saying, though his mention of surgery did set me thinking. I began to wonder more about Mark's comments about psychopaths and how, and if, you could train to be one. Did surgery sort of require a kind of psychopathic tendency? Surgeons cut into people who are usually unconscious and always in cold blood and certainly no threat to them. And remembering my conversation with Mark about soldiers being trained to overcome their natural abhorrence to shooting when they can see the enemy's face, I realised why it must be that surgeons cover most of the patient, just exposing the place on which they operate. Though I have no evidence that I could ever cut anyone, I began to speculate about whether or not I am a psychopath, and how I'd be able to tell, and what it took and whether you were born like that or acquired it. I thought I might, in the future, ask this kind of question of Dr Cross (without, I hope, offending her) but this train of thought was interrupted by Dr Cross herself who suddenly raised her hand to question Duncan.

'The importance of bedside manner, the trust built between patient and doctor? What will happen to that? It is not an insignificant aspect of healing?'

'I agree. It has a placebo effect. No doubt at all, Dr Cross.' He turns to Dr Doctor, sitting beside him. 'I think my colleague has something to say about that, do you not?'

'Yes, indeed. A very good question.' Dr Doctor rose from his chair. 'I'm glad you asked me.'

'Don't patronise me by assessing whether or not the question is good, Doctor.' I can see the colour rising in Dr Cross's face. 'Just answer the question, please.' This seemed to prompt Dr Doctor to sit down before continuing.

'We are currently running tests with the advice of Good Pharma, Good Karma, on a more time-saving method to achieve the same effect without consuming expensive staff time,' Dr Doctor says. 'I'm sure they'll develop a drug for that.'

But Dr Cross was not letting this go. 'That's the height of cynicism. Patients in GP surgeries or hospital outpatient surgeries often begin to feel better as soon as they have explained their symptoms and fears. This is an intrinsic part of the healing process. You cannot believe a drug would be preferable to that trust. Patients need to have their say, to be heard and responded to by a living person. To be able to trust and develop trust in their medical professional.' Dr Cross sounds more confident now, or perhaps she's angry. Perhaps she too had detected what seemed to me to be Dr Doctor's slight discomfort.

'Indeed, you are quite correct, Doctor. No doubt that having the patient feel their voice is heard is good. But so is being in control of the situation, of trusting yourself, as my colleague has already so eloquently put it. The power of patients over their own destiny and health is also highly beneficial and will be an integral part of the new system,' Dr Doctor continues.

'Trust,' she said loud and clear. 'How can we trust the new medical apps, or if you wish, PHUC? How is it to be accountable if it is wrong?'

'I'll answer that question.' Duncan smiles at Dr Doctor. 'If we bring in black-box thinking, then no one will have to be accountable because any mistakes will be used for addressing the problem and dealing with any algorithm needing adjustment, not pointing a finger of guilt towards a hard-working medical employee. Or indeed the poor patient.' Duncan looks satisfied, rubbing his hands together. 'Therefore, as my colleague and I have just made clear, procedures will be put right if they are wrong. The health service will compensate where necessary. No individual health worker will have to be subjected to the inconvenience and ignominy of being sued, as in the past. I don't need to tell you how much this will save.'

'I think you are avoiding a serious problem.' Dr Cross looks directly at Duncan as she speaks. 'As agreed in principle, black-box thinking is beneficial as it resolves problems by taking action to avoid the same errors in future. However, most seriously ill patients would be unable to operate the system. So what you're talking about must be minor health problems. Am I right?'

'I'm glad you brought that up. You are right, of course. A seriously ill patient wouldn't be able to use the service. But as you'll be aware many patients with minor problems and inadequacies are some of the most assiduous timewasters who flood our GP surgeries and A and E departments. You know, the frequent flyers, as we call them. If we could eliminate those people, we would be saving huge sums which could be devoted to helping more seriously ill patients.'

'Eliminate them?' I ask. I couldn't help myself. It sounded sinister, but Duncan ignores me. Just before he turns his attention once again in Dr Cross's direction, he says, as an afterthought, 'Redirect them to our new service,' and then continues, 'serious illnesses can begin with minor symptoms, and if ignored, as you know, they can then develop into something more life-threatening. So a patient's early self-directed diagnostic intervention may save them developing into terminal malfunctions.' He laughs. 'Anyone shy about showing minor symptoms to their doctor can diagnose themselves through PHUC. Another win-win situation.'

'What about mental health patients?' It's Dr Cross. 'Are we really expecting seriously ill mental health patients, those for instance who are already deluded, to diagnose and prescribe for themselves? I think this is absolutely inhuman to expect someone who may not realise they are ill, or how ill they are, to be able to help themselves in the way you are suggesting.'

'The system is only in its infancy, and it is flexible. Once we get it underway, there may be sections of the community who are unable or unwilling to use PHUC. Provision of sorts will have to be made for them, including obligatory treatment. We don't have all the answers yet. The protocol is only in its infancy. Obviously eccentric or dangerous behaviours can be spotted by the CCTV cameras on every street and public building in our towns and cities. No extra capital investment expenditure there, though we may have to train some police observers to help us out.' Duncan sits down. He's clearly tired of standing and being questioned. His gesture appears to mean that the subject is closed for him.

'I really need to ask you to return to the question of the relationship between doctor and patient.' Dr Cross isn't finished. 'Trust is built up over time, particularly through the General Practitioner surgeries where the patient sees their chosen doctor most of the time – when it is possible. This system is already gradually being eroded in the super-surgeries. Patients complain that they rarely see the same GP they saw before. I can see you smile, and guess you think this an archaic principle,' she's looking angry now, 'and you are nodding in agreement, but despite being archaic, the rare surgeries where patients consistently see the same doctor work very well. Trust is the most valuable element and releases oxytocin which makes us all feel better. How can self-directed recovery possibly reproduce this good effect?' She sits down, clearly the fabric of her argument complete and her contempt for Duncan visible.

'Yes. Yes, you are correct, Doctor. I agree, and with this in mind Meds R Us are soon releasing their stats on their research into the effects of the trust drug. You may well have been one of the medics who signed this off, for all I know. You certainly have been aware of our hospital sponsorship by Meds R Us, for some time now. Do not fear. I hear you. Trust me. Though I'm not a doctor. We have trust in hand.' Duncan looks at Dr Doctor who nods in acquiescence. 'Why would we not make use of that wonderful stuff? Why would we waste it? Trust. The elemental property to benefit successful healing. Even if it's just a placebo effect, it works. And it is a natural. When current research figures are released by Meds R Us, we will know how effective it is. If it is as effective as we believe, we will incorporate it in our protocol. Time for a break.'

And while everyone left the room, I caught Dr Cross's eye and smiled at her as Mark led me away but she didn't respond as I hoped. Perhaps she has the same notion as I and needs to keep things under wraps while together we try to unravel where this new protocol can be revealed to the world in all its crazy, annihilating ambition. Can we subversively enrol the whole of the medical profession in a full-on, fast-track down Revolutionary Road to successfully protest against the crazy plans of the hospital management in a major universal campaign? I resolve to have another chat with the poor woman who is clearly a person of integrity and kindness and seemingly isolated. I like the tough, confident way she speaks, all the while keeping her even, gentle voice. I feel inadequate, ignorant and useless in the face of these quite bizarre and crude managers. Perhaps when they are short of doctor representatives, I can invade the management meetings in the white coat Liam scored for me, and report back usefully to Dr Cross, making me a bit of a hero to her. I could obtain ammunition she can use to persuade the hospital doctors to realise the dangers and therefore fight to stop the PHUC protocol being instituted. They are too busy being doctors, I think, to worry about it all. But maybe I'm just deluded, and part of the problem. But fuck me, where's my integrity? Am I partly responsible by being involved in the research? Right now I can play a more positive role, and do some good by doing my own research, and then release an exclusive, explosive exposé. Honestly, how useless and deluded am I? How can things get any worse? They could.

THIRTEEN

I'm amazed once more to find the Soft Day Area has even more amenities. Liam says Mark told him that now we've proved to be a good investment we're being rewarded. It's been upgraded, with small round bijou tables and chairs to match, and a couple of easels, some paints and brushes, and even more plants. I sit with Liam at one of the tables, and notice some music stands folded and stacked against the far wall. I begin to explain my plans to work with Dr Cross to invigorate the campaign to eliminate the PHUC protocol. My resolution is not met with Liam's usual enthusiasm at anything potentially exciting – obviously not engaging his interest filter involving either women, erotica or money. I'm disappointed. I don't want to diss him as he's not without great qualities of charm and consideration for others, though examples of this escape me now. I can see he's bored by my interest, and he questions my motivation, suggesting that my objective is not to campaign, but to curry favour as part of my strategy to pursue Dr Cross. He says he knows I'm determined to get closer to her (he does not put it exactly like this but I am not a fan of locker-room language). He sees conspiracy in everything. If he isn't on a placebo but the trust drug, then it isn't working for him.

'PHUC protocol? What the hell is that anyway? A drink? An aphrodisiac?' he asks. 'You're getting carried away, man. I think all this stuff about getting involved in how the hospital is run is very suspect. A bit above you. Patient Representative? Where are your qualifications? What a laugh! If you are so clever, what the hell are you doing here in the first place?' To which there really is no logical reply, as well he knows. And he is right. I am trying to step into territory I've no right to.

'I have a little something to show you which is way more exciting than anything in a white coat – an insurance against internet malfunction for our new online customer servicing, so to speak,' he dangles a memory stick in front of my face and flaps his hand, 'though if you are partial to a little dressing up, that can be arranged also.' I flap him away, grin and go fetch us each a coffee.

We sit with our drinks, me trying hard to think of something to do which does not require any effort. I'm worried that my imagination and busy mind is getting carried away into a dangerously delusional zone. The buzzing of the holograph bees around the flowers is beginning to get on my nerves, but Liam is laughingly trying to catch them. This just exacerbates my irritation. He asks me which of the doctors I fancied, apart from Cross, and I said, well, I prefer the nurses as they are more touchy-feely and approachable and I hadn't encountered another woman doctor on her rounds or in a surgery yet, as he well knows. And to stop taking the piss, please.

'Tucked is gay,' he says. 'I saw her hugging one of the other nurses at the end of her shift.'

'Really? Are you serious?' Contemplating this idea for a bit – my reactions seem to have slowed down for some reason – I tell him women hug each other all the time, and it doesn't mean they are trying to get into each other's pants. I plan to see if there is a library somewhere that might be a bit more satisfying than sitting around doing nothing. I try doing press-ups, but fail. Liam laughs at me. I feel he views me as pathetic, raving entertainment. He stretches his limbs and then bangs away doing press-ups, all the time making crude suggestions about what the moves remind him of. I wonder what he is on. When he finally gives up trying to shame me, he sits down. Then his eyes begin to falter, lids drooping, and he drifts away, begins to slip sideways, slowly sliding gently backwards to lie on the Soft Day Area couch. He did this once before in the middle of a sentence, so he is practised at landing safely and off he goes peacefully down into ZZZZ Town Centre.

I have developed a nasty sore on my upper leg, and while Liam slept I had a look. It might be why I'm unable to move easily. The doctors have to keep us alive to complete the tests, so I am guessing if I show it to Dr Cross (though as it is pretty gross this may not be the best strategy to appeal to her), then I can get some help. It's an opportunity to have a one-to-one conversation with her.

While I am pulling up my jogging trews, Liam wakes up and in response to asking what I am doing with my trousers down, I show him my sore. 'I think that hospital sores can lead to serious blood poisoning of one sort or another and end up in amputation or death,' is his reassuring comment.

Mark arrives and asks me to follow him as the team want to assess how I have reacted to the meds. He has been aware of my deteriorating physical state, he says, and has mentioned it to the team leader. He leads me to St Sepulchre's to be examined by Roger, who asks if I mind the presence of the new work-experience recruits. When I whisper to Mark that they seem strangely young for medical students, he tells me that they have arrived from the junkie pile. 'Smackheads have to pay their way if they want their methadone or other meds. They earn their keep acting as nursing assistants. Like me!' He laughs. 'They may be experienced with sharps but they still need to have training too. So that's what they're doing now. That is why they are attending,' he says, 'to your ulcer.'

Roger looks sourly at Mark and then turns towards me, asks me how I'm feeling and if he may examine my leg. Of course, I agree and after exposing my leg, he points at my sore and speaks to his audience. 'This is the kind of wound that can be caused by neglect, and you need to see it.' They all peer at my leg. He turns back towards me. 'Roll up your sleeve.' He helps me with the exercise. 'As experienced young Vikings, these fine chaps will shoot you with an antibiotic – don't flinch, they've probably done more jabs than anyone else in the hospital,' and with that he hands a syringe to a keen volunteer who plunges it into me. 'Every day for a week,' he says brusquely, 'that should do the trick.' He turns to the lad. 'Stitching next week. You'll probably find that fun.' I flinch, hoping they're not expecting to practise sewing on me. He returns his attention to me again. 'If the antibiotics don't work, it'll have to be the maggots.' I have no idea what he means. I am sure he is mad. And then as I leave I get it; I guess he means the infection will kill me.

Liam finds me limping up to the water butt. 'We need to talk business. I am bored here and you are getting worse every day. I think we need to be proactive. You are the Patient Rep, so what is your plan?'

'You dissed my radical revolutionary suggestions. Why ask now? I'm on antibiotics for this sore, so for now I don't intend to attend any more meetings,' I reply.

'You've changed your tune pretty fast.' He laughs.

'I can return to the battle when I'm better. Roger has me on a six-day antibiotic regime for my ulcer – which, as he and you pointed out, could be fatal. I'll stay for the duration. After that, who knows? When I say anything provocative or question what they are doing as I did at the first meeting, I'll get evicted and trundled off to be sectioned. It just makes me feel inadequate – as if I didn't feel that already – and that won't boost my immune system. I need rest and recovery. I feel ill, not fit enough to sit through another session yet, though I plan to tough it out when I feel better. Ultimately, I'd like to be there for Dr Cross.'

'Well, how about a bit of serious sleuthing? I have a plan, even if you do not. It involves a toolbox,' he sniggers, 'and a little practical understanding of electronics, but there you go, that's where I can help.' He begins to laugh and dance around, and suddenly sings, 'I am a little busy, buzzy bee, and you are like me. We are going to wing 'em, with our little sting 'em.'

'What are you talking about?'

'When I woke up after my snooze I was wandering around in a daze and nearly went through the glass door into the next room, except it didn't open. As I bumped into it, I noticed a CCTV camera in the centre of the sunflower beside the door. Fiddling around with the leaves I discovered that if you twist the bottom one you can jack up the sound on a mic that must be installed next door. I could just hear people speaking. Looks like they plan to instruct us over the mic, but they haven't used it yet. There's no one there now, but they must be observing us from the CCTV camera when we're in the Soft Day Area. In case they return and hear us speaking, we need to go for a snack in the caff to discuss. Safer to talk there.'

And so we set off together. He is still in an exuberant mood, dancing down the corridor singing his little bee song, but if I look closely, his eyes tell me something's not entirely right.

I put a bowl of soup and a sandwich in front of him. 'I'm not hungry,' he tells me. We sit opposite each other in the caff. 'I don't need to eat,' he continues and pushes his soup across to me, 'I am a hologram. The Holy Ghost. It's a little-known fact that I'm the only person in the world,' he tells me, 'and fucking food, I do not need. I am the Almighty.'

'Steady with the outdoor language, Liam. Don't be so unfriendly. If you are the only person in the world, who do you think I am? Or the rest of us?' I ask.

'You're all figments of my imagination. You don't exist. I'm the only person in the world.' *What a lonely place to be*, I surmise. I realise he's ineluctably slipping towards leaving the planet before shooting off into orbit and if he doesn't come down to earth soon he'll be going through that doughnut, alone in space.

'My poor irrepressible friend, Liam, you are not well,' I say. 'Love you as I do, I also recognise you need to get some help soon or we won't be able to get you back to earth. Your mind is going AWOL. Believe me. It's not your fault, and you cannot help it. And I don't hold it against you, and neither should, or will, anyone. But you're slipping out of your head. Not mentally healthy. Or safe.'

'Get your hands off me!' He slides further away. 'No, please. I'm not like that. You don't know what you are talking about. I am perfectly well. Before I came in here, I had no mental problems and certainly cannot have developed them in a hospital. That would be ridiculous, wouldn't it?' he shouts.

'For sure. Well, calm down then. I have no interest in the way you imply. Have something to eat. Unless you simmer down a bit, I am going to have to ask Mark to call the crisis team. I don't want to do that and I do not recommend them, having been the recipient of their attentions after the meeting. Don't risk going any further out into space, please.' I can see Mark standing in the queue for food and nod towards him.

'You threatening me? A Patient Rep doesn't make you a doc or paramedic.' He suddenly looks anxious and I feel mean saying it but I think he's become manic and delusional. Some memory is bothering me. I'm sure I recognise the symptoms and somehow I feel a solution to bringing mania down is with a carbohydrate loading, though I just cannot access the time and place I discovered this, or who it might have been. I know in my bones that I'd been in this situation before. I want to know more but there is a frustrating barrier preventing access to the context. Was it my own experience or someone dear to me? My memory is letting me down again.

I join the queue, watching while Liam continues to talk apparently to someone beside him. There's no one there. He makes the sign of the cross as if giving a blessing. I fetch some potatoes and cauliflower cheese and bring it to him. 'Jesus! Eat,' I command. 'Believe me, you'll feel a lot better and I love you, man. You bet I wouldn't want any harm to come to you.'

'Mind if I join you?' Mark sits down. We are flanking Liam now, and Mark watches curiously as I continue to encourage Liam to eat. 'My goodness, you're hungry. What are you guys doing later this afternoon? Any plans for this evening? I believe there's a film showing at 7pm tonight. Do you want to join us?'

'Yup.' Liam and I both agree. 'Good idea. Do you know what is showing?'

'No. But you can choose what you want to see.'

'Well, it's better than doing nothing,' I agree and he gives me money to buy some popcorn from the vending machine to eat while we watch tonight. It'll stock up Liam's carb level. Must avoid him obtaining chocolate though. It might send him sky-high. The carbs he eats in front of us seem to be having the desired soporific effect. He blesses the plate of food with the sign of the cross and begins to quickly devour it. After he had stuffed himself with potatoes and cauliflower, and bread and butter, he follows it up, at my insistence, with rice pudding. He's definitely calmer, though he still moves a bit fast.

Eventually he simmers down enough for us all to risk returning to the Soft Day Area. We chat for a while, imagining various movies that might be shown this evening, anticipating enjoying the popcorn and other childish treats while watching, until Liam falls asleep from the boredom of my dull, anodyne conversation. Boring conversation and high carb loading could become a less invasive, more natural and less of a chemical cosh than the accepted treatment for mania. 'There's a thought,' I tell Mark, explaining my theory in more detail.

'Get a grip,' he snarls, 'you seriously think you know more than the shrinks who've spent years learning and practising? His mental state is dangerous. We need to seek help if it continues. We can't just treat it with food. A psychotic event can be life-threatening. And do you want to break ranks and put yourself out of a job testing these drugs?' And before I could protest that I didn't consider myself an altogether willing participant of the drug research programme, he goes off, shaking his head and leaving me shocked and feeling despondent at his splenetic response, when all I'm doing is trying to help.

In my defence I should explain that the environment here is releasing my imagination to freely wander. The slightly surreal and gorgeously engineered surroundings of the Soft Day Area leave one in a state of wonder. Apart from some hologram bees, most of the foliage and flowers around all the walls are painted trompe l'oeil with great skill. Some are in relief and others are convincingly sculpted. The sunflower is one such. I surreptitiously examined the leaves on the sunflower's 3-D stalk, and twist the lowest leaf, trying to avoid my head coming near the centre of the flower where Liam said the camera resided. And he's right. I begin to hear voices.

David and Graham arrive, just as I finish examining the sunflower. I rapidly turn it down thinking to keep this to myself for the moment. After all, it's Liam's secret. But I'm glad of their company. David has a copy of the *Daily Grind* and asks me questions quietly when he gets stuck, until between us we successfully complete the crossword.

I ask Graham how come he's here. He's a big burly chap, with a goodly belly and huge beard he constantly pulls, making him look older than I think he is. He has a strange habit of going *mmm* after he finishes a sentence, and sometimes in the middle, as if he's reassuring himself that what he says is true. 'Well, for a start, mmm, when they closed our local HELP! Hub,' he begins. It dawns on me that some of the other members of The Drug Squad know each other because they've also been sourced from HELP! 'That closure started an unfortunate series of incidents for me. Daily isolation sent me a bit off the path, mmm, ramped up my mental state and so I was turfed out of my lodgings and ended up being not just homeless, but unable to access any financial assistance, as I didn't have an address any longer, mmm.' Now he's happy to have a small sum transferred to his online bank every week he's here, he tells me. He's looking forward to the lump sum we'll be paid on completion of this research, he says, which he hopes will be enough for a down payment on digs when he's released. If it isn't sufficient, he has the option of signing up for another drug programme for more money. So he's happy to have rocked up here. Only three more weeks to wait.

This reminds me that my temporary patient notes will self-destruct in three weeks and I'll also be out on the streets. Unlike the rest of the crowd, I don't have money coming in because, as customer services pointed out when I enquired, no name, no bank account, no spondoolies for me. At the time I wasn't bothered as I have nothing to spend it on. I don't smoke. Liam still unsuccessfully pressures me to earn money from one of his staggering number of extravagant imaginative schemes, but none appeals so far. Yesterday he whispered that he's recently obtained some Chinese balls that he wants to sell to the female guinea pigs and is only thwarted by the lack of female guinea pigs. Should have thought of that, Liam. He started walking around with his legs crossed. I have no idea why, but he leered and laughed. But then he does. Like so many of his other scams, it will not come to anything. I don't care. I'm comfortable here for the moment and without expenses and must finish my antibiotic regime. I'm sure if it all becomes unbearable and I want to leave, I can just walk out through the main entrance. After the end of the programme, of course. I don't want to let the team down and leave them forfeiting their wonga. What can we find to pass the time?

As if to mirror my thoughts, Graham says we need to find something to stop us going bonkers from boredom, as he puts it, and perhaps we should contemplate what we all did in lockdown during the pandemic and see if anyone comes up with some creative ideas. 'I'll ask the other chaps,' he says and asks me what I did before I came in here. When I say I cannot remember, he asks, 'How come you're in here?' I tell him I got fished out of the water, nearly drowned, and can't remember my name or where I live. He doesn't look especially surprised, but murmurs that considering his own experience, he can understand why I wanted to end it all. I explain that I'm not sure it was like that. He looks puzzled and fiddling with his rollie, talks about finding Liam so he can share a smoke. 'We could do with a bar,' he says. I tell both Graham and David about the plan to watch a movie in the screening room this evening, and though we don't know what's showing, we all agree it's worth a toss and hope it's something that'll give us a laugh. We'll have a choice, obviously, as it's streamed and we have all the different channels available to us. So perhaps we can pick something funny, or a thriller. David, who I thought especially shy and withdrawn, surprises me by volunteering to spread the word around inmates of the Phunny Pharm, as he suggests we call our tribal cave, explaining to me how to spell it. Pause for much laughter.

There are another eight in our group, apart from Liam, Graham and David, and myself. So far none of them have dropped out of the programme. We've only really had regular contact when queuing for our meds in the morning, and drinking or eating in the café. I think some of them stay in bed much of the time. The Soft Day Area, so comfortable, beautifully decorated, and both peaceful and strange, is used less than you'd think. I have to admit to feeling a bit antisocial, what with my ulcerated leg giving me grief and feeling tired. Not meaning to be unfriendly. My usual curiosity about people and things has gone AWOL. Most of the other men, apart from Liam, seem subdued, no doubt due to soporific side effects of the drugs we are taking plus having plenty of time and nothing to do. For the last few days, we have been handing in our feedback form every evening. This is the only demand on us, apart from daily workouts in the gym. We need to initiate more activities ourselves, Graham tells me. And that means having a conversation with the others.

Later, just before the screening, I encounter Mark who seems slightly less moody. We go together to fetch some bagged treats and soft drinks. Mark pays. I tell him that Graham and I are going to chat to the chaps about making plans to open up activities between us, after the show. 'Glad to hear it,' he replies. 'You need to get to know each other better, or depression will kick in and the whole group will fall apart,' he says. 'If you don't cooperate you'll be out of pocket, and could be discharged into Community Watch,' he says but will not elaborate on what that means. 'Share an experience, talk about it afterwards and then share other information that might bring you closer. Start by watching something exciting to bond with the team,' he offers, 'we could do worse than pick the latest Bond movie tonight, ha, ha. You have a choice. Run through the menu, have a vote on what to watch. Exchange stuff about why you're here, what you all used to do, who you once were.' He's about to leave but hesitates, turns back to me for a moment. 'Don't forget there's another management meeting scheduled for the day after tomorrow. You're still the Patient Rep. Interesting subjects on the agenda: recycling, work experience for school kids, further solutions to the addiction crisis, and even more interestingly, a new, more muscular pathway for the resuscitation protocol. I'll collect you after lunch for that.' I nod acknowledgement, but tell him I might not attend if I don't feel up to it, what with the ulcer and antibiotics I'm on. 'Please yourself,' he says, 'but I will see you for the film show anyway. I'm not missing that and I bet you're not too!' He slopes off for a smoke, giggling.

I wonder how I can get out of attending the meeting. After my performance at the first meeting, I'm curious about why they've kept me on as Patient Rep. Before this, though, following instructions to get to know the other guys should be interesting. Some ordinary, everyday, incredible stories here, I guess. I have no idea what to expect.

I have myself a quick, upper-body workout at the gym, and after tea slowly make my way to the Soft Day Area, musing on what's ahead. I can see how this socialising plan is to stop the guinea pigs from becoming lonely. As Roger had told us when the tests first started, we need to form a community. I presume he's worried that isolation could make people rebel or become unstable and refuse to cooperate or request discharge. Though we are all together in this, there's been very little genuine connection so far among The Drug Squad. I think I can detect a quiet air of paranoia. Unless we sort this enforced lockdown, the consequential problem of getting bored on our own is likely to end badly. Bit like a pandemic, I think. After all, as far as I know, we've very little in common apart from failure. I can see that attending a movie together will get us talking, especially if we have a few bevvies.

As if he read my thoughts, guess what, Mark saunters towards me swinging a six-pack in each hand. He's a bit glassy-eyed again, smiling and more loquacious than usual, playing the host, trying to introduce everyone to each other again, joshing and laughing. Graham follows him, also hugging a twelve-pack tucked into his capacious arms. As if he's a staff member, Liam helps Mark usher the queue of guinea pigs into the screening room. Mark gives us each a beer, humming and smiling to himself. He gets little response beyond a courteous thanks. Graham says he won't have a beer, but has a Coke instead. In a loud and imperious voice Rob informs Mark that one can is a derisive amount of beer for an adult man. Besides, this wouldn't be his choice of drink. Mark tells him that there'll be more of a selection arriving with a food trolley later, after the film.

When we are all seated, the beer finished and Mark has collected the cans into a receptacle, the fire alarm goes off. As we move towards the door in response, Mark tells us he'll check. A few minutes later he comes back to say it's nothing to worry about and to hang fire! Liam tells me that he knows it's Dr Cross smoking weed again in her room, and that if her insubordination continues, he may have to ask her for a deal in exchange for his silence. What a deluded chancer! We watch the latest Bond movie, have a couple more bevvies and a selection of sandwiches delivered by Mark, and then everyone saunters off to bed.

FOURTEEN

The following morning I relax in the Soft Day Area, until Liam comes rocking up. He's ebullient, obviously hungover – I think he sneaked some cans under his jacket after the screening. If he wasn't still pissed, I'd discuss turning up the sound on the sunflower to record what the voices are saying; I begin to fiddle with the leaf to see if I can hear anything, while he lies down to continue to sleep it off. I hear voices all right, but they're too indistinct for me to discern what they're saying.

I'm preoccupied with trying to record the voices, so don't hear them come in, and suddenly the SDA starts to fill with the other guinea pigs. I swiftly twist the leaf to the off position. My leg is throbbing big time so I guess the antibiotics haven't begun to kick in yet.

Zak sets up an easel in a position that suits him and roughly sketches a shape in grey with a broad brush onto an A3-sized sheet of board. I'm impressed by his lack of self-consciousness. He ignores all of us, quietly working away, using colours from a small palette. Ade shows some interest, but Zak courteously explains that he doesn't want to discuss what he's painting yet. I ask Ade what he enjoys, and he says playing music. Maybe he could play either a keyboard or guitar if only we could get hold of one, he says. Liam suggests sleepily that as we now have an income stream for the duration, we should order musical instruments online. They make a plan to do this. The morning goes on quietly, a couple of the men doing a crossword puzzle asking for help when stuck, and Kev and Scott both reading. I'm still suffering with my leg, but if I keep still and just watch the others, it's tolerable for the moment. I think I fall asleep.

'Ha, ha.' Liam tells me the others had all left. 'Now you see why we need to find a little more to entertain us.' He starts to dance around again as he did before, singing his bee song, exhorting me to join in, but I can hardly stand now. I feel as stiff as an old man.

'I found your speaking sunflower. I'm sorry I doubted you.'

'Aha. That thing, yep, pretty cool, eh?' He goes over to twist the leaf and as he does so voices come through. After a few minutes we agree that we can detect Dr Doctor and Duncan's voices. Duncan is asking where Roger is and the reply was faint but it sounded like, 'Collecting crap.'

We hear him say, 'I see. Good, best thing going. Very useful. Time-saver, yes, yes. All for it. Big money-saving potential. Must instigate.' It makes no sense but I write it down anyway for whatever reason. Maybe everything will become clearer when Roger turns up. I must say I am a bit envious when I hear the sound of tinkling glasses and drinks being poured onto ice, but because Liam is getting jumpy, it worries me that they could turn on their CCTV camera, see us, and hear their own voices – or feedback –

and the game will be up. Before we leave I turn the sound off on the leaf, as we don't want the others to find it and spoil our game. We haven't discovered anything useful yet but I'm a believer in living in hope. We'll have to be discreet.

Later, we join the rest of the team watching an old movie, *Some Like It Hot*. It is funny, but I don't have a clue as to why we all laugh so extravagantly, release of tension, I guess. I'm sure I've seen the movie before, and even with my memory problem it seems impossible to forget some of the images. The raucous laughter helps to disguise Liam's rising mania so that no one notices him savagely attacking the popcorn with total abandon and the mess he's making. I curse myself for handing him not the salty one, but the sweet popcorn. Rather than calming him down, the sugar may be contributing to his state of mind. Distracted by the movie, chatting and exploding with laughter, and pent-up feelings, the audience fails to notice Liam's celebration even when, before the titles roll, he prances around as if he were in high heels, dancing with abandon, and waving his hands like a conductor in time to the title music. I guess to them he looks like a good-natured, slightly camp, appreciative member of the audience. But that was before he starts shouting, 'Fuck everyone, as many times as you can. Birth, copulation and death. Rise up all ye herein, take over Terminal Five, the world and the universe and survive. Fuck off, head honchoes,' over and over again.

I couldn't stop the white coats taking him away. He squealed like a stuck pig as the straitjacket went on. What troubles me most is that, if you believe his account, he was originally only admitted to A and E a couple of days before me because he had fallen and sustained a minor injury that was stitched. But as he was of no fixed abode they couldn't do the paperwork for the discharge without having somewhere to send him home to. As you will know, all homeless hostels have been disbanded through lack of funds and the only reason they couldn't discharge him on to the street was because they still had Duty of Care as long as he was vulnerable to infection – and his then still unhealed wound matched this criterion. That's what he told me, anyway.

As a volunteer for the Trust's drug research project, with his wound completely healed, what are the implications now that he's become unstable again? He's assured me he didn't have a mental health problem before he arrived. Though his manic behaviour belies his statement. I must try to find out if they'll let me visit him tomorrow when they've managed to calm him down. My fear is that the meds they give him will eliminate him from the drug trial programme because it could represent a conflict of interest for the patient. I wonder if I can spring him before the drug monitors know he is missing. I hope he's on an open ward. Remembering what Roger said about completion of any trial, we'll all have to leave if Liam's not on board.

I lie in bed wondering why Liam's mood has become so frantically high. If it is true, as he says, that his demeanour has changed since arriving here, it occurs to me that we could just be testing two different drugs, and that none of us has been given a placebo. Now, while this may negate the experiment if one relied on the drug trial monitors' veracity and integrity, neither word strikes me as synonymous with my impression of Meds R Us.

Every time I turn over, the wound in my leg is excruciating. I am finding it impossible to sleep and I long for the sympathetic ear of Dr Cross. Even if Liam considers her attention to me to be purely professional, how will I know unless I check it out? I cannot refer myself, though you would think that when self-directed recovery is online, it might be possible. But that is no use to me now, or rather, yet. I will have to see if I can seek emergency help tomorrow. Hold that thought.

The following morning I am woken by one of the nurses I haven't seen before. She looks worried, and hurries away to fetch the on-duty senior registrar, who is also a new face to me. He looks at my leg and tells me that he's very concerned at its appearance, and I am led off to a cubicle where the same doctor and nurse, Burt and Sue, clean the wound after giving me a shot of morphine.

'Your wound has become necrotic,' says senior reg, Burt. 'The antibiotics do not seem to have done the job, so although we will continue with them, Sue here will apply some larval therapy. A perfect example of its usefulness.' He left through the curtain and she brought a trolley into the cubicle and opened a small container. Taking a little white squirming creature from the container, she pops it onto my leg, saying, 'Well, this is a nice juicy one and I'm just going to apply a dressing so that there'll be no absconders. It won't hurt,' she says, 'pretty efficient little fellows.' She drops a couple more of the little maggoty things onto my wound, and then bandages my thigh. With a smile she leaves me to ponder what the hell is happening. I realise they have to hold the meds back so they don't interfere with the drug trial regime. Antibiotics not counted I guess. Nor morphine. Too many peeps pumped full of bug-killers or pain-killing stuff already. Endemic in the population, so I hear. Then she says, 'Perfect. Larval therapy is a clean, organic, free-range solution,' and she leaves with her wildlife trolley. I'm more curious than disgusted. Am I crazy?

FIFTEEN

Liam arrives back into the Soft Day Area, closely followed by an impatient Rob. I should have trusted the bed controller. To think there would have been any chance of admitting him to the mental health crisis ward is, to say the least, naïve. He obviously just needed a sharp little reminder of what might be in store if he continues to cause trouble. I dare say they gave him a little shot of a slow-release something to calm him down. Now I'm in the dining area playing blackjack with Graham. As Liam enters, he has a slight limp, so they may have rough-handled him a bit, and his jacket is torn, but other than that he seems to have got off lightly. 'Come and join us,' invites Graham, though Liam seems content to sit quietly in our company while the effect of the liquid cosh subsides.

Liam, trying to be friendly rather than actually keen, tries to help Rob with a crossword. 'Fuck off,' says Rob.

I ask Liam what had happened after he was dragged out of the film viewing unit in a straitjacket. He tells me he can't remember except that Dr Cross examined him thoroughly and told him to breathe deeply and relax, and gave him cake and tea, and she sat with him, gently stroking his back while he ate and then kissed him goodbye. I realise he's trying to wind me up. He says she told him there were no beds in Resurrection Ward where the mental health patients in crisis hang out. This I judge to be true. She said that since Terminal Five is only a short leg away, if he feels a crisis developing again he is to come and see her for comfort and reassurance. As if! She told him that part of the problem is the lack of activities for people who have no reason to lie around doing nothing while on drug trials. 'Let's try to sort out activities,' Liam says, 'that's her suggestion. What's your expertise, Uncle Rob?' he asks.

'I am the best salesman of Aubusson Tapestries for reproduction furniture, suites and things, and I import Persian rugs. Very expensive, very beautiful. Any use to you?'

'Maybe not today,' replies Liam. 'What sort of price are you talking? Could we do a little trading? By the way, I hear there'll be a delivery of musical instruments soon. What have you ordered? Might be room for a deal.'

Rob ignores him, returning to his crossword.

'You think you're great, don't you.' Liam stands up, walks closer to Rob. 'Well, you can bugger off with your fucking carpets and furniture. Salesman for Carpetright? Yes, I thought so.'

'You ignoramus. No.' Rob stands up and I realise we're in trouble.

'Seconds out,' I say, trying to lighten the moment. 'Come on, fellows, we're all frustrated as hell in here. Don't let's pick on each other. What Liam means, I think, is that we could try to entertain ourselves with activities we know about. Although the gym is great it's hard to get up the enthusiasm to keep up regular exercise. Apart from specialist furniture and stuff, what is your interest, Rob?'

'Antique musical instruments,' he replies, and I think it would be good to have a course, maybe he could teach me, us, anyone who is interested. We discuss this quietly for a moment, and although Rob calms down, Liam is getting worked up again and tells Rob he's a snob. To defuse, as usual I choose the default and bring Liam with me as I go fetch coffee or something to eat.

So here we are, standing in an orderly queue and looking around the room. I see that Dave is at a table near the door, gesticulating as he talks to Graham. Dave is a quietly spoken soul and Graham is half-deaf. I can understand the need for primitive sign language, but there seems to be some kind of crisis going on if the wildness of the gestures is any indication. When we return to the table, Rob has pissed off. Liam lingers a while, eating slowly and at my suggestion he had piled his plate with not just two eggs and sausages, but with half a loaf of bread. I reckon that though he seems subdued now, it's wise to hold this mood steady as long as possible and he agrees, acknowledging that if he became overexcited he might blow our cover. He follows me around while we put our trays in place and I'm a bit worried he'll lose patience with me because I'm so slow on account of my leg. I tell him he won't believe what's under the bandages, and he winks and says he guesses I have a woody.

It seems Graham is feeling a bit worked up, or perhaps suspicious of our furtive whisperings, as he follows us into the Soft Day Area. As we sit on the sofas I ask him what he was discussing with Dave but he's says it's nothing. We start a game of blackjack to pass the time and I'm hoping we can bore him so much that he leaves, so we can spy a bit, but he seems determined to stay.

While we play, I ask Graham what he thinks is going to happen with the NHS now it's in such a crisis. He looks quite worked up at this question, so perhaps that's what he'd been discussing with Dave. 'Funny you should ask,' he says, 'it's screwed, in my opinion, beyond repair. While I worked as a nurse, it was already in trouble. And that was before they brought in yet another large-scale reorganisation. It was as if they believed that by adding yet another tier of highly costly management and restructuring the whole institution it would solve the financial crisis. It made for more work and less efficiency. It was all window dressing. We need to start all over again.' He looks downcast. I can see it's too painful for him to discuss further. So we continue to play in a desultory way. I make no effort either to win or lose. By the time Graham decides to go for a stroll along the corridor, Liam has, infuriatingly, though perhaps conveniently, fallen asleep.

I slink up to the sunflower, conscious that Graham has left his cards and could return any minute. I tweak the leaf to boost the sound. No sound. Except now Liam is snoring. I'll wake him or they'll be able to hear him. If I do, I'll be left with a problem of how to subdue him for the afternoon. I could try to persuade him to take a mid-afternoon workout as he'll need to keep moving when he's awake, to absorb and control his manic energy. I realise I've taken Liam on as a responsibility, and thinking about it makes me slightly resentful. But as you know, we need to keep together to complete the trials or we all lose out and Liam seems to be the weakest link. On balance, I decide to leave him sleeping to give myself a break. I abandon the surveillance for now.

I think we could make some plans to entertain ourselves, maybe ask permission to go swimming in the rehabilitation pool, then I realise my ulcer precludes me. I want to check in with the others for suggestions, and think we could organise poetry or writing groups, as there's no shortage of paper and pens. I'm convinced that there are some really interesting stories among this cohort of peeps. I'm enthusiastic to listen to any info Rob can give me about antique musical instruments. Though I can predict a groan from Liam at this thought, I plan to put this to the others this afternoon and ask for activity ideas from them.

My leg is still giving me grief, itching and hurting. It seems a good time to take a peek at it while Liam's asleep. If I shift around and squat, pull at the bandage a bit, I can just lift the edge enough to perhaps see the wound and visit the maggots. I am a bit nervous of hurting myself and of trying to explain the disarray of the bandage to Nurse Sue or Dr Burt but then, if they notice, I could try putting it down to normal daily ablutions and other activities. Ye gods, I'm a wimp. I can't see anything at this angle. I fruitlessly glance around in the hope of finding a mirror. Little by little I pull off the dressing and lay it on the couch. I twist my body and pull enough of my leg around to be able to see it. There they are, three plump wriggling maggots.

I watch them for a while. They wriggle their heads in the air, rolling about a bit in the juicy playground of my wound. Not one of them is feasting on me, though it is clear that I am their favourite flavour, plumper and rounder as they are. I am surprised not to be repulsed. I like my little pets. As I watch them I murmur reassuring noises to them, telling them I have no intention of disturbing them again, but am delighted to see them so happy at the sustenance I provide as they feast on dead tissue, or *debride* my wound, as Dr Burt calls it. I am disappointed not to catch them in the process of eating but perhaps I'll get luckier another time. Okay, I agree, I'm sick.

Suddenly I hear voices coming from the sunflower at the other end of the room. This could wake Liam, which wouldn't be so bad if there was no danger of Graham realising he'd left his cards behind, or any of the team returning at any minute. I scrabble along to the flower, tweak the lower leaf down, but not before I hear Jeremy being greeted by Dr Doctor and then Liam stirs at the sound. 'Don't turn it down,' he says, 'we need to hear what they are saying.' And he slides across the couch from where he is lying, oblivious of my dressing, and knocks it onto the floor.

'…we'll spray the wards. I think it can be done through the air-con. Can you check it out, Jeremy?' It is Dr Doctor's voice and Jeremy mumbles agreement in reply. 'Most cost-effective method. And though I don't wish to pre-empt the trial results, they will confirm this I am sure. We can buy oxytocin in bulk at a very competitive price. Another thought; we could mix it with the disinfectant gel at each ward's entrance. Oh, good, here comes coffee.' And their voices recede a bit and are masked by the sound of crockery so I have to listen more carefully. 'I have some speculative figures here. Duncan is obtaining more, I believe. So you might like to factor that in when deciding what shares to buy.' And Liam suddenly gasps as he notices my unwrapped wound.

'Fuck it, JA. What has happened? Ugh! You're covered in maggots.'

'Don't freak,' I tell him, indicating silence with a finger on my lips and I turn down the sound with the leaf. 'Not covered. Just a few. They are my little pets.' And I educate him in the cost-effective method of wound debridement, how it requires little or no antibiotic.

'How can you bear it?' he asks. 'It's totally revolting.'

I explain this is not a cool thing to say. 'They are made of me, innocent creatures, who do no harm. Love me, love my pets,' I say. He seems to mull it over, and asks with a prurient wink if they have sex and are able to reproduce and will there soon be hundreds of baby ones squirming about on my person?

'Idiot,' I say to him, 'they are babies themselves. Basically, they are fly larvae,' which only makes him cringe more. And I must say, with that thought, now I'm afraid they may turn into bluebottles. This would not especially endear them to me and the thought is frankly giving me palpitations as I imagine the little creatures developing wings and flapping about under the dressing trying to escape. How long do they remain larvae? I'll have to check this out. Hello, Google.

We agree to leave the maggots to their business and to go back to our reconnaissance task, turning the sound on again. We hear coughing and then after a bit of murmuring neither of us manage to understand, Liam turns up the leaf further and the sound becomes clearer. We high-five in delight and Liam begins to dance around the room again.

'We've got 'em,' he laughs, 'we can find out all about their plans. Maybe an opportunity for a quick buck. Lean on 'em, threaten to go to the press?'

'Hold on,' I say, 'stop shouting or they'll hear you. And remember we're not just their house guests, we're at their mercy. Ask yourself who the press guys will believe, the Terminal Five NHS Trust management team, or you and me, homeless, out of work nutters? Shut the fuck up so we can hear what they're saying.'

There's a commotion at the door to the Soft Day Area. 'Hit it! Turn the bloody thing down before they come in and discover us.' The door opens as I pick up my dressing to try to put my pets to bed.

Mid-dash to drown the sound, Graham enters the room. I try to distract him by shouting a stream of loose, inconsequential questions, and ask him did he notice he's forgotten his cards and does he still want to play again; he must think I'm crazy. He doesn't seem to notice anything, but asks if he can join us. I realise the maggots may disgust him but they serve as distraction from our spying. So you could say they're useful again. In any case I need to put them to bed and so I pick up the dressing from the floor and try to rebandage my wound. I'm making a bollocks of it. Graham bends towards me, he's a tall bugger, and peering at the bandage, says very quietly, 'Allow me.' He seems to assess the wound, asking in a sympathetic tone, if I realise that 'There's a couple of wildlife folk set up home here, we need to clean the ulcer, or would you like me to accompany you to a professional?'

I tell him, no, that's just fine and repeat once again about my maggots, but he shakes his head. 'Sounds odd to me. Are you sure?' I tell him yes, and it's because antibiotics are ineffective from overuse, and he agrees he knew that and tells me larval therapy was used during the First World War. 'Remember I used to be a nurse,' he says, but though he's not working now, how to dress a wound is still fresh with him. He isn't happy replacing the old dressing and only reluctantly does so when I promise to let him obtain a clean one. He agrees we have to cover the little maggots or they might escape. Liam is dancing around making vomiting noises while Graham attends to me. It's difficult fastening it, but he wraps the end and tucks it in, tells me to hold it tight, that it needs tape and he'll go fetch some. He comes back a few minutes later with a fresh bandage he's managed to obtain from goodness knows where, and completes the job, dressing the wound properly without my little pals escaping. 'Are you as bored as I am?'

'We have the news on a TV in the patient day room upstairs, and football has dominated much of the watching, but it seems like a good opportunity to take advantage of the hotel services so to speak, and learn something new,' Graham tells me. 'What would you do if you weren't here?' he asks.

'Well, apart from meeting my mates in the pub between six and seven in the evening after work, I'd probably take a walk around the local park or meet up with an old girlfriend and have a meal with her. But someone significant to me died, and the girlfriend and I split and she's nowhere near here,' I reply.

'Sounds like you've hit a pretty bleak time in your personal life right now then, mmm, nothing else?' And now he asks if I see how empty my life sounds and how dependent I was on work, which I told him I resigned from. I could have been offended, but his solicitousness makes me recognise he's just trying to help. I realise my own part in this, and I truly miss the two people now unavailable to me through death or my own self-destructive nature. I tell him that since I've been here, yes, I find it difficult to replace the company I enjoyed, and I knew work was a displacement activity. And that was one reason I resigned from it. 'Your life was not entirely exciting even then, was it?'

'If you mean, was my life filled with action, risk, power, status, decisions, laughter, covering world-shattering events and life-changing discoveries, wealth, beauty, love, deep philosophical exchanges, influence and a bon-vivant lifestyle in my Manhattan pad? No, not quite.'

'Ah!' he responds, 'that's your idea of fulfilment then?'

'No, of course not. High achievement sounds like far too much trouble and doomed to failure because death will ultimately get us all and win however successful we are.' I ask him what he used to do apart from nursing, what interests he has, and why he has stopped working. He looks a little sad, and I feel bad questioning him but it doesn't stop me, so why am I being so insensitive? 'Why did you give up nursing?' I repeat, and wonder if my insensitivity is connected to telling the truth, ergo, having been coshed with a truth drug not a trust drug, have I gone a bit all frontal-lobe broke? Is my capacity to edit what I say depleted, am I becoming disinhibited? It's not the first time I hear myself saying something I didn't expect or truly intend to.

'Don't get me started. I had my reasons to quit nursing – I've already sounded off about pointless restructuring. And other reasons too.' And I wonder if, despite being an apparently gentle soul, he might have got into trouble at work in some way. It's clear he's not going to elaborate, so I ask if he watches films or television and he tells me he likes things to be quieter when he is relaxing because increasingly deafness has demolished his previous great pleasure in music so much that he avoids listening. He says he's cool now about the resulting silence. He likes reading and walking. He says he never goes to pubs anymore because they're too noisy and he can't hear anything anyone says, and he doesn't drink. He isn't forthcoming about why he is here. I can't imagine what he did to become homeless despite his apparent explanation that the HELP! Hub closing turned him crazy; he seems far too together and measured for that. I ask him about his previous nursing experience again, where he worked, and, as he is too young to retire, why he isn't working here in this hospital. He doesn't reply so I don't know if he's avoiding the question or thinks it impertinent of me to ask again when he's already indicated he won't answer. Or didn't hear me.

'We need more physical activities than are supplied by the morning exercise,' he says and Liam nods in agreement.

'Do you think the drug trials might damage our health?' I ask. He is slow to reply, mumbling first that I seem to be in unexplained trouble with my leg, and that we all need to stay together in this to protect ourselves. He tells me that he thinks the idea of taking elaborate steps to organise many small groups in isolation, to then extrapolate the findings instead of testing on thousands, is something he's not heard before. And yes, it saves money but how can it be reliable? Then he says he'd like to know this: who are the beneficiaries of the drug trials? Is it only the drug company and their shareholders, the patients or the hospital, or even the government who may have put up the cash? He thinks it's impossible to discover, and it's troubling because anyone with a vested interest may distort and not be impartial in interpreting the results. He thinks patient confidentiality can be used to mask the results of these complicated statistics. He says that apart from my leg problem which might be the side effect of the trial, so far no others have suffered, but we can't know what long-term harm, if any, may be done to any of us. I can't work out whether or not he doesn't know or if he is trying to protect his own privacy or avoiding commenting specifically on Meds R Us, because he knows something we don't. He's reluctant to expand further and maybe he's simply self-effacing and shy of appearing too clever because he has some medical experience, though it occurs to me he could be a plant by the Meds R Us management. Liam is becoming agitated again, anxiously looking around, not paying attention to what we are discussing and jigging his knee and searching his pockets.

I want to turn up the sunflower, to not lose this opportunity to hear what is happening in the next room. As an ex-nurse, Graham could enlighten us about the meaning and consequences of what we hear, and, if he is to be trusted, he has a right to know. But I don't feel that I can include him without Liam's agreement as it is our secret and besides, we don't know for certain that he isn't a management spy. I missed the opportunity to discuss telling Graham when he left to get the new dressing for my leg. I will have to create another quiet moment with Liam, not an easy ask. He is now very agitated. I say I will take care of him if Graham gets us coffee, but he wants me to come with him to help carry them, so that's what I do. Of course, a stimulant is the very last thing Liam needs.

Graham is silent and thoughtful while we wait for the machine to dispense. He asks if I want something. I'm not hungry, I tell him. He moves slowly so I wonder what he is on. This is becoming my default assumption, whatever anyone's perceived fault lines are, and it proves to me that I am not on the trust drug. So that leaves Liam on it, so what are they giving me? I ask Graham is he on trial A or B, and he grins for a moment, seemingly weighing things up, and then he says he never swallows the meds and chuckles. 'So you'll inadvertently be the control group then!' I declare. 'Whatever they've given Liam, it seems to have caused him to be a bit manic,' I suggest, 'and he's imagining things, hearing voices, I mean. I don't know anything about it, but perhaps he's becoming a bit psychotic,' and I fill him in with the grandiose delusions Liam has expressed. 'I don't want him to make another trip to the mental health crisis ward but I don't know what to do to help him but feed him up to calm him down. What do you think?' I ask, hoping to be enlightened, and to test how much Graham has observed.

'Well, if he's having a psychotic episode and hearing things, delusional in any way, imagining he's God or all-powerful, or that the news is all about him, that sort of thing that you describe, you'll not persuade him otherwise. You don't have to agree with his delusions though. Just be neutral. There's no point in arguing with him – you can say you don't think the same way. What exactly makes you think he's hearing things?' And he's got me there. I don't know how to prove he hasn't heard what he says. I suggest we pick up the drinks and hurry back before Liam gets into trouble. By the time we reach the end of the corridor outside the Soft Day Area we can hear him shouting obscenities and stamping.

The sound on the sunflower is turned up. Liam is directing his cursing towards it. I watch Graham's inscrutable expression as much as possible, in the chaos. If Graham hears the voices coming from the loudspeaker he makes no indication, but rather, gently persuades Liam to sit down, which he does, though he continues swearing. 'Hold my hand, buddy.' Graham sits beside him. 'Not a good time for you, is it?' He passes Liam the coffee, though of course it isn't the best idea to give caffeine to someone already high as a kite, but if Graham is thinking like me, he'll assume it's the better of two bad options and withholding it will likely cause an escalation in Liam's mania. Either way it's a loser. I suggest we take Liam to the canteen for a carb loading and Graham agrees and asks me how I know this helps. 'Experience,' I tell him.

Sounds of an indecipherable argument are being channelled through the sunflower, so before we leave, I turn down the sound via the leaf, and strangely, Graham shows no surprise. Does he already know about it through the management, did he discover it himself, or are the voices a figment of my and Liam's imagination? There seems only one way to find out, but I'll first need to get Liam's agreement in a discreet conversation. That's going to be a difficult ask. Discretion just might not be Liam's overriding distinguishing feature right now.

But he does cooperate in the café, especially when I remind him what happened previously when he lost control. He loads up with carbs until the desired effect is achieved. Graham and I support him while he staggers back in a soporific stupor to the Soft Day Area. Along the way we speculate about what the second simultaneous drug trial might be for, if that's what's happening, and accepting that one is for trust and that no one is being given a placebo. Graham leaves to use the toilet, I ask Liam how he feels about including Graham in the discovery about the sunflower. 'Keeping it to ourselves limits the opportunity to listen in,' I say.

'What do we have to lose by including him? He's sharp enough,' says Liam. 'I'm all for letting him in on it.'

'You would say that, wouldn't you if you're on the trust drug. If he is a spy, then he'll tell Terminal Five management that we have discovered the sunflower if we tell him about it.'

'Then we'll know they know, when they dismantle the mic so we can't hear any longer,' he replies.

'Dickhead,' I retort. 'We could lose all our advantages. But we can't keep him out of here, and he could be useful in interpreting what the managers are saying.'

'It's a high-risk strategy but, on balance, I think we should trust him.'

'You would say that.'

'Listen, man. You're crazy. He didn't hear a thing. Remember? He said he is half-deaf.' Liam is sounding impatient.

'He is. But maybe he's kidding. I realise that his trip to the toilet could be to let the management know that we know and it's already a done deal. They'll turn it down their side if they know we know. And if he comes back and we can still hear the guys through the sunflower, then that proves he hasn't informed on us but is on the level. We can also see if he shows surprise or not if we turn it up.'

'He'll still be deaf!'

'Well, boost it more then,' I tell him.

'You don't know everything.' Liam turns to Graham when he returns. 'Listen to this.' Being a cool customer Graham says nothing. He doesn't seem unduly surprised at our revelation, which is baffling, but maybe it's just his manner of quiet confidence. He just listens for a moment while we hear Dr Doctor say that they may as well wind up the discussion because they've covered everything.

'See you at tomorrow's crisis meeting,' it's Dr Doctor's voice still, 'hope all goes well. Plenty to tell them.'

SIXTEEN

Any remaining suspicion about Graham being a management spy is immediately dispelled when he informs all the Drug Squad guys about what we've discovered. All our comrades seem interested except Rob, who doesn't believe him. Rob has returned to the Soft Day Area, says nothing but shakes his head while I explain and try to demonstrate the powers of the flower. As there's no one in the next room, it is silent and he smirks smugly. Not the best demonstration on record.

Graham backs me up, saying, 'Okay, no more news from there for now, but it'll be interesting to discover more of their plans. Let's see what our buddy here, JA, brings us from the crisis meeting tomorrow when he reports back as our very own Patient Rep. In the meantime we need to continue to form a good strong unit, mmm.' David nods in agreement. They appear to have resolved whatever it was that earlier caused a problem between them. 'To defeat boredom we can exchange what we know to steer us through this ordeal. Any special skills, anyone? Something useful to share? Something to lift the spirits?'

Liam claps his hands. 'Sticking together is your only chance to rediscover our best lockdown strategies, eh? So mine's a double.'

'I'm not sure getting rat-arsed is the very best solution, but it's a nice thought so I'll have a pint too if you don't mind, mmm.' Graham laughs at his empty request. 'Later!' He heads off with the others to the caff.

Liam is absorbed by playing solitaire with Graham's cards, so I've turned up the sound and now hear Duncan, Jeremy and Dr Doctor having a heated discussion in raised voices. Sod's law! Too bad the others were in such a hurry that they're missing this. 'Government bailiffs are threatening to take action if we don't comply with the Green Protocol Solution immediately.' The voice sounds like Jeremy's. Crackle, crackle, bang of cup on saucer. 'Because despite all the policy and procedural changes,' he coughs, 'we are still not keeping within budget. Let me make this clear again – any department which is in deficit will be closed. We'll not only have to cut our services, but at the same time, we're in the process of cutting repayment of overspend accrued during the last few years. It's the only way for our hospital to remain open. GPS will show us the way if we follow instructions! You'll have to think up something to fill the coffers.

'We need to make use of vertical integration and develop strategies, policies and procedures which incorporate this possibility,' it is definitely Jeremy speaking now, 'if the capital expense of a crematorium is doable, it would be going in the right direction. It may be that during the re-engineering of the site, closing part of the campus might mean we can evacuate a building we no longer use, such as the emergency mortuary and allocate it with minor adaptation. It's a long shot.'

'Highly unlikely. But thanks for the suggestion. I don't want to deter you; this kind of creative thinking is invaluable. We have nothing left in the new-build budget either. We've three months left to make the hospital viable. We're up to our necks in old debt, but thank the lord, Volvo have promised to continue to sponsor A and E for another year, and there's a possibility being floated that Saga will take a punt on the geriatric wing, but they'll only do so if someone else takes half and they're not so viable themselves, so we're looking at hearing-aid sponsorship or even Specsavers. And it's also been suggested that some pension providers might take a long shot at short odds. I'm not overly hopeful. Gordon's and Jameson's have agreed to sponsor the hepatic department, though we are still negotiating terms. Heart and lung disease departments are both still in crisis with no official sponsors even vaguely on the horizon. They're a hard sell. We need to be proactive in advertising this unique opportunity among rich philanthropists and cigarette companies. Well, it's in their best interest now they're losing so much custom without traditional advertising and plain packaging plus the rise of vapes. Any advertising opportunity will help them out.'

'Since Truman brought in guarantee-based health, every department has had to struggle to find the correct balance between adhering to the law at the expense of common sense,' Dr Doctor chips in. 'Truman seems relentless in his demands. Surprisingly for a doctor he seems somewhat lacking in compassion.'

'He's an academic, not a medical doctor.'

'Aha, that explains it. GBH sounded great when he outlined its benefits. But I do have one idea that we haven't looked at for a while; we could use the resuscitation policy more efficiently by lowering the age at which it automatically kicks in.' He continues, 'There's a lot of people who, by the time they reach sixty-five, really are not Fit for Purpose. And they're usually not earning and their lifestyle is worth interrogating. I can see that we can't continue replacing parts for free and as a doctor, I'm not sure it's ethical to keep them going long after their lives have any meaning or comfort. Especially if treating the old and infirm threatens the closure of Terminal Five. The bailiffs will have no difficulty flogging our capital equipment off to the private sector, where some of the better-off patients can be treated. I don't see what other choice we have except to lower automatic resuscitation age for unfit patients.'

'Now you're thinking clearly, Doctor. I like the sound of that. Yep, we could fly somewhere with that one. Give me and Duncan a day or two to get creative with it. I'll see what I can purposefully add. Resuscitation? I thought we had agreed to call it reanimation?'

'Yes, yes. We have. And I agree. Heads together, Jeremy. Drinkies tonight? Have you had any further thoughts about the recycling of body parts? See if you can get back to me with promo ideas pronto. I believe there's an export opportunity there, what? Yes?' For some reason Duncan is chuckling in a prurient way. 'Yes, yes.'

'Sure. I need to check out more about export licences as well as ice-cold technology. You know this is always a problem, the crucial temperature line between preserving and destroying. And we may be able to find a way to lengthen the short viability window. If we can find a procedure we can patent, we'd seriously be in the money.'

'What about cryonics? By the time reanimation is viable from frozen, we'll not be around to take the flak! I'll talk to the freezer boys and see what I can extract from them.'

'We're doing well with mental health patients, without resorting to unnecessary sectioning, or outsourcing. Currently another twelve have been volunteered for the latest research programme with Meds R Us. They tell us that one drug that they're trialling, a trust drug, could usefully come on stream immediately. It might solve patient dissatisfaction problems. Well, so they say. As I said before, we've begun to distribute it via the air-con system, and also with antibacterial gel. We're keeping an eye on the feedback forms for our regular patients. Might already be working. Watch this space. We'll be informed as soon as the stats are ready.

'We'll continue recruiting from Resurrection Ward when we have appropriate units, that is, suitable individual patients. The good news is that even adhering to strict and appropriate health and safety protocols, an increasing number of mental health units from St Sepulchre's and Resurrection are self-supporting with these trials and they're not complaining. Meds R Us will take as many subjects as we can supply. It's been a nice little earner for us so far. I still think we could consider taking advantage of more volunteers and work-experience units. And self-directed recovery is going very well as we constantly update the technology. AI is proving excellent at the job we've set.'

'I like the sound of that. You're making my day, Doc.'

'Good. Glad to be of service. But I am concerned that the online service is not going to pick up cases of serious illness, especially with the old and infirm, or the deaf or blind, and dare I say, those that are not the full shilling or without an advocate. They'll not be accessing the service in the same way as healthy younger members of society who are familiar and happy to use media and any IT. The GPS protocol sounds horribly familiar.' Dr Doctor has raised his voice, a slight tremor and fear is detectable. 'The territory of the eradication of the weak could be seen as euthanasia with echoes of the Final Solution. My family came from Eastern Europe, their name was Doctorow. My grandparents were victims of purges in the forties and they managed to dispatch their children, including my father, westwards, eventually landing in the UK. By the time he reached England at the end of World War Two, my father, as soon as he could, while still a young man, was forced to change his name, hoping to begin a new life with a new identity.'

'Sorry if the process offends you, Doc. And I do see how it relates to your past, and believe me when I tell you I am upset also, please believe me. And I am not without some similar but not identical refugee history. With a system that year on year costs more, without radical changes, how are we to keep a system going? Deficits and debts pile up and the population is expanding. Which is why we're using unemployed, work-experience units and addicted people to help keep the show going. Now *that's* vertical integration.'

'It's pretty obvious, really. Recent events have sadly culled some of the obvious candidates,' Dr Doctor says. 'I'm very disconcerted about the way that happened. Grim to think of the vulnerable being traded in again.'

'I wouldn't want to put it like that. We can't keep all the people alive, all of the time. We have to prioritise. I don't wish to offend you, but to paraphrase Truman, our job is to keep the hospital viable, but not all of the patients. So yes, some of the more vulnerable and less Fit for Purpose members of the population may thus be let go, so to speak. The alternative is to close down the NHS.'

I look at Liam, he is looking very confused and unhappy. 'Christ, there's no hope for us.'

At this point we hear the fire bell. 'Turn down the fucking leaf. You'll get feedback,' shouts Liam, 'you're nearest.' So that's what I do. I have taken at least enough notes to show Graham if we choose to. How could he otherwise be expected to believe all that we've heard? And there's plenty here for a press release, a real beaut of a sting, a seriously big story, a worthwhile reveal that Megan would be so cool with. I think if I also reassured her that her service users from the HELP! Hubs up and down the country were – relatively – safe it would make her happy. Anything would be better than thinking they were all on the street. Wouldn't it? But at what unknown price to their health and without informed choices? She'd have mixed feelings for sure but she would be impressed by a truly valuable exposé. Then I remember my own words – who's going to believe a nutter like me? I'll need to change my status to be believed. I stagger out. The siren is still urgently calling.

SEVENTEEN

We meet Graham in the corridor just outside the Soft Day Area. He is smiling, and solicitously takes my arm as I'm limping badly now the painkiller has worn off. Liam is seriously biting his lip; I try elbow-shoving and severe looks to encourage him to refrain from unburdening himself by catastrophising. It doesn't work. He gives a scattergun precis of what we heard about prioritising treatment only for those people whom they consider Fit for Purpose.

Graham looks at him, kind of puzzled. 'Why so surprised? We've been here before. Is there any time in history when there's been equality?' He sees me wobbling, about to collapse. 'You really need to see a doctor, JA. If you have a serious infection like blood poisoning or MRSA you could lose your leg. Take advantage of being in a hospital.' I tell him the larval therapy hasn't had a chance to work yet so I'm going to be patient before asking to see a medic. I now have a bit of a conscience about letting the maggots go, well, die, as they've been good to me. So I would like to keep them a bit longer.

'And it's a little high up, sort of near your buttock and your dick, so it might be a tad more incapacitating in that area than you'd like, as well as life-threatening.' He swipes his hand across his neck. After what we have just been listening to, I swiftly deduce that I am not especially Fit for Purpose. His gesture is a grim but real possibility. We stagger our way along with the throng of peeps pushing towards the fire exit. I spot a couple of other guinea pigs, but soon lose sight of Liam in the crowd moving swiftly along the way to the fire exit too.

Outside the building, in soft rain, four fire engines congregate. A group of tooled-up firefighters push past us, smiling and hurrying, but there's no smoke. Is it a fire drill? The firefighters don't look too serious nor are they anxiously moving especially fast, and within minutes we are filing back in. 'One of the doctors smoking again,' says Nurse Remarc as she's just about to sail past us but changes her mind and stops to ask how I am. I tell her I'm not too bad but one of my legs is giving me grief still, and Graham interrupts and tells her that I'm pretty crook really. She tells me that I look very disabled to her and it's best to seek help before my leg deteriorates further. I ask how she knows one of the docs set off the alarms and she laughs and says, 'Well, it's the weed,' and I think she winks at me. I don't know whether to believe her, though I can see no reason for her to lie but her face says she's kidding. 'We don't mind,' Remarc continues. 'Nice to see hunky firefighters with their hoses.' And I think what an absurd stereotypical idea she has for someone so smart, and down she goes in my estimation. Although I do hate cigarettes of any sort, I kind of see why some of the medics, and especially Dr Cross, would be frustrated by everything she talked about on the night when I eavesdropped on her. She would be even more perturbed if she knew what the management team are now planning. Could I risk taking her into my confidence? If I tell her, what could she do about it? Answer? Nothing. Furthermore, in the unlikely event that Dr Cross caused the fire alarm to go off, possibly incurring a financial penalty for the hospital, she isn't in a strong bargaining position. All in all, it might lead to her needing someone to comfort her or a little something stronger than weed to relax.

Liam has suddenly appeared beside me wearing high heels that I hadn't noticed him ever wearing before. He offers to score just the right thing for her. I tell him not to take advantage of her vulnerability, that we can't assume it was her and she wouldn't be interested in class As, and to fuck off. I am beginning to recognise that as far as she is concerned I am seriously unbalanced and working towards crazy. Graham laughs and tells me to sit down and he'll take care of me. I don't want to hang around and so I limp slowly away from him, surprised that his few kind words seem to have eased the pain a bit but also made me well up. He says he's going to get me some water and then heads quickly back into the building.

As I turn to go inside, I realise Liam isn't with me again, and then after a loud gasping sound from the people behind me in the designated fire assembly area, I see he's atop one of the fire ladders, screaming and shouting. He's dropped his trousers and is standing there in fishnet tights and high heels, waving. A firefighter follows him up the ladder. Liam tells him in a false, screeching falsetto to 'Stop flirting, you naughty boy.' I love this guy. He doesn't seem to have noticed that the firefighter leading his rescue just behind him is a woman.

I'm laughing so much it hurts. Much as I'd like to see what happens next, my legs are collapsing and I stagger back inside just as the experts bring him down. They won't want to keep him. I limp towards the Soft Day Area, looking for Graham, and resolving to find Dr Cross, thinking about commiserating with her. I speculate about the false fire alarm being a ruse to keep us out of the building while they dismantle the connection between the Soft Day Area and their secret meeting room? The idea does seem a bit extreme. They could simply turn it off. Fuck it, is my paranoia getting worse?

Graham is aghast at my suggestion that I try to find Dr Cross. 'If anything, you'll antagonise her. She's been good to you, given you her confidence and trust by suggesting and endorsing you as a Patient Representative at management meetings. If you suddenly turn crazy, how is that going to make her judgement look? Being a rep gives you the opportunity to report back any grim stuff without it being personal. And you have already tried to champion the good lady with being outspoken in the meetings from which you had to be removed and sectioned; you're lucky she didn't tell you off. Besides, it's pointless and patronising to think your words will make any difference to her. You think the comfort of a crazy man is what she needs? Really, young JA, this is not the way to go. You hardly know her. Pleeeeze! Dr Cross is a crush, not a friend.' And he takes my arm and pats my hand. He's beginning to remind me of Megan. 'Now let's see if we can find young Liam and give him something to do, which doesn't offend anyone.' I tell him I last saw Liam on top of the fire ladder being brought down dressed in drag. He laughs and tells me not to fret, the fire peeps are used to attention-seekers and will return him pronto to base.

We walk towards the Soft Day Area, grabbing a coffee each as we pass the dispenser. He seems too sensible to be a St Sepulchre's patient, and quite the gent. To my surprise, but not Graham's, Liam follows us up the corridor, and I can see he is not happy. I fear that he is getting out of hand again, as he shouts obscenities to everyone he meets, then passes on before they have a chance to reply or work out what is wrong. Then he shoves me from behind with his arm, nearly making me trip. 'Show me the way to go home. I'm the only sane person here. If you don't get it, you can fuck off,' he says.

'You can't do anything for him except be kind.' Graham pulls me to keep me upright while we walk together. 'I can see you mean well, your carb-loading theory might calm down a normally edgy person but it's laughable as a solution for his mania. He's too far gone.' Graham guides my arm and helps me walk away from Liam who sits down with his head in his hands. 'I'm more worried about you. They'll take care of him. He's in the right place. A quick spell in the bin and a shot of antipsychotic will sort him. Mmmm.' I nod. Sure, I feel I am betraying Liam by leaving him crumpled into madness in the corridor, but there are other people around and I am feeling nauseated by the pain in my leg.

I stagger, leaning heavily on Graham who insists we visit Dr Burt to see if he can reassess my leg wound. When we arrive at his surgery Burt's not there. Nurse Sue obliges, examining the wound carefully, telling me, 'You can't just turn up here and expect immediate help.' Nevertheless, she takes a peek. The ulcer has spread a bit, and looks inflamed and wet and raw still but the maggots are doing well by debriding it efficiently, and sufficiently for us not to worry, she tells me. She re-dresses it and sends us on our way.

Back in the Soft Day Area, I ask Graham how he thinks he knows so much about how Dr Cross feels? He tells me he doesn't, of course, any more than I do, and that's the point. I ask if he's married. He tells me he was, but not anymore and doesn't elaborate. I don't know why he is so secretive, if that's what he is, but how would I know if I'm paranoid? I want to talk to him about Megan, but if he doesn't confide in me a bit more, I don't know if I have his permission to raise the subject; and then, wouldn't you know, this guy sets the agenda. 'What about you? Ever married?' he asks.

'No. Nothing ever worked out. I mean, it's not lack of opportunity, it's that I cut and run before *they* do. Pathetic. No courage to wait until they push me first. Just before I rocked up on here, I walked out on the best woman I ever had.'

'That did you a lot of good then!' Graham laughs.

'Yep. Always the same story. After a romantic walk in the park, I was about to suggest we move in together, maybe find somewhere between us. I don't care if you laugh. I do too. It would be funny if it wasn't so pathetic. I get all romantic about her, and then I find out she's been heading off with someone else. She said something which showed me she'd been playing away.'

'Boo hoo. And you? You squeaky clean?'

'Well, no, not if I have a chance not to be. But I had just decided that, all things considered, I wanted her enough to keep it just for her.'

'Lucky Megan! I'm getting a warm fuzzy feeling just thinking about it, mmm. And had you told her she'd won the lottery?'

'Sarky bastard!' And I tell him I'd reached the time in my life when I need to assess things and again he's taking the mick, saying that it's my mid-life crisis not hers, and why did I want a long-term contract with her after so long freelancing? I tell him that I was fed up with everything about my life; that Ben dying brought it into sharp focus, especially since his death was mirrored in the grief I witnessed in my job every day. And then it all came tumbling out. 'You've never been to a crime scene, I take it?' He shook his head and asked who was Ben.

I ignore his last question. Just keep blabbing on. 'It all haunts. Unavoidable images that I can't get out of my head. The police and firefighters have a harder job of it, of course, and the trauma team in A and E. Truth? I'm a bit of a coward. You're very easy to talk to. I think you understand. I guess that's part of being a nurse.'

'Thank you. I take that as a compliment. But when you resigned from your job, was there a final straw?'

'Yeah, man. But I'd also got myself in a hole with Megan, so walking away from the job was part of that, I think. Though there was one final story that would break anyone's resolve to keep working on reporting. But then if I tell you, it will be shit-dumping and you'll be stuck with it too. As I said, there was this one story that got me in the end. I think it broke me. Just one case. The final one. It involved drugs, and the desolation of a toddler. I'm not going to burden you with any more than that. Just to say, there was no justice and no resolution and the whole court was affected.' I put my head in my hands, trying to dispel the images that wouldn't leave me now and probably never will. 'It was in the papers. It was on my watch. I reported it. But do not look it up, and in any case I will not give you the date. It coincided with Megan's betrayal, so you know it was recently. I'm glad you'll never get to read it.'

'If it was so bad, why did it not help you get things in perspective about Megan? You haven't told me how you discovered Megan had betrayed you, as you call it.'

'She had someone else stay the weekend before the weekend we had – the one when I was going to suggest we move in together.'

'Yep, that's difficult. How do you know?'

'She pressed a pair of men's shades into my hands, thinking I'd left them behind at hers. They were not mine!'

'Easy, man. What a crushed little petal you are. Perhaps your feelings were still raw from reporting the horrendous case of the little one left wandering around the flat until he died, with both parents already dead from an overdose? Don't look surprised, I read the news too. It was only a few weeks ago. That was the case you are referring to?' I nodded. 'It's an indelible image of desolation, as you say. And no, I do not want more details, but I think if you had to listen to what happened before they found the baby's body, then anyone would flip. No wonder social workers at the sharp end burn out. And by the way, the specs could have belonged to some other friend. A bit of a flimsy reason to suspect infidelity. It could be that this is an excuse for you to avoid commitment. You were looking for a reason. And half knew it, and that's why you got so worked up. The anger may be a way to distract yourself from the truth; that you wanted yet another excuse to bail out. You gave her no opportunity to give you an innocent explanation. You didn't want that, mmmm? And you didn't confront her with your suspicions? No, I thought not. Just a lot of flailing around and shouting. I am finding it utterly impossible to imagine how you can expect to have any sort of lasting relationship without intimacy.'

'We were intimate.'

'I think you mean you were physical. If you didn't tell Megan how you felt, then you were effectively lying to her. You blocked any possibility of emotional honesty and therefore true intimacy. Truth is often painful. But without truth there is no trust. Without trust, who are you? It's not surprising that you can't remember your name – who you are. Think about the significance of that. Or can you remember? You are recalling a remarkable amount of information if what you say is on the level. How's that working? Have you honestly lost your memory? It seems highly improbable to me.'

'Are you a shrink?' I ask and he shakes his head. 'Psychiatric nurse?' He begins to shake his head again, then changes his mind and nods. So he knows something about mental health. And a helluva lot compared to me. Then again, being smarter than me, it wouldn't be too difficult. The evidence tells him I'm lying about being an amnesiac. Does he surmise that being a journo, my motivation is professional?

'I want to be friends with you, buddy,' he tells me, 'but

how's that going to work if you're not honest with me?'

'Okay, little blobs of info have come back to me since I've been stuck in here. Though I still can't remember my name or how I came to be in the water. It is true I've picked up some massively wild things going on, industrial levels of shenanigans which could be useful if I was bent on writing an exposé. Yep, you are right, there's a temptation to sound off to the press about how drugs are being trialled among groups of mental health patients, or service users as they call them. Megan would be well pleased with me for telling her where her patients are since they've been ejected from their HELP! Hubs now they've lost their funding and had to close. She may be able to track them down at the nearest large hospital. Maybe she'd think more kindly of me after the unfair way I treated her.'

'You'd have saved yourself a deal of trouble if you'd only come clean with her. So, what would be your motive for going to the press, John? To save your comrades from being exploited, or to gain Megan's goodwill?'

I chuckle with embarrassment. 'Bit below the belt, that one,' I tell him. 'I'm not trying to avoid the question, but I can't leave here anyway, so it's academic. I haven't said I'll go to the press. My credibility might be in question. Now I'm feeling so ill, I need to go lie down. How the hell am I going to take a peek at the meeting tomorrow when I feel like shit? I sure ain't Fit for Purpose.'

'You wouldn't want to miss out on a crisis meeting, John. Would you really want to pass up the chance to discover sensational information?'

EIGHTEEN

'Can you feel this?' Nurse Sue touches my foot and I tell her yes, but that's not where the problem is. My thigh is giving me great grief. 'I'll replace the cannula for pain relief. You're familiar with the SAS, I guess?'

'Sure.'

'Well, I am sorry it has come to this, John, but it is bed-rest for you.'

'I have a crisis meeting to attend,' I tell her, 'I'm the Patient Rep.'

'No more wandering around for you, pal. Forget about attending meetings. You'll change nothing anyway! I'll get one of the research team to bring you the meds you are trialling. No need to interfere with the drug regime. We'll take good care of you. I'll send off a swab to ascertain the best antibiotic for your problem. More antibiotics I'm afraid, so you'll just maybe have a little less energy. You'll have to learn to tolerate that. And I've made your dressing more extensive. We have crutches for you if you get worse, but after that, if you don't improve, then I'll authorise complete bed-rest.'

I tell her, 'I was fine before I was admitted,' and she replies that sometimes happens and at this stage she couldn't predict when I would feel better.

'I need you to take it very easy for me, to listen to what the doctors tell you to do, comply with the medication regime and generally be a good boy, and then you'll be fine.' She laughs, pats me on the arm and summons Mark to take me back to my bed by wheelchair.

'What about the maggots?' I ask as I am loaded onto my new wheels.

'Gone. You were too much for them.' I have heard that in another context, I tell her, but she didn't laugh. I wonder if anyone else on the planet has ever been rejected by maggots. When Mark shovels me into my bed I grab a paper someone has left on a chair beside it. I suspect it is out of date. I have no idea what's happening in the world yesterday or today. But I can't focus. Sinking into another world inside hard or soft covers will take more concentration than I can muster right now. I wonder how Liam is. I miss the intermittent delights of his madness; it adds a bit of texture to the day and he's the only chance I have to find out exactly what are the implications of the Green Protocol Solution. So unless Liam rocks up, bang goes any chance of exposing the buggers.

* * *

I awake to find Graham standing by my bed and grinning. He's holding a bucket of popcorn. He could deputise for me in the meeting if he wasn't so deaf, I think. 'Sit down,' I tell him. 'It's great to see you. What's happening in the outside world?'

'I know nothing,' he giggles, 'no one tells me anything. But I think you'll be moved soon.' He continues, 'You look much too ill to stay here.' I ask him how he knows. 'Training,' he says. He can see. I want him to reassure me by telling me I'll be fine, which is something most nurses say whether or not it is true and it's all relative anyway.

'What's happening down at the Phunny Pharm?'

He tells me Liam has somehow locked himself into the Soft Day Area, won't let anyone else in which doesn't particularly matter for now as all the guinea pigs are watching a film. 'I wish I knew how to escape. It's doing me no good remaining here. I feel I'm rotting inside.'

'You know the stats are useless unless completed with the same cohort they began with. So just finish the programme which is nearly done. Shall I check your hospital notes for you?'

'I don't have any proper hospital notes,' I tell him. 'That's why they couldn't discharge me from A and E when I was first admitted. Remember? You know very well I don't know my name or, of course, my date of birth, though I think I'm about forty.'

'Well, of course I know that, but I've never entirely believed it and still don't despite what you say. What happened to you, buddy?'

'I fell into a river and nearly drowned.'

'How did that happen?'

'I don't know. I told you. Being submerged so long without oxygen has shattered my memory, they say, so that I don't know my name.' He looks askance at me and then asks, if I have no memory, how can I possibly recall all I told him – about Megan, the pub where I got hammered, the death of Ben, whoever he was, and the job I used to do, the cases I covered, and so on? I try to explain again. It does seem odd that I recall so much, and perhaps all the things I think I can remember are false memories. He agrees that's possible but unlikely. Maybe I have a good imagination and just make things up. I tell him the only serious information I cannot remember is my name and age. Until my memory is jogged back to normal, my hospital notes can only be raised as John Anon on temporary notes which are at this very minute accessible on the iPad at the end of this very bed I now inhabit. He is welcome to have a peek as far as I am concerned. 'So now you have all the information about my distinctly dubious adventure leading me to this current soul-destroying predicament, what about you?' I ask him. 'What's your story?'

'Nothing as exciting as yours, mmmm,' he says enigmatically, in that infuriating way he has of drawing me in to confiding in him and yet again avoiding his own personal information. I'm curious. He briskly changes the subject, asking if I want Liam to visit me and yes, I do. I suggest leaving Liam to re-enter from outer space and then when he's landed back on earth, yep, great if he could ask him to drop in, but no hassle. He parks the popcorn beside my bed and tells me he'll let me rest and, as he's about to replace the iPad, he checks it out. 'It just has your name, John Anon, and a few words describing your leg ulcer and what treatment you're having and the drugs you are on.' He brings it over. 'Check it out. You have somewhat limited notes for an adult. Nothing recorded before this last month!'

I feel dizzy. He tells me to lie down again and to rest my leg as ordered by nursey. I tell him that if my patient notes have recorded the history of the current damage, I may in future be able to sue them for the harmful side effects as a result of their drug tests. They've probably covered their backs by keeping a record somewhere else, he tells me, clipping the thing back to the end of my bed. Then I remember that they'll self-destruct at some preordained date soon.

The grossness of my situation reminds me of Ben and I tell Graham I'm cursing myself for allowing all this to happen to me and that if, like him, I don't swallow whatever drug I'm on, I may have the strength to get myself sorted enough to escape.

'Your best bet is to be transferred to another ward, say acute surgery, where they might patch you up and then there's a chance of being discharged from there, I guess. You don't qualify right now, and you'll have to deteriorate further to go in that direction, you know, of amputation. Which would be very risky. I'm sure Meds R Us will not agree to you quitting the trials at this late stage. I mean, even Liam couldn't remain on the mental health crisis ward and he's *really* in trouble. There are no beds. They're cutting down all the time through the new Green Protocol,' he says. 'I should know.' I wondered then if a little self-destruction might be desirable and apart from strong drink, which Liam might help with, nothing else appeals and to be honest, I'm too much of a coward to cut myself and I don't think starving is an option I'm particularly drawn to, I tell him. He tells me that I won't need to do anything more if I want to top myself, because if, as he suspects, I'm suffering from blood poisoning, it's only a matter of time. I think this is pretty cruel of him, and it surprises me in one so compassionate. Though it's not his intention to be harsh, I'm sure, he's just being honest with me or, possibly, taking the piss. 'And really,' he says, 'you're not that uncomfortable so that if you do respond to the antibiotics and get your strength back and your mobility – is it really so bad? Would you then be any worse than when you were first brought in here half drowned?' He has a point. 'With all the budget cuts, that's more than most patients can say. Considering your current state of health, you're being well cared for, so perhaps a little gratitude might be in order. The truth is, the side effects of antibiotics and any illness can make you depressed so perhaps that's why you feel such despair. Have you filled in your daily obligatory questionnaire Meds R Us gave you? No, I thought not. Have a rest and fill it in, and I'll drop it off for you later and let them know why you can't do it for yourself. Perhaps they'll take you off the trial if you are sinking too low, though it will bugger up their stats. They don't want you to snuff it; that would certainly screw up the results. After all, these small groups of guinea pigs are only cost-effective if there's one hundred per cent attendance, so no wriggle room. As the results are then extrapolated to larger figures which would not work if *anyone* dropped out, there's no contingency for anyone leaving and as you know we would all lose out. There are a dozen groups involved before results are consolidated. Get better soon.'

'Thanks for everything,' I mumble.

'What would you like me to do?' he asks. 'I can bring you something to eat, or a drink, or perhaps something to read?' I tell him I'm not hungry and can't focus enough to read so he insists I drink some water before he leaves. He stands over me, watches me take the pop and asks me how my leg is now feeling. I tell him the morphine seems to be doing the trick and I can't feel much except being cosily snuggled down on cloud nine.

'Nice,' he says.

'I hope Ben felt like this when he was tucked up.'

'Ah, the mysterious Ben. Who he?'

I tell him he was my dear friend whose hand I held when he died. I shut my eyes. At last Graham feels free to leave me alone.

And there I lay, suppurating and stinking in a putrid mess of my own making. Thinking about Graham's honesty, and what he said about truth and trust. It is not lost on me that there is a connection, and the irony that both drugs are probably being tested on us covertly has a nice, cruel shape to it. And then I remember clocking something significant he said just now about the Green Protocol. I'm too out of it to understand. I should have asked him to explain when he mentioned it. But I'm too caught up in my own problems. Typical.

* * *

When I wake I have one of those eureka moments; I'm feeling stronger after the rest, and realise that if I stay, I'm on a journey to oblivion. I can stay and take that route or, now the time seems right, I can just walk out of here. Although this might compromise the stats, it's not beyond management to falsify them to mitigate my absence in which case nobody will lose out. The bottom line is that I cannot continue to risk my health deteriorating. I look around the corridor outside and it's pretty quiet. Everyone is usefully occupied. What a bonus. I will miss my comrades, but if I leg it now, and really take a turn for the worse later, paramedics won't ask my age but will treat me outside the hospital. And I can make up a name, or use Ben's. At least, using his name, I can score some patient notes, though it might cause a bit of confusion if Ben's records show 'time of death'. I'll come to that hurdle when I have to. I must just avoid being taken to A and E again. Brilliant. Here I go, no white coat needed, just crutches and determination.

NINETEEN

The noise of the alarm generated by the implanted microchip Dr Doctor had installed in my arm alerted not just security, but all the guinea pigs, all the medics on this level and probably woke up everyone in New York. By the time security decked me, they'd injured me enough to apologise as I sat trying not to sob with frustration and pain. 'If you're determined to make a run for it, why didn't you leave when the fire drill was happening?' Graham sensibly asked, while helping me back to bed. 'You know about your alarm implant. Is your memory deteriorating further? The alarm installed in your person is always turned off during fire drill.' But it hadn't occurred to me, and now thinking about it, I can see that if I want to escape again, I can try setting off the fire alarm first, which would disable the microchip implant. But I'm under enforced additional monitoring now, so may have less of an opportunity. This adventure hasn't done my health any favours and I find myself in bed again, frustrated, angry and feeling desperately stupid.

A few days later I have improved sufficiently to meet the other peeps in the Soft Day Area. Through a fog of delirium

I remember Graham visiting daily to collect my feedback forms. I miss the maggots, I tell him; they were made of me, so that's little bits of me destroyed, and he tells me I'm nuts to have an identity crisis over a few insects. 'Food chain.' He laughs. During the period before I recovered, Nurse Sue told me I'd been hallucinating, so perhaps that's why I'm overreacting. I can only remember snatches of that time. On the whole, it is reassuring to recognise that though it's unconscionable to imagine my own death, had I just slipped away it would have been very simple and easy. I do realise it isn't so comfortable for everyone. And truthfully, had it been possible to feel rage after death, I would have been irked to have gone without enough warning.

Liam has plenty to report. Being less than discreet, he is sitting in the café telling everyone, that is, Graham and four other guinea pigs, about how Duncan has purchased a Stingray. He says he heard Duncan boasting to Jeremy that he'd been testing it by racing around the ring road and, according to Liam, taking it through the sound barrier. Liam tells us he is planning to blackmail Duncan into letting him have a go. I'd like to hear that conversation. 'So what else have you discovered then?' I ask him pointedly. My question goes smartly over his head to the other side of the road.

'It's four hundred and fifty horsepower, nought to sixty in four point four secs and bloody hits one hundred miles per hour in ten fucking secs. What's not to like about that? I'd give anything for a go.' He's bouncing up and down in his chair. I do love that man! 'I wonder how I can get the keys off him.' And he launches into more details about the motor; to me he might as well be describing the complexities of rocket science or brain surgery, or indeed, how to form intimate relationships. The others are sitting open-jawed in awe but understand what he's talking about, so I'm obviously the odd one out.

'Did you find anything more about hospital re-engineering plans?' I try again, quietly.

'Very interesting stuff about the Green Protocol Solution. Sounds radical.' He winks at me, at last on the same path for a moment, but he doesn't expand on it, and it's fun watching him enjoying the vicarious pleasure of driving a sports car and comparing engines and all that stuff with the other guys. I am worried that he may try to steal the motor and get into trouble, though I'm sure Duncan keeps it well locked and the keys safely on his person. I hope. And Liam is security tagged like me.

Graham is searching for a book in the library when I wheel myself in. I have decided that the crutches are more awkward and more effort than wheels for getting around and I rather like the deference shown to me when I'm in the wheelchair. Graham is looking for something about caterpillars and butterflies, and though he can't find a hard copy, he says he'll check out the one he wants online later. He asks me how I'm feeling now and I tell him not bad. As we talk I deduce he's up to speed with the secret of the sunflower, because he says that while I was ill he heard more news about what they intend to do with patients they describe as 'Not Fit for Purpose'. They're planning a system where patients who are disabled, or single – i.e. have nobody to care for them at home, or are without an advocate, or elderly or not working, will not be resuscitated. I laugh and point to myself.

'Three out of four, that's me finished,' I say. 'I don't believe you. You're making that up.'

He is upset by this and says, 'The reason I resigned as a nurse is because there was no trust from management. Everything we did we had to prove we had done by ticking boxes. So we spent more time filling in these forms than nursing. It's untenable. I couldn't nurse patients properly like that. It wasn't the way I was trained. For everyone except management, nurses are among the most trusted people on the planet,' he says. 'It sent me crazy. I mean that. How do you think I ended up here?'

I'm shocked that my throwaway comment elicits such a heartfelt response. I can see he's genuinely upset, and he tells me that trust was one of the most satisfying elements of his day. He said that before it all went out the window it felt good to be trusted and those doing the trusting felt good too. I realise he's echoing exactly what Megan has said. And yes, he did know what he was talking about and he'd been a mental health nurse for over fifteen years. I try to ameliorate things by telling him that I didn't mean I don't trust him personally, I mean, what he is telling me is so shocking it's hard to believe.

'Of course, of course, of course I trust you, yourself. It's what you are telling me that is so unbelievable it's hard to believe it is true,' I reiterate.

'You don't trust me. You're hiding something from me,' he says.

I tell him, yes, but not really. 'We tried to tell you earlier about how we got our information, Liam and I, but I didn't think you believed us and then the thing didn't oblige when I tried to demonstrate it. Now you know how we obtained daily information through the sunflower and how it works anyway. It is hard to believe the Green Protocol Solution and what management plan to do regarding resuscitation.'

'I get it. I didn't believe it at first. I have a hearing deficit, so I'm not always sure that I hear everything correctly.'

'Well, we kind of realised that hearing was difficult for you. Anyway, as a journalist, would you believe me?' I josh, hoping to change the atmosphere, lighten things a bit. 'Journalists aren't trusted.'

'And politicians even less. Only fifteen per cent of people trust politicians,' he replies.

'That much! What's wrong with people? Look, it's not that I disbelieve you about your job and the demoralising effect of the destructive power of relentless creeping bureaucracy. It's the other stuff you say that's hard to get my head around. The cost-cutting by not resuscitating disabled, unemployed, single or old people or what you describe as people who are not Fit for Purpose.'

'I don't describe them as such. The management executives do. To save money they're also lowering the age at which resuscitation will automatically be applied.' And he's only satisfied when I've accepted what he says is true and apologise for doubting him. I tell him, no one has been kinder to me than he has and I couldn't get a handle on why he'd been made redundant when he is clearly a great nurse. He retorts that he wasn't fired, but walked for the reason he has just given me. I ask him how they justify cutting services to the vulnerable groups he describes. He tells me not to be so obtuse, that I know perfectly well the depths they will stoop to. If management do not comply, government bailiffs will be corralled to collect stuff to the value of overspend if the hospital goes any further into the red. The new Green Protocol Solution is coming on stream in order to save more money. Yes, even with a rising population. They also have to save. You remember what it means? When I tell him not entirely, he says it's about making the NHS self-sufficient. Ecologically sound, as in 'Green'. GPS, he says. Way to go. And I think well, way to go home then. Where's the fire alarm? Best check out locations asap. Graham and I decide to head off for a bit of quiet and comfort in the Soft Day Area.

By the time we rock up, Liam has turned on the sunflower and is listening to Vivaldi through the speakers. He tells me he discovered that, curiously, when they're not having a meeting they sometimes play music – so you can always tune in, he says. 'Very convenient. Perhaps it is an IQ test of some sort to see how we operate during the drug trials. The fuckers may be monitoring us to see if we react to lack of stimulation by exploring our environment. Could be other stuff here we can entertain ourselves with if we only explored a bit more.' Graham nods in agreement. He's picking at his nails in an odd way that I've just recently noticed. 'Although there are geographical and material limitations to possibilities,' Liam observes. I think I've underestimated him; the talk of scams, blue movies, his manic behaviour, borderline delusional behaviour, as well as the plan to nick Duncan's motor, kind of puts me off taking Liam seriously. I'm thinking now I've taken him too much at face value. We turn off the music and listen and explore the walls and tweak and rummage around the flowers and plants, sculptures and holograms of bees and other insects, looking for clues about what secrets the room holds, hoping to find a pop-up screen or something but without success. The only new thing we hadn't noticed before, nor its significance, is a fine perfumed spray emitting from a little fountain in the corner, but we agree we don't see how this can affect anything or take us anywhere interesting. We said that. Didn't know then that there was something in the air.

We are just about to leave for the café when Dr Truman arrives at the door with the rest of the guinea pigs trotting along behind him. Mark pushes in a trolley loaded with refreshments. 'Please help yourselves.'

On Dr Truman's instructions, everyone sits on the seats along the back wall. He's smiling as he surveys the seated guinea pigs, his head sweeping from side to side in an odd way. 'When you hand in your completed feedback forms, please let Mark here know if you wish to be included in the next set of trials,' he says.

'You getting a taste for hazardous combat missions on the road to recovery, with an altruistic purpose?' I whisper to Liam and he looks at me as if I am mad. I realise that I need to sign up as a decoy for my plan to escape. While we eat sandwiches and snacks from the trolley, Dr Truman circulates the room, thanking and shaking the hand of each guinea pig, asking how they feel, encouraging them to continue with the valuable work, and handing a card to each of us with a code on it, telling us that of course it's our choice, but if we sign up everyone who benefits from the research will be in our debt.

Behind the row of chairs, he tells us, is a drop-down screen, operated from just outside the door and with a memory key slot at the bottom-right-hand corner for watching whatever we want from the library. *Ha*, I think, *we missed that when we explored the room.* What else did we miss? Are they keeping tabs on our abilities in other areas like cognisance? He tells us to pull back the chairs for the moment, and asks Mark, who is smiling benignly, to demonstrate the screen descending. Mark is looking a tad glassy-eyed and constantly grinning, asking what else we would like and pointing to the trolley, telling us to eat up, and I swear I saw him wink at Liam. What the fuck are they up to?

Dr Truman tells us to spend more time in the Soft Day Area because so far we're not using it sufficiently to justify the expense laid out to ensure our comfort. He looks for a while at the fountain, and sniffs the air rather like a hungry bear, commenting how lovely the perfume is. Dr Truman says that a further condition of the programme we will join is what he calls lockdown research, by educating each other in our own areas of expertise and interest and feedback details on our forms. Otherwise we are not sufficiently exploiting this opportunity. This is not a suggestion, it is an order! He smiles around the room, then leaves with Mark.

TWENTY

Graham invites us to put forward ideas about extending our activities. Liam volunteers to teach tattoo skills. He says he tattooed his mates as a teenager, improvising with alcohol, using his sister's sewing kit and cordless hand drill belonging to his older brother. He'll order a professional kit online. He also fancies running art history workshops using the screen, accessing BBC programmes on iPlayer and other information via the Tate and Royal Academy websites. Now I would not have predicted that. Zak tells him he doesn't know what he's talking about and should stick to teaching us about car engines, Liam's other consuming interest, apart from porn and football.

'This is going well,' Graham says sarcastically. 'If we're to avoid conflict, let's have a system. Shall we zip around the room and start with Liam? As he's the noisiest one!' Laughter.

'There'll be nudes in the art he's talking about,' Rob says. Liam retorts that he'll show us a urinal that's called art. I tell him he's taking the piss and he tells me I'm a coarse bugger and that the art is in perceiving a found object as art. 'We'll not be getting anywhere with this kind of talk,' Graham tells us, 'let's open our minds to learning something from each other, not just competing with each other and showing off. We need to quit dissing other people's suggestions. Everyone has something to offer, or to tell us, that we didn't know before,' he says. 'Even just our own personal history would be interesting.'

Dave's gone quiet, sitting on his own. Graham sits beside him, tries to draw him out, asking, 'What would you like to do, buddy?'

'Not much,' is his reply. 'I like watching birds. Twitching it's called. No chance of that as the only birds we can see are holograms.' He seems to thaw out under Graham's undivided attention and especially when Graham suggests that we access information about birds online; coupled with his own experience he could give us a wildlife education talk. Nodding, Dave thanks him, saying the thought appeals to him.

'And who else has something to contribute? Kev?'

'As a postman, I can't deliver on that one! I have an English lit degree though, so I could do a couple of sessions on mid-twentieth-century fiction if you like.' To which there's some agreement that it, too, could be interesting. 'And I play drums.'

Ade looks pleased at this. He tells us that although he is an advertising man, he plays classical music and can adapt to all sorts. 'Piano,' he smiles shyly, 'I'm not sure I have the confidence to play any longer. Had to play too many concerts as a child. My parents were disappointed that I didn't take it up professionally. Found myself a job in an agency as a copywriter, advertising products that I didn't really believe in. I don't value consumerism, and the wasteful aspects of manipulating people towards the compulsion of excessive consumption. Advertising didn't go comfortably through my ideological filter but I was stuck with it.' Steve nods agreement and tells Ade he knows exactly what he means. 'Thanks,' says Ade, 'good to have someone get it. I could teach you Latin, except there isn't really a long enough time frame. When I was four, my father insisted that I only speak Latin at the dining table from then on,' he looks uncomfortable for a moment, 'the price of privilege! But if Kev plays the drums, then I could have a little tinkle with keyboards in a band if you like, I'm quite adaptable. Often played jazz, and well, ragtime.'

'Thank you for sharing that. Fantastic, Ade. I'm sure a band will benefit from a trained muso,' says Graham. 'Well, someone who can play a musical instrument properly. Steve, do you have something you want to contribute?'

'Not sure. I was a pharmacist from a big hospital. So although I'm interested in what is happening here, I can't see how to convert my knowledge into something appropriately useful. There are also ethical considerations.' I notice Liam showing great interest.

'Would you tell us about your experiences as a nurse?' I suggest to Graham, but he puts his hand up to resist. And suggests that art lessons would be a great contribution – he's looking forward to hearing about that if anyone can help. 'And you, Zak? You can paint?'

'I can. But I don't like talking about my work. It's a visual language, speaks for itself.'

'I was thinking more about telling us what you know

about drawing or painting?' Graham says gently. 'I'm sure you have some knowledge you can pass on.'

'Let me think about it,' says Zak, 'I'll let you know when I have the time.'

Ryan says that as an insurance agent, he wouldn't really want to divulge the tricks of the trade in case he ever finds employment again. But he's happy to conduct short poetry readings. We sit around considering more suggestions in turn. Adam says he never had time for anything in his demanding job farming, except music. He once had a rock group. He plays guitar and is happy to pass on what he can about string instruments, he says, and perhaps start with the ukulele for anyone who doesn't play anything. He thinks it's very useful to have Ade on board with keyboard knowledge as the main man. Scott, who mainlines on footie, says he can play the recorder and is prepared to upgrade to a guitar on which he can muster a few chords. He'll leave it to the rest of us to decide what we want him to do.

Adam offers to score instruments online, subbing us until they arrive. We can reimburse him from funds dumped into our banks each week. The thought of us making up a scratch band is voted the best idea so far. Ade brightens up, he's excited at the thought of converting his skills to rock. So there is general agreement about at least having a go. Assuming that I'll be fit enough by the time the instruments are in our hands, they're counting on me to play percussion. The Soft Day Area will be our practice dive. We now have to think up a name.

Graham is subdued and I wonder what it is that is troubling him. 'I'm fine,' he tells me. 'I can't play anything, is all. Always wanted to.' I ask him why he agreed to continue with another drug trial programme and he tells me he has his reasons and taps the side of his nose, which is irritating as I'm no wiser. I suggest that he teaches us first aid and he nods in agreement without much enthusiasm; but murmurs of approval about how useful it would be come from everyone else. While the rest of The Drug Squad head off to the café or to see what movies they can obtain, Graham helps me back to bed because I'm beginning to feel unwell again, but I detect a slight distance. He doesn't make eye contact, and is less warm than usual.

He hangs around for a bit, brings me water. 'Have any of the doctors diagnosed what's wrong with you?' I shake my head but tell him they've sent off swabs to the lab for a proper diagnosis. 'You're foolish to continue. The next trial may be just as toxic. Why did you agree?' For which there's no intelligent answer. Something about the atmosphere in the Soft Day Area is reassuringly harmonious and conducive to agreeing to anything, I tell him.

'And I'm the most pathetic person when it comes to being decisive.'

'I find that worrying.' He continues, 'You've had no valid diagnosis of what is almost certainly the side effects of whatever drug you're currently on. Now I have a code to the library computer and can look up what your condition could be. The good news is that I can hack into your patient notes from there without a problem because everyone's notes are available online. If that's okay with you.' I nod agreement.

'Right. You're on. We have a couple of days then. I'm not happy with this situation. You could just vanish along with your notes, you know, be discharged or die, and there'd be no accountability. No chance to sue for damage sustained in the trialling. I'm suspicious that although you've been treated you've been kept in the dark about why you have deteriorated so much. It's unacceptable.'

'Thank you,' I say, 'you always cover my back. My guardian angel. You're so good to me, Graham, I love you, man. And frankly, I may high-tail it out of here before the next programme begins. Please keep it to yourself – I want to give the impression that I'm up for another programme. I can't get discharge papers, so may have to find another way to scarper.'

'Well then, how about confiding in me with your real name? I won't divulge it to anyone else.'

'Don't ask me again. If it sounds implausible, considering my memory for my job, my old girlfriend, memories of Ben's death and other details of my life, I can't help that. As I said, these might even be false memories.'

'Ben? Who's Ben?'

I begin to cry. I don't know why. 'I can't tell you much, except that he died in my arms in a hospital bed.'

'Do you think you're responsible for his death in some way?' His arm is around my shoulder, the big man comforting me, like a father.

'Possibly. I really don't know. It sounds ridiculous, not to be able to remember something that elicits such extreme grief. I'm hiding in some dense tangled bush, in a strange land where I cannot reach the past, and even when some of it returns I'm not sure it's real. I feel it's all fuzzy, glimpsed and slippery. Am I avoiding confronting something?'

'Probably. But what are you avoiding? You say you trust me, but I'm not feeling that, John. So how does it work? If you don't confide in me, what's the point?'

'Okay. I'll tell you what I can remember. Ben was a friend for twenty years. I met him on a walking holiday and discovered we lived only a mile away from each other. When we returned we often used to meet for a drink after work. He worked in a bank. We used to share stuff together from time to time, you know, just puff. I think he wanted a settled life, so then he married and had a kid, and at that point he checked out of my orbit. I know that can happen when people couple up. I didn't see him for ages. Maybe eight or nine years. Further along the line he scarpered down a hazardous fork, fell hostage to alcohol and drugs.' I take a deep breath and hesitate. 'I was taking a walk along the embankment when I encountered him again after so many years – he was begging. He was filthy and I remember his fear of violence in the ghastly conditions where he lived under a bridge. I used to bring him beers but he knew we'd never share a pint in a pub again. Not in his condition. And then he got ill. It was too late by the time he obtained medical help. I'm feeling slightly dizzy. I can't give you the whole history, but let me just say that we did experiment a bit together before he married. He died a few weeks ago.'

'You were very close, then, earlier?'

'As close as mates can be before he married and disappeared. We hung out together a lot, shared holidays twice, had each other's backs. I think he might have been gay, you know, he hadn't come out or anything. It was harder to do a few years back. I just sort of thought that, even though he married. But that's not my thing.'

'Why didn't he tell you? That must have been a lonely place for him to be.'

'Yes. Maybe.' I coughed to prevent myself choking. 'When he lost touch I knew he'd lost himself. I'll always feel guilty that during the years we were apart, I didn't try to find and help him. When he was dying he'd described me as his next of kin. It was on his hospital notes. I was surprised that it didn't help when I first brought him in to Accident and Emergency. I didn't realise he'd named me. But they wouldn't give me information about where he was for a bit.'

'Maybe A and E didn't realise that any more than you did. How's it work that you're his closest friend but he doesn't confide in you?'

'It cuts me up. I can't believe that he died without saying anything to me. I know he loved me as I did him. Though it's not how it sounds, now that I say it.'

'How did he die?'

'What do you think? He was on the street for ten years, homeless, addicted to just about everything. I remember sitting beside his hospital bed, laying my head on his pillow to catch what he said. His poor bent hand coming up to stroke my face.' I begin to cry great big uncontrollable tears.

'Okay, okay,' says Graham. 'There, there. We can talk more when you feel a bit better if you like.'

'Look at the state of me!' I wipe my eyes. 'And here I am fantasising about playing in a rock band. My motives are not exactly edifying. We all know, well we think, women find musicians, especially rockers, a turn-on, though my physical condition makes any serious action impossible. What a joker. I'm going to sleep now. Please don't be offended.' Graham pats my arm, changes his mind, envelopes me in his big arms, and leaves me to slip down to Self-Pity City once again.

I lie in my bed dozing and then I'd weep some more, remembering Ben's last week. I do deep breathing, mindful exercises for a while until I'm calmer, then take a hike down to that sweet place, the interstice between waking and sleeping where unexpurgated thoughts take flight. Ruminating about having guys to rock with in the Soft Day Area, about the various drugs we're on, and suddenly it comes to me. Eureka! We have a band name: The Day Trippers.

I'm woken by Mark trundling in a sort of trolley topped by a nice new laptop. 'Not for long,' he says as I eye it. 'It's for you to attend the crisis meeting,' he laughs, 'virtually. Unfortunately you won't be able to contribute, because they've muted you. But at least you get the lowdown.' And off he went.

Now I'm in possession of a hoard of new information. What transpired at the crisis meeting is worth a few bevvies. At last I have something new to tell the other peeps. Unfortunately, though I can listen in to the meeting, as Mark had already told me, there's no comeback, no way to let them know what I felt about the revelations. No amount of pressing buttons on the keyboard removed the mute. So there's no way to comment or give feedback. But that works both ways. They cannot be certain that I heard any of it.

Later that day Graham wakes me with a drink. It's distressing to know that nursing has lost someone so gentle and decent. 'I've news. Not good.' He doesn't seem interested in what I have to say, but wants to talk.

'I don't want to worry you but the blood tests show that you've some kind of serious blood condition. And here's the problem, you're not for resuscitation.' He looks forlorn. I ask him how he knows, and he says, 'Well, it's here on your notes; "Not for 222" means "not for resus",' he explains. 'In the old days, with dialling telephones, 111 or 222 were the fastest numbers to dial. In the US it's 111.' I nod in recognition. 'And in this country 222 summoned the crash team so it became shorthand for resuscitation; and "Not for 222" means no resus.'

'I have worse news for you,' I say triumphantly. 'I was able to watch and listen to the crisis meeting. Apart from lowering the age at which resus automatically kicks in to sixty, the patient still has to prove that they're Fit for Purpose.' He looks at me, clearly puzzled. 'You know the criteria: able-bodied, no mental health problems, no additional underlying health conditions, having accommodation, a significant other or advocate, and working, et cetera.'

'Are you sure? How did you come by this little gem of info?'

'Well, we know it's been going in that direction. They've extended the principle. Mark gave me a laptop to watch the crisis meeting. I bet the management executive team change the resus age limit upwards a year at a time before they reach sixty. They'll want to keep pace with their own age.'

'So our Management Team best not take too many risks on the ring road with their glitzy new motor and become disabled. That reminds me, Liam told me he's going for a spin in their Stingray. He's obtaining a key online if you can believe anything he says. How are you feeling now, buddy?'

'Marginally better.'

'And Ben? Any more memories of Ben that you want to share?'

'I gave him his first line of coke,' I say, 'I feel pretty bad about that.'

TWENTY-ONE

The next day, Graham collects me, easing me into a wheelchair, looking pleased with himself. He tells me there's a surprise for me in the Soft Day Area. I tell him I've thought up a name for the band: The Day Trippers. What does he think? 'Love it. Perfect. Great name. Hope the others approve.'

Adam, as good as his word, has had musical instruments fast-tracked to us. Within twenty-four hours we're in business. The optimism is infectious. The fact that most of us cannot play a note is not a problem, Adam says, it only takes a couple of strong band members who really know what they're at to carry the rest. He'll test our singing voices too and has scored a nice-looking electric guitar for himself. Everyone wants to try a few swanky cords. Kev has a go at putting the drum kit together, and then surprises us with an impressive, cool Phil Collins drum roll. Some of these guys look happier than I've ever seen. Ade can hardly contain his excitement at seeing the keyboard, his long, delicate fingers rushing up and down the keys like a demented mother hen looking for her chicks. Graham tells them I've come up with a name for the group: The Day Trippers, you know, Soft *Day* Area, *drugs* combination, that sort of thing. 'Yep,' says Ade. 'Brill. Couldn't have come up with a better name myself, and I'm a copywriter. It will do.' And then he plays a swift few riffs of 'The Entertainer', smiling and bringing good feelings to all of us. We sit watching those that can play something set up their instruments, test a few riffs, laughing and joshing together. Things are looking up, but I still feel crook.

After our band practice, when everyone leaves for the day, Liam and I realise we have forgotten to check what's going on in the next room. We tweak the leaf, hear a bit of Vivaldi, but no voices.

With all the excitement, I've reached a bit of a dead end. Sitting in the caff, too knackered to queue, we use the dispensing machine for coffee, shredded cardboard flavour with an aftertaste of dead dog. Graham looks solemnly at me. Even though I have a raw-looking rash he takes my hand without flinching. 'I can't find any more clues in your medical notes. Nothing of significance recorded. In my experience it's probable that your immune system has been compromised by whatever drugs you're on. Or you could have a new virus. Or an infection that is antibiotic resistant. Welcome to the land of the damaged. Maybe time to seriously consider quitting the research programme, buddy.' He looks down. I can tell he's upset. I'm just getting to know this sensitive soul. I tell him that I do have plans to leave. 'I notice that all your joints are a bit swollen,' he gently strokes my knee, 'probably inflammation of some sort that's making it difficult for you to shift around. I don't really know. Cannot help you, buddy. Look, you need to insist you get checked out by Dr Doctor before it gets worse. As you are so far gone you may not qualify for treatment, never mind resuscitation. However, Meds R Us will have a Duty of Care regulation under their terms and conditions, under which you can access treatment. Or sue them. Maybe it's a toxic rash; what do I know? Did you show Dr Truman your skin?' I shake my head. 'I thought not.'

I'm not liking the idea of leaving someone and somewhere comfortable where my SAS provides something close to a feeling of bliss. But I only have a couple of days to sort things out before my notes self-destruct and I become invisible or a non-person. If I'm too far gone to sign up for another set of trials, what options are open to me? I think I'm entitled to ask for an extension of my temporary patient notes from Dr Doctor if he wants me to sign up again. If I can get him to admit I'm disabled by the research I reckon he owes me one.

Graham helps me move to a long table at the other side of the café where we see three of The Day Trippers planning what tunes to practise. Adam points out that serious band practice is a little premature, because apart from Ade few of us know how to play anything except air guitar, and that, badly. Ade offers to write out notes in tablature for the ukulele, and explains this system. It's a form of notation for the fingering on the instruments, sort of key stage one music reading, he says. When we've grasped this he tells us he'll teach us a few useful chords.

Liam saunters over, beaming and hardly able to contain himself with news he says he's heard from the sunflower. It's an oracle. The others look puzzled when he tells us that there's going to be one more variation of the resuscitation policy called OPTIN. 'The Final Solution,' he triumphantly says.

'So how does that work?' Graham asks. 'The managers decide on a policy and then announce the new OPTIN subversively via a sunflower? I don't think so. Don't look so worried. Don't panic. People hear voices. I should know. In any case we already know that the new Green Protocol Solution will navigate anyone with a serious or terminal illness, or anyone who is elderly or disabled, away from being resuscitated. I believe the unemployed and homeless are under review to be included on this route. I mean, how can they discharge someone if they've nowhere to go? Hey, Duty of Care! That would be irresponsible, yes?' He laughs grimly.

'I've been speaking to Nurse Sue who outlined the whole thing for me.' He's looking at me intently. 'So, yes, young man, he's absolutely right, you will need to leave if you can't get medical help immediately – and before you get any more disabled. If you have a bit of a turn and collapse outside the hospital, paramedics won't ask how old you are, or whether you have a serious illness and they'll ignore the fact that you're disabled, unemployed or homeless and guess what? They'll resuscitate you. Terminal Five staff are the only ones who are forced to agree to the new terms under GPS. So far.' Some of the others are looking seriously worried or maybe just confused. 'I think it might be a good thing if our John here leaves after he's finished this round of the current drug trial, and while he can still move about before he becomes seriously crook,' says Graham, affectionately putting his arm around my shoulder. 'I've told him that already. He's half agreed. Unless he gets urgent help he's in serious trouble. Please back me up, fellows. We can't have our friend keeling over in front of us. They can send another person in to replace him when the next programme begins. He needs to get out to protect himself.'

'I'm changing my mind about whether or not to get the hell out of here,' I say. I'm shocked he's confided my plans to the guys. He's determined to pressure me, to save my life. 'I'm not homeless or unemployed, as long as I'm signed up for drug research here. We all have somewhere safe to live and a job to do. Let's start doing a bit of band practice while I can still get about. I don't want to think about it all any longer. Thanks for being so concerned, Graham, but I have to disagree with you. Anyway, it's giving me a headache. I can't decide to leave while I feel so sick. I'm sorry to be so indecisive. I've always been like that.'

Liam looks as if he's about to explode. 'Are you all crazy? Take control of yourself, John. Graham is right. You don't get it, any of you. Listen to what I've heard. They've gone way beyond age and disability, marital status or work criteria. You have to OPTIN.' And he looks around at us. He's shouting it out to get our attention, and as a result the entire clientele of the café is watching him. 'OPTIN. Opt in. Get it? If you want to be resuscitated, you have to opt in. The default setting is that everyone automatically opts out. Unless you opt in.' We're all staring aghast at him. He is so excited that it's infectious, though I certainly don't fully comprehend what he is saying. 'Everyone who is admitted to hospital automatically opts out. The only way for anyone to be resuscitated is to sign to opt in.'

'Where's the problem?' asks Graham. 'We can sign for opting in. Can you score the forms for that?'

'No. You can't. There's the catch. You can only sign to OPTIN at the time that you need resuscitation. Not *before* you need it and certainly not on admission.'

'But if you need to be resuscitated, you'd be unconscious.'

'That's the point. If you're unconscious, you can't sign anything.' He's laughing grimly. 'Resuscitation is a medical procedure, so requires an agreement with a signature. Being unconscious is no excuse. I rest my case, or rather, their case.'

'How does that work?' Graham is still looking very worried, and shifts in his chair.

'Simple. No one gets resuscitated, or reanimated, as they call it now. If there's a code on your patient notes: Not for 222,' says Liam, 'you're in trouble; and NFFP, Not Fit for Purpose, no one can remove that.'

Graham agrees with him about what the code 222 stands for and tells the others what he'd already explained to me about the history of dialling for the crash team. 'John,' he turns to me, 'you really must get Dr Doctor to check you out as soon as possible, and before the new OPTIN policy kicks in.' I nod in agreement.

Liam has noticed the whole café population is staring at him and shifts uncomfortably. Rising from the table with a little flirty gesture, he suggests that we all live a little right now and the best way to do that is to make music. And so we retreat from the café, to the place of safety, the Soft Day Area, to calm down and check out who can play what, and who is really keen to learn an instrument if they have the capacity. Talk about optimistic!

Is Liam having delusions about OPTIN or is he trying to outdo me with shocking information? I could challenge

Dr Doctor with this on my visit but it'd be hard to do so without giving our source away. Everyone's mood lifts as we enter the Soft Day Area. We laugh and josh at last, all paranoia left at the door. Now why is that? My suspicion is that it's not just the little ivory-coloured diffuser, but that the fountain too is emitting the trust drug. We fiddle around trying out different instruments. Adam sits looking pretty smug as we admire what he has managed to score. He picks up and demonstrates all three guitars – one acoustic, two electric – keeping one for himself and handing one to Graham. He gives the bass, a Fender, to Ade, who immediately demonstrates a few chords, his face alive with pleasure. Kev is checking out the percussion stuff, the electric keyboard and a mouth organ and recorders and Graham is showing how he can play both of the ukuleles – a tenor and soprano. Adam's fingers scamper up and down a few chords on each instrument in turn. He finally gives an impressive, hasty riff on a five-string banjo; 'Foggy Mountain Breakdown', he tells us – leaving me feeling how impossible it will be to ever reach such a standard. He puts to one side the kit for boosting: mics, stands, speakers, cans and a woofer and other electronic knick-knacks. Ade says he's going to audition each band member in turn. Kev, Adam, Graham and he can at least play something, but Liam and I are pretty useless. 'Time to start at the beginning; here are your chords,' Ade says as he produces sheets with the tablature marked for both guitars and ukuleles, and shows us how to operate a tuner he attaches to each instrument. If we two novices practise the chords everyday he'll guarantee that by the end of the next research programme we'll be up to speed enough to accompany the band members who can already play something. He's forgotten I might not be here. 'And don't forget vocals,' he's grinning, 'one of you must have tried karaoke, and emptied the pub.' Liam says that's him, and yes, he'll be giving singing a go if Ade gives him enough bevvies, but I'd rather eat maggots than sing. Having a bash at learning some of the sheets of tablature seems like a possibility if we can just suspend disbelief in our adequacy and get started.

Having raw, rotting hands isn't going to assist me, but in the Soft Day Area, perhaps significantly, perhaps sinisterly, I get the feeling things might change for the better. The atmosphere in the Area is brilliant, full of laughter and the smiling faces of The Day Trippers responding to music Ade cannot stop practising. I know the music has enhanced our mood, but this level of exhilaration, I suspect, is because we are receiving a double shot of oxytocin through the fountain. Six of us: one brilliant, one pretty good, two learners who could do better, and two totally ignorant, all convinced we can successfully make rock music together. As Graham might say, how's that going to work?

TWENTY-TWO

The music put off the hour when I knew I had to do something. When I left the Soft Day Area, my mood scarpered so resolutely downwards that I retired to my bed for the afternoon but could only sleep intermittently. How had rejigging or recalibration, or whatever it is of my life gone so horribly wrong? If I hadn't forgotten my name, if I hadn't fallen, jumped or been pushed, or whatever, into the water, none of this would have happened. I continued backwards with these thoughts; if I hadn't left Megan, my job, my flat, if Ben hadn't died, and all the rest of it, then where would I be now? Somehow I'd taken a wrong road. Reaction Road? Resignation Road? If the latter, was this a character flaw, an inability to see any positive possibilities in the future or now, or make decisions based on sound thinking, all of which has allowed me to end up in a cul-de-sac of a pulsating, rotting body in Self-Pity City? What kind of fissure in my soul, fracture in my spirit, and fault line in my DNA has left me so out of control of my own destiny? My head is throbbing so resolutely that I cannot rest or desist from negative thoughts that just will not take a hike. If I try to get back into the Soft Day Area, I may have to engage with the others and I'm not in the mood. When he helped me into bed earlier, Graham told me that he's going to see if Dr Doctor can be persuaded to call on me.

He returns from his mission and sits beside me, looking forlorn. He's come back with the news that Nurse Sue will page the good doctor on my behalf.

'What is the matter?' I ask him.

'I think we're going to lose you, mate.' And I tell him I'm a useless musician so the band won't miss me as much as I'll miss them. He tells me I'm an idiot, which I already knew, and then says he thinks I should settle my affairs. I don't have much to leave, I tell him. But that's not what he wants to hear. He wants me to put my affairs in order, emotional affairs, consider how my lack of sensitivity had affected Megan, and maybe put that right if I really thought I was important to her.

'Yes, a shitty thing to do,' I agree, 'must have hurt her.'

'You assume she was devastated? I'm getting the impression that you think her world fell apart when you left. Was she really so dependent on you? What makes you think she is such a victim of convention, or of her need for your affection, or a hostage to her libido?'

'She always made me feel that she cared. That she enjoyed being with me. *Knew* me.'

'And that's enough for her, is it? And then when you were upset – because you imagined she'd played away – that became a capital offence? And to confuse her, you didn't let her know she'd grazed your knee? No. Or didn't you know how to tell her the devastating news? I notice she hasn't come claiming you and let's face it, you being found floating in the river, an unknown man, will have made the news. So why didn't she search for you? You'd have been easy to find after the accident. Police have records of found people whether injured or dead or with memory problems. Do you think you might overestimate your importance to her?' He laughs quietly, shoulders shaking up and down, until I nearly punch him.

'Fuck you. You're a bit of a loser too. You think you don't avoid stuff yourself? Look, you encouraged me to divulge sensitive, personal stuff without any reciprocity,' I say, 'and what you just said is hurtful. But you don't tell me your innermost thoughts or reasons why you left nursing – except for the lack of trust you felt they had towards you – which you blame them for, and for your breakdown. You've disclosed nothing about your private life. You've avoided all my questions about yourself. You pretend to be concerned about me, and sit there in your grandiose way, manipulating me to reveal things to you. And then take the piss.' I notice him sit upright. He stops chortling, and his eyes change. His mouth hardens into an expression I don't like.

'Trivial. The hospital is so understaffed now with one emergency after another to attend to that patients from all recently closed hospitals in the area are rocking up here. Mmmmm. Some of the medical staff are looking for jobs abroad. This means a massive equity loss as each doctor and nurse leaves our shores, each one representing hundreds of thousands of pounds' worth of trained and Fit for Purpose adults. And you lie there complaining,' he barks, 'at least I did my bit to help.'

'Hang on,' I say, 'that's a bit below the belt and we guinea pigs are *all* doing our bit!' I laugh. 'And you're still avoiding answering my questions. Most of the medical staff are immigrants anyway. So it seems to me that we owe their country of origin big time. The only valid and humane reason for stopping the influx of medical peeps from Third World countries is because it depletes the qualified stock of people from poorer countries who can least afford this loss of human equity – the brain drain. You were part of that equation and didn't complain when you worked as a nurse. So, you're right, what the fuck am I doing lying around taking up a bed when I don't believe I needed it before the drug trials fucked my health? I'm having stronger thoughts now about suing Meds R Us or Dr Doctor for advising me to take part. If I can prove it's the cause of physical damage. But here's the rub – I need his help.' I sit up. Anger giving me strength. 'And what are you really doing here?'

The look he gives me doesn't feel safe. I feel I lost him when I accused him of manipulating me. He gets up, and without another word quietly exits left. I'll bet that after my dissing him he won't be looking to check if Nurse Sue managed to persuade Dr Doctor to visit. I lie back indulging myself in self-pity and then slightly more creative thoughts about litigation, when I am startled by the bright, boozy arrival of Liam dressed in a white coat, stethoscope around his neck, grin on his big, ugly face.

'My dear fellow. Do not fear. I am here.' He pushes my bedclothes back and begins to listen to my heart. 'It's working,' he announces, 'time to sign up for your tattoo. We need to find an area of your chest not covered in unsavoury spots or pulsating zits.'

'Ever your charismatic self,' I say. 'What the fuck are you doing dressed like that? And where did you get the outfit?'

'Less of the outdoors language, John. Stethoscope off the peg. Well, internet. I have another one for you in case an emergency demob is needed. Have a big syringe too, ditto, for via a different route to the exit.' He pulls a lurid face and produces a syringe the size of the Eiffel Tower from his pocket. 'But we won't be needing the hypodermic today. You can always hook up to your very own SAS for pain relief. You know I used to do tattoos when I was a nipper? Well, I have a professional kit now too. Internet again. Ha, ha. We'll foil them yet. I have signed up all of St Sepulchre's Ward for treatment. There's a waiting list, John. But I'll give proper priority to anyone with a serious, life-threatening illness. For my good buddy who ain't Fit for Purpose. You can jump the queue. No need to drive a Volvo. You'll still be fast-tracked in the A and E sponsored by Liam. No extra charge. Just there for you from cradle to grave. Here, I'll give you a cuddle. Now, was that nice? No pathways to death via obscure euphemisms, no excuses, just unconditional one-to-one care from a professional you know and who knows you and most importantly,' he hesitates for a moment for dramatic effect, 'someone you can trust!' He finishes with an emphatic flourish, arms akimbo, and a massive smile on his face. 'That's me!' he says and then beats his chest King Kong style. 'And that completes the case for the procedure I am offering you today. Do you want my help?' He flashes the syringe in a circle around his head.

'You going to kill me?' I ask. 'I might like that. Imagine – you'll be the last person on earth I'll see.'

'Whatever makes you think that? My, my, you *are* feeling bad. How can you think I would ever do such a thing? For why? And what about your commitment to The Day Trippers? The band needs you. You'll be fine. All you need is a sponge and press, John.'

'But I can't play anything.'

'When was that ever a problem for the pros?'

'The syringe. Look at the size of it. Liquid cosh size. Only useful for dispensing a gin and tonic straight into the vein if you are not intent on delivering me from this nest of horror. Put me out of my misery without some long-drawn-out pathway or whatever.' I begin to roll up my sleeve.

'Not so fast. I can do that too, if you like. Reluctantly, though. Terms and conditions apply. Signature required. Full printed version of services available on request. I can deliver whatever you want straight into the corridors of life itself. I have all sorts of other solutions on tap – just say the word. Did you know the mark-up on prescription drugs is about eight thousand per cent? I thought not. Well, they have been open to – I'll try to put this delicately – to a little of what you might call blackmail. If you want a special delivery at six pm every evening straight into the eye or vein, just tell me your preference. Pretty near anything illegal or legal available. I am here to please. And at no cost for my personal delivery directly to your person. First, I think we need to secure your future, well, okay, your survival. Without that guarantee, no you, and no customer for me.'

'What are you talking about?'

'Tattoo. I'll tattoo you. But we need to get some more alcohol wipes before I begin, and I think Graham will help by guaranteeing everything is sterile. Must make sure I don't make you worse. It's a once-in-a-lifetime opportunity. You won't need it repeated – it's a lifelong solution. Lasts as long as you do. I only use edible, indelible, vegan ink. And of course, you'll be fully anaesthetised for the whole procedure with the very best oblivion pick 'n' mix. No expense spared on the cocktails. Your choice.'

'Dear Liam, I have too many problems to look for anything as frivolous as a tattoo. In any case, the shock to my system of so much junk we've been testing has left my health sorely depleted of any strength, even to get to the john on my own. So I don't want to risk what's left of my tentative hold on life with a noxious cocktail streaming through my person, nor do I relish the pain of the bloody tattoo, thanks. But no thanks.'

He looks downhearted. 'I only scored this kit because of you. And as I said, I'll knock you out, you won't feel a thing. If I guarantee that you'll be resuscitated if necessary, will you agree? For a small consideration, I'll ask Graham to stand by with a defibrillator and all his own expertise in CPR and life-saving skills.'

'I'm in Graham's bad books right now. Besides, none of this makes sense. I've never expressed any desire to have a tattoo. Never. Whatever possessed you to think that I like the bloody things? Look,' I pulled up my sleeve, 'if I was a devotee of such self-decoration, don't you think I'd have had one by now?' I glance at my spotty arm. 'Dear God, you aren't offering me this to cover up my rash, are you? You funny man. A tattoo will only make it worse in the long run.'

'Hell, no. I am offering it to you to save your life. I had no idea the rash was all over your arm. But that's not a problem. It's your chest I need to tattoo. Nobody would notice it on your arm. Let's have a look at your body.'

'Please tell me this mad idea is not connected with The Day Trippers. Are you suggesting that we play bare-chested and tattooed to excite the girls? Are you? You may have a physique to die for, but I am a weed.' He's pulling up my shirt.

'Nobody's perfect,' he says, peering at my chest. Perhaps not the reaction I wanted.

'Thanks. Your powers of perception never fail to astonish me.' I pull my shirt down again.

'I hadn't thought of bare-chested musos, but it's a great idea. Thank you. When we all have tattoos, it would be kind of good to have our bare chests exposed as an advertisement for the service I'm offering. And a kind of passive but powerful protest. A big thanks for that clever thought, John. I'll cut you in.'

'I thought you said the service is free.'

'Well, it is for you because I love you, man. For anyone else there are some slight charges to cover the cost of equipment and medication, but my service is free at the point of need for you. Good policy, eh? Can't think where I sourced that idea. What do you think?'

'I think you are certifiably mad. No offence. Lots of good people are. Don't take it personally.'

'I'm sorry you take that attitude, John. This tattoo will save your life. And all my customers on St Sepulchre's Ward are in agreement too. They've promised to form an orderly queue. You want to live?'

'As Graham would say, how's that going to work?'

'As I said, it's a guarantee that you'll be resuscitated

if you need it. If not, when the coroner hears from your lawyer, I wouldn't like to be the doctor picking up the tab for a lawsuit after refusing to resuscitate you. Ha, ha. I'm going to tattoo everyone's chest with "hashtag Fit For Purpose". It's not too late. Got Special Brew anaesthetic here. How about you roll up your sleeve and I'll give you a free sample? No? Okay. I'll be back later.' And he kissed me.

TWENTY-THREE

I managed to escape Liam's nurturing ministrations, telling him I'll put off the procedure until after band practice. I'd require strong anaesthetic meds to blot out the pain of surgery. And I couldn't play stoned. He seemed to accept this with a slight reservation, asking, as we staggered towards the Soft Day Area, something about what state did I think The Rolling Stones and all the other top bands were in when they played? The rehearsal was a model of the comedian's art. Never have so few produced such a racket in the pursuit of harmony.

During an intermission, I quietly mention to Graham that I think the fountain in the Soft Day Area is emitting a double oxytocin dose, and is why we all feel so positive, trusting and somehow confident enough to expect great things of The Day Trippers. He agrees. I'm glad he seems to have forgiven me for my slight gaff about his sensitivity regarding his personal and professional life. I didn't mean to discourage anyone, and I'm disappointed when he informs the rest of The Day Trippers that the oxytocin is contributing to our delusion that we can have a successful fundraising gig. Liam retorts that fundraisers aren't expected to achieve professional standards.

Liam reports that all the wards, waiting areas and Accident and Emergency are being adjusted by a swarm of engineers who arrived and tinkered with the air-conditioning system, adjusting it to deliver the oxytocin. Now that the corridors are used as waiting and medical areas also, the chemical is being circulated to the whole population throughout the hospital. As you can imagine, this is pleasing everyone; nurses, doctors and patients alike, and now there are very few places where the trust drug is not in the air. It's an interesting equation that if you want to know the truth, then you'll need to find an oxytocin-free area. According to Liam there'll soon be a black market in information about drug-free areas of the hospital. Mark is on board to discover the places where you can safely roam freely to experience paranoia at your heart's desire. You have to admire his capacity to exploit every opportunity available.

I don't know the mark-up on the purchase of oxytocin, but if rumours about an eight thousand per cent hike on other medication is true, one can only hope the cost to the hospital covers the cost of what they are saving in expensive patient care. 'A nice little earner,' Mark says as the hospital has shares in Meds R Us, but I don't know where he obtained this information. He says they plan to export for profit. 'I'm glad to know that the research, and the risks our combat team are taking to bring about this radical solution of vertical integration to plug the shortfall in health funding will not only benefit the drug companies but will fund NHS Trust Terminal Five,' comments Graham.

'Now that we've done a good job helping develop new meds,' he points out, 'it's time to protect ourselves from side effects.' I'm glad he seems to have forgotten our row. He suggests I take a rest while he checks out more about my symptoms online. Back in my room I remember Ade has marked up chords on paper in tablature form and that I must practise the chords daily if I wish to remain in The Day Trippers. He had explained that using the correct fingering is vital for easy transition from one chord to another. I pick up my ukulele and strum a bit, trying out the fingering as instructed. Mark arrives and tells me that Dr Doctor has been looking for me, and that I need to meet him in the caff at 4.10pm this afternoon. 'But that's now,' I say, reluctantly putting my ukulele carefully on the end of the bed.

Mark leads me to my appointment. Dr Doctor is already drinking coffee and a nice-looking Danish pastry sits untouched awaiting his long, soft, white talons on a white plate. He offers to get the same for me, but I decline as I am still feeling a little nauseous after the effort required to get my fingers nearly around the sweet tenor ukulele tuned to G, C, E, and A. I can see the whole band sitting comfortably at the long table, laughing and relaxing. They're better than me. In every way you can think of. Every single one of them.

'I'll take John to my office, and then back to his bed when I've finished our consultation,' Dr Doctor tells Mark as he dismisses him.

'I'd rather have the initial talk here in the café with you and, if we can agree a course of action, we can go to your consultation room later,' I say. He tells me that he understands I like to keep my buddies in sight. I realise that he's trying to shame me into going with him and almost relent. But he cannot force me to leave this public space.

After a slight hesitation he says we'll have our initial chat here, and then move to his consultation rooms. Under patient confidentiality rules this environment is not acceptable. He reminds me also that his time is precious.

'In view of my limited life expectancy, so is mine,' I say, in the mistaken belief that I have all the cards. 'My rules or nothing.'

'Now, young man.' He turns to me, insisting that I drink some water, handing me a glass. 'You're looking a bit wobbly,' he says, 'I hope you're not too uncomfortable.' I reassure him I'm getting used to it, but will welcome a diagnosis as to why I feel so bad, why my skin feels uncomfortable with a burning rash and why I can hardly move about. He tells me he really wants to help me as I have kindly obliged him by enrolling for drug trials that will provide great benefits to many people.

'I see from your temporary patient notes that they'll go offline in a few days,' he says, 'and so now your health is deteriorating, we need to do something urgently.' While he speaks he is taking my blood pressure, checks my pulse and heart, and smiles benignly. 'Good, good,' he says as if I have passed a test. 'Excellent. After hearing the reports from Nurse Sue, they're better than I expected. We'll need to take you upstairs for more tests where I have the correct apparatus.' And when I demur, he says, 'Later then. Just relax now. How are you feeling?' When I look over at the others, I see Liam smirking.

'Shitty,' I say. 'Sorry, pretty rough. Haven't ever felt this bad before. I wasn't ill like this when I was admitted. So I guess the drugs you have been trialling on me have caused my health to deteriorate,' I suggest, the public environment filling me with confidence, 'so unless you can help me recover, I think it might be time for the lawyers.'

'What an extraordinary idea. I am disappointed you even consider this type of action, John. The drug trials are not responsible for the state of your health. If that were the case all the other guinea pigs would be in the same state, but the other participants are all fit as a fiddle.'

'What is wrong with me?' I am not ready to let the idea of litigation go. 'I need some proof that the drugs are not responsible for the state of my health.'

'Blood tests prove that you were given only a placebo. No drugs have entered your system through the hospital channels except when we saved your life soon after admission.' One point to him.

'What about the oxytocin?'

'Goodness! I cannot imagine why you ask that. It makes no difference to anything. None in your bloodstream. I have checked the bloods my assistant, Mark, took this morning and I am sorry to say I think you will not recover any of the health you had before an unknown virus took hold of you. Probably before you came to the hospital. It's surprising that it didn't show up in your health check before you enlisted in the research. Still, whatever it is, it may be the cause of why you fainted into the water from which you were extricated by our wonderful paramedics who saved your life. It seems to me that you can only deteriorate further as the virus is one so far unknown. We are all now familiar with how that can pan out and take millions of lives. So far, none of your team have contacted it, which is a great blessing.'

'If I have a virus, the rest of the team would have it too. And they don't, so that's not the problem.'

'I really am very sorry to say that sometimes life kicks at us unexpectedly, and there's little or nothing we can do to improve things. I can offer you counselling. You know, end-of-life counselling if you like. You just have to say. And you can be sure that in recognition of your valuable contribution to the NHS you will be treated with the highest level of palliative care available. I hear you are part of a rock group formed by the guinea pigs; commendably resourceful use of your time.'

'They're planning a fundraising gig for the hospital. I would like to discharge myself.' I must get out and find Megan, she will know what to do, whether I have a case to sue the fuckers for breach of Duty of Care or anything else. It will be an opportunity to make amends to her, explain why I disappeared. Acknowledge to her that to protect my own feelings, I neutered hers. What a shit I am.

'I'm sorry but we cannot discharge you in your present state of health,' I swear he is smirking, 'we have a duty to make sure you are Fit for Purpose first. In any case, as we know, you have no hospital notes to self-discharge.'

'I have the temporary notes,' I say, 'at least for another forty-eight hours.'

'We couldn't get you fit enough in that time. You have signed up for another set of drug trials and cannot let your *Team Fides* down.'

'I've nearly completed the first set. You could get a new guinea pig to replace me for the next programme. Someone less likely to let you down by having side effects leading to their death on your watch.'

'There's no proof the meds affected your health yet.'

'It's my life. My decision. You can't detain me. I know about the OPTIN policy.' I detect a mini-blink, though otherwise he appears impassive.

'How's that?' He hesitates and looks around the room. 'What do you mean by OPTIN?' he asks quietly.

It's a rumour around the hospital, I tell him. To admit that Liam heard it over the sunflower would blow our source out the window, and it sounds so absurd I think he'll have me sectioned for hearing voices if that suited him. Then I remember the bed controller. No beds in mental health. I'm safe. 'It means no resuscitation without signing in writing to OPTIN at the moment you need it,' I say smugly, 'when that is impossible. You'd be unconscious.' My voice is rising.

'Calm down,' he says, glancing across the room at the others, 'I'm in the business of taking care of people, not wishing them dead. How else,' he asks me softly, 'are we to cope with the overwhelming numbers coming to A and E? We've cancelled all elective processes and surgeries, but without beds to transfer resuscitated or high dependency patients to, what can we do? These near-death patients consume a disproportionate portion of our funds. Meds R Us already sponsor all the medication we use and the export profit on prescription drugs helps to fund our wards. We need the OPTIN policy to begin to function again as a hospital. What you need to realise is that with a rising population, diminishing resources and all the best will in the world, we cannot keep the hospitals running without recourse to terms that make me uncomfortable too. As a Patient Representative you'll know that if we go over budget, then we'll be closed under the rules of the Green Protocol Solution. What decision would you make in these circumstances, John? As a doctor, do you seriously think that I would not wish to save every life possible? Every patient matters.'

'It seems unconscionable that the medics are put in this position,' I agree, 'I often hear protest groups outside the hospital demanding better funding.' I guess Liam will be offering the tattoo service to those guys too.

'Yes, yes. This is not a new problem. I have mixed feelings about them to be frank, though grateful that they feel the need to support us.' He's silent for a moment and I sit staring at Dr Doctor while he shifts around in his chair and finally says, 'I'll leave you to have a think, then come to my consultation rooms. Don't miss this opportunity, John. I will explain about a life-saving and exclusive idea I have that might resolve your problem. On one condition. I'll be taking a risk helping you without official, permanent patient notes, and I'll be using scarce hospital funds in order to save your life. So I trust you will keep our decision confidential. I see your predicament and am responding to that need, exactly as I was trained to do. All I ask is that you use discretion to protect me from my best self, the one who wants to help and cure the sick. Not a big ask, John,' and he takes my hand in his. It is warm, and comforting. Across the room Liam flaps his hand in derision. 'What I hope to do is an expensive procedure, but it's your only route to survival. In return I want your confidence, John. Can I expect you in half an hour in my consultation rooms?' I nod assent. 'I'll send Mark down to fetch you when I'm ready. You'll need to say farewell to your buddies here as you'll be in quarantine for a while before we operate.' And then he's gone before I can ask any further questions.

TWENTY-FOUR

When I join the long table, Graham and Liam are arguing about what sort of music to play – if they *could* play. I try to drink a cup of coffee but have to ask Liam to take me urgently to the john where I throw up. 'Don't worry, I've seen worse. Done worse,' he tells me as if to comfort me. 'When do you want your tattoo?'

'If you look carefully, Liam, you will note that I'm in no fit state for anything,' I wipe my mouth, 'and am in such pain I'd ask for an overdose if I could keep it down,' I say with some venom and then I feel sorry for being so abrupt with him especially when he leans down to my level and gently wipes my mouth with a tissue.

'Sorry, matey, I know it's shit for you,' he says, hugging stinking me, and that just makes it worse and now all I want to do is cry; but I'm stopped by his suggestion that he can produce an overdose if I just give him the word. He has a cool line in Brompton cocktails which, he says, is a good way to go.

'Piss off,' I tell him, 'don't take me so literally.'

'Make up your mind. I love you too,' he retorts. After taking a paper towel from the roller thing he wipes my mouth again, gives me water to drink, clears any smears of vomit from the bowl and standing back to appraise the state of me, and seemingly satisfied, he finally pushes me back into the café. When we return to the table he rattles something in his pocket. 'Got a sweet set of car keys for the Stingray here,' he tells me, 'ready to head off in style when discharged at the end of the drug trial. You can come if you like. I've scored another white coat for you to escape in.'

'Look at me! Seriously? You think I'd last the journey?'

'I don't drive that badly. Okay then. When you recover. No car sickness, though. It's a new motor.'

'*If* I recover,' I laugh, 'what's wrong with your memory? We've already established that I can't leave dressed as a medic without setting off an alarm that would wake Europe,' and then it comes to me. 'Can you let me have the Brompton cocktail?' I ask. 'I'll only use it if I'm in absolute need.' He looks worried. 'You do have it?'

'Sure. I just don't want to lose you, old fellow, is all.'

'I'll only use it in extremis.'

'You'll say goodbye before you go?' he asks.

'Sure. If I need to use it, I will tell you and leave you my ukulele!' He pushes me to his room space, and in a locker beside the bed is a package from which he extracts something in a small glass vial. He gives it a shake, dancing around, flinging it into the air like a flamboyant flairman. 'Cocktail time!' he exclaims, then brings out a syringe and puts it all together in a blue plastic bag and forces the whole lot into my jacket pocket. 'Instructions included in the bag. If you wake up from this, there's more if you still want it,' he grins and raises his eyebrows, 'it would knock a rhinoceros out, so you should be fine. You know how the hypodermic works? Do you know how to inject?' Then I notice the tears in his eyes. Or perhaps he's taken something.

'Sure. Never injected myself before. Not a user. Not interested in drugs, just like a bevvy occasionally. But I've watched the medic, well, the junkie experts like Mark administering injections to other patients as well as me.'

'Make sure you push the air from the syringe before using.' He adds, 'Health and safety!' and I laugh at the absurdity and incongruity of his words.

And now we are sitting at the long café table where the rest of the band have joined us. There's some laughter when I tell them about my discussion about litigation with Dr Doctor, but I suspect they overheard much of it. Liam tells us that at 11am tomorrow he's setting up his tattoo clinic in the Soft Day Area and he outlines again why the tattoo is a life-saver.

Scott looks keen. Perhaps he already has tattoos. Liam continues to try to sell the idea of the tattoo as something both beneficial for themselves but part of a greater organised protest at the gap in the health budget. 'A good publicity stunt. Visual. Standing in solidarity with the mass of vocal protesters outside the hospital.' He promises that he has a new embellishment to the usual tattoo inks, bright Day-Glo colours. When Graham suggests they could be toxic, Liam convinces most of the group that the ink is going to do them good. 'With added vitamins and other essential oils and healthy mineral elements.' Zak, who has been quiet until now, begins a conversation about what to play again, and as usual it ends in an argument. Which is not surprising as we're not in the Soft Day Area where anything and everything seems possible as long as the fountain gently plays. I ask Mark to bring me there for some peace to think. I want to be alone for these last few minutes before decision time. To think about my life. And death. Trusty cocktail in pocket. As Mark pushes me past them I just touch fingers with both Graham and Liam who I will miss most. In retrospect, it occurs to me I've disappeared without explanation like this before. I did it to Megan and all the crowd in The Flounder. This is part of a pattern of behaviour which may need to be addressed, as Graham might say. Is it too late now?

TWENTY-FIVE

I sit in the Soft Day Area checking out what I know. Dr Doctor hasn't divulged the options but some procedure is on the cards. The mystery embargo is not reassuring. It sounds like a fait accompli. He's obviously playing a control game. In truth he already has all the cards and I have none, so it's not exactly an even match. So far. And in any case, I have the final say in my jacket pocket. I've been slow, half believing him when he said I'm suffering from a new virus. He didn't argue when I pointed out that the same argument, for it being a side effect of the drug, was also true of the virus. As in, nobody else was suffering the same way. Either way, where's the proof? I feel so ill that I may have trouble gathering a coherent question to ask him.

The real question is, am I dying? The slow, soft flow of the fountain's water soothes me into a reverie about my state of mind before I entered the river, when I slowly sauntered up the towpath ruminating on the recent loss of Ben. Remembering the many years in our early twenties when Ben and I were pals, bad boys, he risk-taking me, his anchor, his fan club, his wing-man. We were an incongruous pair – his interest was politics and he was loud about it. As a journo, I could never sum up the passion required to engage much in debate about anyone I didn't actually believe in. The decisions politicians make are responsible for the deterioration of all our national institutions, and the inequality gap. Ben ridiculed me for sitting on the fence. What frustration hid behind the release of his venomous torrents of invective directed at opposition politicians? What did he expect? I mean, how can you believe any of them, particularly after the ghastly Iraq war fuck-up? We did enjoy watching sport together, particularly cricket, and a stream of abuse from him was initiated by the Beeb losing control of test matches to Sky. I agreed with him on that score. We'd even gone on holiday a couple of times, but it was a bit of a nightmare as we didn't have a lot in common when thrown together for a fortnight. Except for a sense of the ridiculous. He was insanely funny. And he was kind.

I remember once we returned a couple of days early, ready with funny holiday stories, to find a sea of devastation in my flat. My flat-sharer, Tim, had left for a weekend break, and abandoned a dog alone. Hungry and lonely the dog had left a mess everywhere. The place had been trashed, and there was evidence of industrial levels of Tim's compulsive catalogue ordering. Ben told me to take the catalogues and ring around to cancel any more products in the pipeline, while he fixed all the physical damage and dog mess. When the culprit later turned up at the door, I heard Ben tell him in a quiet, steady voice that he, Tim, had betrayed me, had behaved like a prat or worse, and was to go away and come back in an hour. He'd make sure all Tim's stuff was in black bags on the doorstep for him. Tim didn't argue, though I couldn't legally throw him out. While I'd been on the phone, Ben, without complaint, was kind to the dog and cleaned up the poo. Then he took the bucket and scrubbed all the floors until perfect. Returning as requested an hour later, Tim made off with his dog and his belongings. Never saw him again. Gratitude never left me for Ben's heroic levels of kindness and loyalty.

Not long after Ben married and disappeared from my life, I came across him two years ago, sitting outside the supermarket, on the ground, cap beside him. Told me he'd been divorced and had lost contact with his son. I never met the lad. Ben didn't seem to know whatever secret it is that others have about how to sustain a long-term relationship, which seems such a settling and good thing to do. All my lovers evoke in me a strong sensation of tenderness and gratitude, and in the end love, and finally regret. I'm always searching for a woman with whom I could be intimate, have a companionable relationship, but not fall in love.

I consider again what I should have done for Ben, to help him, to make time for him, and then I ask myself why he'd deteriorated so much so rapidly. His trip down Chemical Avenue would have damaged his health of course, and his drug intake is why Megan had little time for him, I think. Understandable, especially remembering what she saw when she handled the case of the toddler alone while his parents overdosed.

The look in Ben's eyes in the last week frightened me. But you have to stay in there. I know his ex-wife was called Marion, but they'd divorced after a couple of years and Ben said he didn't know what became of her. I thought someone should really try to find her and their son because they also had a right to know he'd gone.

On the day before he died, a commotion started in the bed opposite. Someone was shouting and cursing. A nurse finally arrived and pulled the curtains open but the noisy patient was so abusive, despite reassuring words from her, that she left him and he continued his aggression. After an hour of relentless loud interruptions, a young doctor approached Ben's bed. She's shaking her head and I ask if I can have a word with her outside.

'Ben hasn't got long, has he?' I ask softly; the door to the ward is still ajar. She shakes her head in confirmation. 'Oh dear,' I whisper, 'I'm just glad he won't survive long enough to remember this terrible, nerve-shattering day in here.' I indicate the noisy patient. She nods in an absent-minded way. 'Have you just come on duty?' I continue, denying her a chance to elaborate on his condition.

'No. I've been on these wards for the last twenty hours.'

'You have? How can they do that to you? It makes me doubly grateful that you are taking the time to discuss him with me, through your unconscionably long shift.' I smile at her.

'It's not over yet!' She sighs.

'Really? I'm sorry to add to your problems then. I'll be as quick as I can.'

'Only another four hours to go!'

'How do you do it?'

'Speedily.' She raises an eyebrow. 'Good ticker.' She's tapping herself over her heart. I get it! She's on amphetamines, I conjecture. Good grief! Yes, she'll need a sound heart for consistent use and I can see why she needs it, of course; a twenty-four-hour shift would warrant speed in the newsroom on a major news story break – but the authorities turn somersaults trying to ban athletes taking drugs. So, docs on whizz! Now there's a story, I thought at the time.

'My friend is a very sensitive and quiet man himself, and it seems sad to think his last experience of this life will be the sound of that angry patient shouting unending invective to all and sundry, including the overworked staff. Is there any chance at all that my friend, er, brother, could be moved to another ward? Or maybe a room of his own, please?' And I only just refrain from reaching into my pocket and offending her right there and then.

'We just lost a patient in a side room twenty minutes ago.' I think what a funny way to put it. 'I'll see what I can do.' An hour later Ben was moved into a small, quiet, single room with two chairs and a window.

I keep coming back to that last day. Ben didn't appear to be conscious when I stood beside his hospital bed. Megan arrived with small treats for him but he's too ill to know or care, I tell her. Then she holds his head, gently strokes it, holding a glass of water to his lips. 'Time for a little bevvy,' she says. 'A nice cool G and T tonight, Ben, dear? Can you manage a little sip for me?' And he does seem to swallow some water while she reassures him. 'Well done, darling.' I don't know what's got into her, because I didn't think she cared overly for him, but he seems to relax. She showed me how to rehydrate his mouth with water on little cotton wool covered lollipop sticks, and then she left and I sat staring out at the world outside the window for the rest of the day. I was still holding his hand as he lay on what would be his deathbed with the curtains drawn around it. Sometimes I'd stroke his forehead, and remembering what she said, feed him water on the little lollipop-stick things like she showed me, which Ben sucked as if he was a tiny baby. 'There, there.'

He didn't open his eyes all the rest of the day, so I couldn't really know what he knew or if he suffered, but I think he felt something because he looked sad in his sleep. He moaned a bit whenever he was turned over. Late in the evening when the sun shifted to the horizon a nurse did something to the drip in his arm and said, 'He should be fine now. Let me know if there is any change or if he gets distressed.' And when she left, I asked him if he could hear me.

'Mmmm,' Ben mumbled. 'Yes. Please don't leave me. I'm dying.'

'I really hope that's not true.'

'Don't argue with me. I know what I'm doing.' I thought he made a little chuckling sound.

'Okay, okay. But I hope it's not true. You're enjoying all this! A bit of a cabaret act!'

'You better pay for your ticket then,' he mumbled.

I thought maybe I should ask him what he wanted.

'A last request?' he asks with a slight chuckle, and I think this sounds too melodramatic, too much like a cliché to be true, more as if he is playing a part, that the whole thing is a terrible mistake and isn't really happening; that I'll wake up and find it's all a nightmare. Is Ben playing to the gallery after all? As well as dying? Is this his last act, his last big performance? When he was a teenager and into his early twenties, he'd been a bit of an actor, or more accurately, a bit-part actor, well, amateur stuff really, a very small-time one but that had impressed the girls and been a way of meeting them, so maybe that is the thing, maybe there's not much wrong after all. What would you say if you thought you were going? How on earth are you supposed to do this? Has he suddenly reached the end? Is there no more time left? No. More. What must that feel like? I shiver all over.

'There's no right way to do this,' he said, as if reading my mind, 'please lie down beside me. I'm cold,' he mumbles, his eyes still shut, a drip on one arm. I speculate how I could fit in beside my friend on the narrow hospital bed. On the other hand, I cannot refuse the last request of a dying man, if he really is dying. So I pull up the chair and bend over and gently rest my head awkwardly on the edge of his pillow and hold his hand. The other arm, with the drip attached, moves towards me, and his fingers come up to my face and I feel a slight, tentative, stroking movement on my cheek. Honestly? Yes, he's trying to comfort *me*.

'Thank you,' he says, 'thank you, darling.'

His breathing is becoming shallower while I lie awkwardly beside him, one of his poor, white hands in mine. 'There, there.'

Later, with the dark showing outside the window, the city lights sparkling, and after I think I dozed for a while, I notice he's quiet. I raise my head off the pillow to look at his face. I panic that he has stopped breathing and see that a tear has slid down his cheek and lies frozen there. 'Ben,' I say, 'Ben.' He doesn't react immediately, but suddenly takes a deep breath. His hand feels cold. 'Are you okay?' I ask absurdly. But there's no reply, only a continuous, steady, slow, shallow breathing for a while. I didn't do anything else; just stayed beside him, still holding his hand, mine cramping a bit, so occasionally I'd have to remove it and stretch my fingers, though he doesn't appear to mind, and when I replace my fingers around his I think I feel a gentle pressure. I stroke his hair, matted and fine, for probably an hour or so. I glance at my watch. I don't remember what time I arrived and my mind is feeling a bit confused and I'm finding the silence and inactivity difficult. My leg's gone to sleep. I need to move, but am nervous to leave his side. He suddenly gives a deep breath and says in a clear voice, 'If it's any consolation, I'm quite happy.' It is his last, generous, perfect gift to me. He didn't breathe again.

TWENTY-SIX

I await my fate. I'm pretty sure Dr Doctor is afraid that if I survive outside the hospital I might bear witness to forfeiting my health for Meds R Us research. And looking at the equation dispassionately, I can sort of understand. We are basically on what Liam calls a combat mission, designed to test meds to keep people fit, as money-spinners for pharmacological companies, and most significantly, to top up the hospital budget so that some folk will ultimately benefit, and we too, perhaps. The group of animal rights protesters, who so vigorously championed the campaign to end animal research programmes, may turn their attention to us, and garner forces on our behalf. We are just guinea pigs after all.

In my case, whether I am fit for anything at all is not even debatable any longer. I have in my possession Liam's final solution, the Brompton cocktail. It's comforting to know I have some control over my destiny. But I have things to settle, stuff to put right. I'm not ready to walk the plank into oblivion yet. Any minute now, Dr Doctor will present me with my choices. *Houston, we have a problem.*

I'll be forced to make a decision. As you know, not my strong suit.

Mark arrives to take me to Dr Doctor's consultation room. He makes a joke about how much he will charge to push me in the wheelchair down the hill. He tells me that he and Liam plan to leave together in the fast lane with the Stingray. While we travel the corridors and lifts – such a long journey, a satnav would be useful – towards facing my fate, he says he has some sort of financial pact with the teenage junkie on work experience who fixes his sharps. I realise that he's trying to distract me from the terror that must be showing on my face.

Dr Doctor's office is pristine except for dirty coffee cups lined up neatly on the edge of one side of his desk by the window. When we enter, he's in the process of taking his own blood pressure. He stops doing it and smiles at me, thanks Mark and waves him away, shutting the door after him. 'Good. Glad you've made it up here safely.' He helps me from the wheelchair and into an upright position, supporting me by the arm. Guiding me by my elbow, he insists that I look out of the window. 'Life,' he says, and he stands beside me, surveying his domain from this top floor of Terminal Five. The penthouse suite. From here we can observe small uniformed figures scurrying about attending to the ambulances arriving at the entrance. All the windows are sealed, except I see he's contrived to open a transom window. From a length of metal, which can only be fashioned by himself, as it would not go through the health and safety filter, a bird feeder is hanging. I think he clocks I have seen it, but making no comment he ushers me to an easy chair on the opposite side of his desk so my back is to the door and facing the enchanting sight of little birds feeding. 'Life,' he repeats, nodding towards the window, 'that's my aspiration. To save life. To live life. To help life thrive.'

I begin to speculate about why he is emphasising this. He asks me to please have a glass of water, handing one to me. When I finish drinking he asks, 'Better? Good.' And what I suddenly think is a ghastly thought: that his kindly nurturing gesture of feeding birds here, as high up as treetops, but where no trees exist for cover, could be a trap. Could it be a place where raptors feast on them?

'You're smart enough to recognise that there are very few options open to you, John. But I want you to make as many choices as is possible about your treatment.' And following that fiction about possibilities and choices remaining to me for the end of my life, he regurgitates information about my mysterious medical state, with no known treatment except that he will prescribe something to relieve the symptoms as they arise, including a better unguent to relieve the discomfort of itching skin, and an inhaler for shortness of breath. Oxygen is available if and when I inevitably deteriorate.

'What evidence do you have about whether I'm suffering from a new virus or as the result of the drug test programme?'

'That's the conundrum, John,' he smiles, 'there's no time left to be certain either way; in the end, the result will be the same.' Now I'm on red alert. Sparks of suspicion course through my ragged veins. He doesn't know. Time to hit the road. Best start another pleading session to be discharged. Plan A: maybe find Megan.

'So it's goodbye from me then,' I say. 'I'm grateful to the paramedics who saved my life, and you've brought me a long way from my admission in A and E, through to the Soft Day Area via Meds R Us – an interesting and novel experience – and as you're a consultant clinical manager, I'm guessing at some considerable cost to your precious time.'

'Thank you. Yes, but here's the good news, there's more help to come.' He nods as if agreeing with himself, that odd gesture that some people make to help you to agree with them. 'Every patient counts. We don't want to say goodbye while we can still assist you.'

'I hazard a guess that End of Life is not the favourite specialty for doctors. In addition you have all the decisions on protocol to make in your role of clinical manager. I'm sorry if this sounds insulting, but why the interest in saving me?'

'No offence taken, John. I'm glad you asked, the truth is that I do have what you could call an ulterior motive. Though not for personal gain. And of course, it'll be your only chance of recovery.'

'How can I be of any value to you or anyone else? I mean, seriously? Take a peek at me.'

'That's a good question.' He looks steadily at me for a moment. 'You've been very cooperative, apart from a couple of outbursts that I put down to mania brought about by frustration at your situation. As we have not been able to prevent your illness and deterioration, and taking into account your cooperation with our drug trial research, I feel I owe you an opportunity not open to some other patients.'

'Right. Thanks. The thing is, Doc, I'm not quite believing in all this altruism. Please do not be offended. I'm grateful, of course, for anything you can do to help me. But why are you offering me treatment when so many deserving patients, ones that are actually valuable to society, await your care?'

'You're right to be cautious. All patients should consider all aspects of their treatment and make informed choices. And in this case, if all goes to plan, I believe I have a solution that will grant your wish and result in a healthy you, ready to be discharged.' This doesn't answer my question, but rather than interrupt again, I let it go for now, though the juxtaposition of 'solution' and Dr Doctor does not sit comfortably with me.

'As you know, if you leave in your present condition, you are not currently Fit for Purpose as a functioning person. I have been searching around for a solution to your complicated case. As it happens, a timely answer has arisen. Serendipity, I think you could call it. What I have in mind, John, is something that would benefit both yourself and the hospital funds.' I am definitely not trusting this now. 'If you will agree to one more medical research project, a "first" in the world, I think that then we could find a way out for you. A solution that has the added attraction for yourself in that with it will go a set of new hospital notes. At best it will result in a fit you, ready for the discharge that you so desire.' And he leans forward and begins to move the line of cups around; changing the position of each one but keeping them in a straight line.

'If you could produce new hospital notes now, why not previously?' I cannot understand how he has the effrontery to be continually controlling.

'That's complicated. Don't think we are not grateful for your contribution to the research programme, my friend. It's just that if you are really keen to leave, and you seem to be consistently complaining about the conditions here, then we must find an amicable solution without breaking the law. You do not need me to reiterate that without your known identity, there are no patient notes, and without patient notes we cannot discharge you. As I say, you didn't need me to tell you that.' And he has knocked over one of the empty cups, using a tissue to mop up dregs that spill onto his desk, and in silence he puts the cup back in its place. 'However, the hospital has been designing a yet untried procedure as part of our bid to be the most up-to-date centre of excellence. To complete our plans we need someone whose condition is such that they can only benefit from it, someone who would otherwise perish. And believe me, you will benefit. In many ways.' Hearing this should have raised a red flag, but curiosity and impatience overcame me, as usual.

'Let me know more.'

'It will be what you might call a massive makeover.' He looked directly at me and held my gaze in silence for a moment. 'And it will leave you Fit for Purpose and therefore ready for discharge. I warn you it is not without very serious risk. Although it will bring extraordinary advantages for you, we are not yet certain of what the side effects will be.'

'Risks? Ballpark figure?'

'Not entirely known. We estimate forty-nine per cent mortality with the procedure, one hundred per cent if nothing is done.'

'Okay. I get that,' I say. Running these figures swiftly though my mind, I realise it's a no-brainer. No procedure; death. Procedure; fifty-one per cent survival. 'I'll try anything to break this stalemate,' I say. 'And you base these figures on?'

'One hundred per cent? Experience. Medical knowledge.'

'Forty-nine per cent?'

'Unknown territory. Worst-case scenario. Oxford statisticians.'

'So let's go for it.' My mind taps the pocket containing my Brompton cocktail. Is it really me making this decision? Yep. I can't stay here and may as well take a punt on a trip down Experimental Street. 'What are you suggesting?'

'A whole body transplant.' He looks closely at me for a reaction as he says this, but I hold steady while digging my nails into my palms. OMG, that took some effort.

'Sounds interesting. Tell me more.'

'Well, of course with the new body you'll have a new identity and,' he hesitates for effect, 'drumroll...' Am I imagining this? Does he really say that as he raises his hands out towards me in a ta-da sort of way? '...a new set of patient notes!' He seems pleased with himself, and though cooperating with him sticks in my craw, I don't fancy cutting off my nose to spite my face, so to speak. A cliché so apt it's funny.

A whole body transplant, now that really is an original concept. 'Fine,' I say. 'Shoot the truth.' My heart is beating so fast I'm not sure I'll even survive long enough to rock up to the operating theatre at this rate.

'Ask whatever questions you may have, and I'll answer.'

'What are the main dangers? What about all the technical problems?'

'Oh, the clockwork? Well, that's what we've been working on. Making sure all your nerves, blood vessels and muscles et cetera will be linked up correctly, you might say.'

'A once-in-a-lifetime offer then.'

'More like a lifeline.'

'Okay, but can you confirm what, if anything, of me you intend I keep?'

'It's your body that is not Fit for Purpose. We'll abandon that and you'll keep your head of course… well, er… your brain's the important bit. So you will still remain yourself in here.' Dr Doctor taps his own head. 'You'll keep your own personality, and so you'll keep any memories that you can dig up, er, retrieve, bearing in mind that you've lost your memory.'

'That's less of a relief than you think. My personality could do with a makeover too.'

'Ah, that's a step too far for us,' he laughs, 'something for the future perhaps. Well, of course, you can *perform* in your new role in your new body, and be whoever you want to be. Do a bit of acting,' he says and then laughs again, and I'm thinking this is also a bit suspect, but perhaps if I *look* different, I might behave differently. Perhaps have more confidence to be less indecisive. Rehearsal starting right now!

'Great,' I say, testing out my new persona to see how it feels. This is exciting. 'Terrific. I'll be able to remember everything then?'

'Everything you already know. Sure.' Dr Doctor shifts in his chair. 'But you may remember that, as I have already pointed out, you have a memory problem which will not be altered. Though in time, with a healthy body, your memory just may recover from damage that seems to have occurred when you were submerged. You told us you cannot remember who you are, is that still the case?' I notice he isn't making eye contact now – is he sparing *me* embarrassment? He moves a set of notes from one side of his desk to the other, absent-mindedly, and keeps looking down.

'Yes,' I reply, 'I still have some memory problems.'

'Good. So a *new you*, and a new set of patient notes ready for your discharge after the surgery.' I nod assent. 'You're on then? Good, good, I'll print out the terms and conditions. The usual protocol, but for an unusual operation!' he exclaims cheerfully. Shifting in his chair and picking up his phone, he hesitates and then puts it down again. 'Anything else?' He presses a button and I hear the quiet hiss of a form printing. He removes it and places it on his desk.

'You bet. But is there anything I should know that you are not telling me?'

'Well.' Dr Doctor is looking shifty and leans forward and looks me straight in the eye, but I can tell it's a strain and he's determined to look truthful and not to blink. God, he's a sly one. 'There's a slight catch.' He stops for a moment, seeming to think about it. 'We have to make sure that if things go wrong you'll be young enough to reach the resuscitation, er, reanimation criteria. We need to justify the huge expense of saving you if you become unwell during surgery or after.' He laughs. 'It's a hugely costly procedure so we'll want you to last a while.' He laughs some more, in short huh-huh sounds that I'm finding disconcerting and, quite frankly, a bit cruel.

'How can this benefit you?' I ask.

'Channel Four are lined up to make a film of the whole operation. As it will be a first in the world, we will be able to sell the technique all over the globe and have signed an agreement to this effect. We will retain the copyright on the procedure and so very rich souls who wish to be kept alive in this way will be able to contribute to the health of others through paying a royalty to our hospital. So, win-win for you and for the hospital. This extra money will keep us running and we'll be able to provide more beds and staff, and of course a new reconditioned body for wealthy recipients of future operations. Added to this direct advantage to us will be the fact that it enhances our status as a centre of excellence. A flagship hospital. This last element will ensure that despite the Green Protocol Solution whereby all the smaller hospitals go out of business, we will remain open and operating and attract additional funding. This will also make deep inroads into our existing financial deficit. And you, John, will be a hero, able to write your own story and benefit financially from that too. What do you think?' What could I say? I'm reeling from his revelation and shocked to recognise that if he has all the agreements in place for copyright and filming, he has obviously been planning this for a long time. So when was it exactly that I became the fall guy? I sit speechless for a moment.

'You seem a little worried,' he says, 'what are your concerns?'

'This is a major life-change with no time to discuss it.'

'Yes, of course. In medicine we have to confront this all the time when saving lives. You'll get over it with some therapy.'

'I will?' Again I mentally tap my cocktail pocket. 'Maybe, but it's a big decision, and I'm very uncomfortable with that. I think I need more time to consider all the implications.'

'Well, I can understand your concerns, John. Very understandable. But time is the problem. We need you to be in as good a condition as possible for the surgery and you're deteriorating fast. And the donor body has a finite life too. The tissue match is excellent. No issues there. We couldn't ask for better. So to delay might mean we miss the opportunity and another donor might not arise before you succumb. Would you like to have a chat with our donor nurse about any of your concerns?'

'I'm not sure that's the direction I need to drive down. Tell me more about the donor.'

'Of course, the identity of the donor is protected by our confidentiality clause. Sometimes donor families are happy to meet recipients of loved ones' organs. But this procedure takes time and anonymity of this particular donor is at the donor family's request. Our intention is to provide you with a young body – as I say, young enough to warrant resuscitation if you become ill and that is what is on offer now. And of course, a young body will bring certain benefits to you.'

'And do you have any doubts about how this will pan out? Any concerns about failure, disablement of any sort?'

'Not really, John. We've done so much research and many experiments in preparation. We've a real confidence in our surgeons and all the medical staff involved.'

So, it's come down to the Brompton or this. And the Brompton still exists if this op fails. There's my choice. And get-out clause. 'Okay. Do you have anything else you want to tell me?'

'Only that there might be a slight incongruence between mind and body.' He stops talking and gazes at me, awaiting a reaction.

'I'm not that old,' I say, 'young at heart.' I wish.

'Well that's fine then,' he replies.

'Cool! A young body sounds good to me. I think I can live with that. A reconditioned me! You have me. It'll be a pleasure to sign up, just give me the consent form.' He is looking suspiciously pleased at my reaction, and although I am now sure I detected a whiff of the trust drug when I entered his consulting room, I find myself in a strange situation. I have encountered this feeling before – you know, the one where you should hesitate, your instinct says hold on, but then you rashly go ahead anyway. And then there's a disaster. Self-sabotage. Something like that. Not that I was often that decisive before, but occasionally I succumbed to taking a dodgy punt. Was there anything in the glass of water he gave me when I first sat down? It seems to me he perhaps wasn't expecting me to give up my old body without a fight. Me neither. Something perverse in me thinks it might be fun to take the wind out of his sails too. 'What a unique opportunity.'

'I'm glad you are taking that attitude.'

'What about the pain of the operation?'

'We'll take care of that. Plenty of pain relief lined up in case you need it. You already know how to operate an SAS. Though we anticipate there'll be surprisingly little pain relative to the benefit to you and the scale of the operation.'

'What age is the body you have in mind?' I ask. It all seems a tad surreal now, and I cannot quite believe my luck. Maybe there's some trick in it; a lot of pain to be sure, despite what he says, but thinking quickly through possibilities I begin to see that, with luck, news media will be rushing to press large cheques into my hand if I survive, so that I'll also gain a decent chunk of change for my life story.

'Twenty,' says Dr Doctor.

'Twenty what?'

'Twenty years old.'

'Oh great. So my libido, how's that going to be?'

'We don't know for sure. We think there will be some compromise. After all, you know, sex is to some extent in the mind.'

'Speak for yourself, Doc. I've no problems there,' I say, and watch Dr Doctor crossing and uncrossing his legs, 'I mean, okay, my head is sometimes ahead of my body, so to speak. You know the mind is willing but the flesh isn't always up to it right now.'

'Precisely. Well, an opportunity to put that right. I think you should be fine on that score then,' he coughs and rebuttons both cuffs, 'I mean, given the opportunity, well, I'm guessing you'll have some fun.' He smiles.

'I certainly hope so.'

'I certainly do too. If we get the clockwork right and connect everything up in the correct order, then you should be okay. Be reassured we'll do everything in our power to make you whole and Fit for Purpose. Our goal is yours too. Remember our motto. *Every Patient Counts.*'

'And I'll look good, eh?'

'Yes. We'll give you a face and scalp transplant while

we're at it. It'll make for more congruity between face and body. If we didn't do that, the join on the neck might just be a little difficult to explain.' He chuckles. 'You'll look great when the temporary swellings go down and after the stitches are removed.' Dr Doctor pushes towards me a clipboard with the consent form he'd printed clipped onto it. 'We've listed all the likely risks here, and it only requires that you read through them carefully and when you've thoroughly understood, then you can come right back and sign just there,' he indicates, 'take your time.'

'No problem, Doc, I trust you. Terrific. I'll sign right now.' Is this really me speaking? Have I changed personality already? I lean across his desk to take the form. 'I can't wait to get into some cool gear, check out all the talent, go on the pull, maybe, you know, have a great time with the chicks…' I stop myself, I think this doesn't sound like me. Chicks? What kind of word is that? What is happening to me, already? 'I mean I'll have a normal, fulfilled life.' I correct myself as I sign John Anon on the dotted line on the consent form and return it across the desk to him.

'There's just a small catch.' The doctor takes it, smiles, puts it in a folder, and looks down at his flies. Surely he isn't grinning.

'Yes?' I stop moving and hold my breath.

'I'm not sure you're going to want to chase the girls.'

'Eh? Sure I will. What's the point otherwise? Never had a problem in that direction before.'

'Well, you might now.'

'Listen, Doc, you just said my libido would be in good shape and…'

'You just might not want to... they might not want to... I mean, you know, the body... the best tissue match we have for you is already earmarked and on a ventilator.' He leans towards me and smiles.

'Yes? What? Where's the problem?' I'm beginning to sweat.

TWENTY-SEVEN

I lie for a long time hearing the sounds of life around me but far away, and then Nurse Tucked appears with a lovely smile and a cool glass of water that she carefully feeds to me through a straw; and once more I have that comforting, soft, cosy feeling of being like a little baby, all warm and cuddly. Looking at her now takes me back to the moments before they began to operate. She was pushing the head-end of the gurney, taking me down to the theatre, when I felt her gentle hand massaging my head. It was perfect. I look at her now, and thank her for being so sensitive and recognising my fear before the first cut and calming me down with a head massage. 'No problem,' she says. Smiling and leaning forward she clutches my hand for a moment of girly intimacy.

Tucked says I've been in an induced coma for three weeks. I was all bandaged up while my wounds healed. She tells me that they removed the stitches this morning after giving me a shot of seriously powerful, what Liam calls Thanatos cocktail. I feel quite woozy, though I think the effect is wearing off. Tucked gives me a small piece of buttered toast. Delicious. 'Cup of tea?' and she helps me drink through a cup designed for toddlers. She leaves me to rest and before long, memories of my last thoughts in a man's body return and I think of how confused I was and still am, and may continue to be.

I didn't have long to wait before the operation, but having signed the form and being so incredibly physically weak gave me little choice, I thought. I lay with a drip on my arm thinking about this haunting and terrifying decision. I remember considering that it was all too rapid, that I'd never adjust to looking in the mirror at someone else's face and body. But then the question of survival kept nudging me towards acceptance. I knew I'd die if nothing was done. One hundred per cent. On balance, I didn't want that. My old body was useless and not Fit for Purpose. And then there's the story in it all. Pretty exclusive. How often do these chances drop by? I haven't taken a peek at the new me yet as it all seems too intimidating and scary to see my scars.

A few minutes ago I turned over slightly and thought I was dreaming because there in my bed was a pair of very lovely, long smooth legs, the sort that would look very well in stockings and suspenders – and as I put my hand – tentatively – on one – after all, to lie naked there beside me is to invite such a thing – I felt a gentle stroke on my own leg and was glad of the reciprocation. It was at that point the realisation hit home that they were my legs and would continue to be so. After I explored a little further I discover my fanny and then my breasts and what fun they are! I have a lovely set of pins, nicely turned ankles and smooth, lovely-touchy skin and great boobies. What more could any guy want? I guess I will have to be careful about developing acute narcissistic personality disorder as I really do not want to develop a gross mental health problem. Wait until Liam sees me! Ha, ha, ha.

Awaiting the op, I do remember thinking that being a man has become a very tricky thing to get right. How we are supposed to behave is a conundrum I struggle with and hadn't been able to resolve. Attitudes and life as a man changed too rapidly for me to adjust. But there are advantages about being a man, a slight edge in the food chain and a deference that I'm used to. And we earn more, on average. This is not something I want to let go. If I remember all the delightful experiences in the sack too, I wonder how much I'm going to miss those experiences as a man. There are so many things I need to think about, with so little time left to do so. I need to take control and close down these thoughts about how much I've sacrificed or I'll drive myself mad. Perhaps I should go over the disadvantages too. Men have a shorter lifespan, and there's still the expectation that you'll be decisive – which I'm not, and I'm pissed off about getting caught in all sorts of difficulties about offhand non-pc comments. We're expected to be strong and silent about our feelings, though this seems to be changing. What is the point of men now that the traditional roles of breadwinner and boss of the family are disappearing? Did I really ask that? Women have kids if they want them and are in control of family life and their own finances and can manage without men. And there are increasing numbers of women who decide to set up as a couple and live a contented life. Life is much harder for men now. You only have to check out the suicide statistics among men to realise how lost and futile young men feel. Maybe I could write a piece about that for the *Daily Drag*, though I think it's probably been done to death already.

If I think about it too much, it makes me sad to realise what I have forfeited, but also how frustrated and sad the position of men is becoming. And here's another thought. How on earth am I going to remember that I'm a woman? Will my new body simply adjust my brain into moving the right way? I wish I'd had longer to think about the cost of discarding my male body. Transgender women do it – but then their mindset has already adjusted and it's their heart's desire to be a woman. But for me, it's the price I've paid for life. I'll need counselling to work out who I am. I think that now there are probably more decisive roadmaps for being female. Living life as a woman has to be easier. Surely? Megan, if you are reading this, please stop the derisive laughter. Forgive your old mate and come advise me! And is there anything else you want to do?

I'm thinking about what my next move will be after my release; maybe pitching up at The Flounder and Lemon to see how Megan is getting on, and wondering if anyone will believe my story or even recognise me. My voice has changed, never mind my radical appearance. How can I prove to them that I'm me? Of course, my new makeover has taken me out of the running to return to my old physical relationship with her, I think, and this strikes me as a bit sad. I'm pretty certain she would disapprove of the bargain I have made and the brake it will put on our old activities. There could be other possibilities but my head hasn't recovered enough to think what that might entail.

I could say nothing, but become her friend without any suggestion of who I used to be. Would she recognise me from my eyes still watching her through my new face? Perhaps after a while I could elicit in some gentle way a picture of what she felt about her old boyfriend who had left her without any explanation. That'd be a bit sneaky after all she has done for me over the years. And what would be the point in deceiving her? She'd never trust me again. Where is my integrity heading with that idea? The betrayal of trust I've been trapped in – because I feared rejection (and that they'd leave me first) – is finally over. I hope. No, I will start where I intend to continue. I have an important job to do.

I imagine writing my story and flogging it to a publisher. And film rights? And who knows who could play me? Well okay, both of me. And now it occurs to me that somewhere along the line I might not actually own myself, that is, my new body, and there might be a problem with copyright. I can see how the hospital will benefit because they have intellectual property rights over the procedure that I know was filmed by Channel Four. And they can, of course, franchise the story for different countries and make a mint with pics and film too. But me? Do I own myself? I will need a specialist intellectual property rights lawyer to discover the full implications here. After all, now I think about it, put one way, it could be asserted that I am whoever my body is, with just my brain transplanted. A little bit me, but mostly her. I will have to check this out. And as muscles have memory, I can imagine making some interesting discoveries in the sack. And the possibilities of experience too confusing to comprehend at present. Hormones? What triggers production?

My hospital records are another conundrum to resolve. I don't think there are paper notes any longer, just the electronic pad awaiting my new identity clipped to the end of my bed. In order that a doctor anywhere in the world can access them, hospital notes are available online, in case of emergency. Before they can discharge me I'm asked to designate a new name and elect at first for *Josephine Daphne*, though I have to say I am not entirely liking this. It appeals to my sense of the absurd, something I have in spades as you may have noticed; and having watched *Some Like it Hot,* it brings up happy, falling-over-funny, filmic memories. Just in time, by rejecting this name, I save myself from pure humiliation from Liam. Oh, he would love to try to make out with me and then push me away and say, 'Not tonight, Josephine.' But the choice of name is obvious, really. Only one will do, I guess. I can probably employ Liam's help to go into 'enable editing mode' and change the name in future if I feel like it. Always indecisive. Hold that thought, me. Can't wait to see his face when Liam sees my body upgrade.

So I am now Florence. Dear little Florence can live again. Reach twenty years old. Have back her life that had been cut short by water. And be someone. So I have a responsibility towards my sister, to live her life fully. I will be young enough to train. Seven years I think it currently takes. Seven years and endless further learning, a lifetime of experience and demands. Soon I shall apply for her birth certificate, and though I may have to get working with Photoshop to change her birth date to match my new body, hell, nobody's perfect.

Liam has come in to see me and he can't resist flirting and clicking his tongue against his teeth in approval. I tell him I'll visit him after I leave and will keep in touch. 'No need, darling,' he replies, 'when I've scored that bad-boy Stingray, I promise to come fetch you and take you for the best spin you've ever had.' He minces around the bed, joshing and laughing as usual, and then after raising his eyebrow in a suggestive way, says, 'I don't think I could quite get it up for you.' He looks deep into my eyes. 'You know, knowing who you really are.'

'I thought that was the sole purpose of your visit,' I reply, at which point Nurse Tucked mysteriously appears. She suggests that as I am probably tired after the serious trauma of the operation, he might like to leave, because, she says, he's being inappropriate. That's too subtle for Liam and he continues prancing around and flirting with me and saying he'll take me for a very special ride, until she's had enough. 'You bad lad, off you go.' He's so surprised he doesn't resist when she takes his arm in a vice-like grip. I swear that she tosses him over her shoulder and through the door, telling him, under her breath, to piss off.

Dr Cross comes to see me and we have a lovely girly chat, as you do. There's no point in flirting with her now. My indignation on her behalf, my resolve to expose the shenanigans of hospital management, my fixation on the retreat of trust in the face of the relentless march of bureaucracy, and use of homeless addicts and mental health patients by Meds R Us, were not evidently welcomed by her in the meetings. In any case, soon I'll have an opportunity to reveal all about it. I still think she'd be really good to know if I wasn't once her patient. Who am I kidding? She'd never want to know me. But we may encounter one another in the next chapter. I have ambitious plans for Florence.

Two weeks later, on the morning of my final day at the hospital, Dr Doctor accompanies the cameras and the presenter, unknown to me, but whose appearance was oddly familiar – but you know what my memory is like – and gives a commentary. At Dr Doctor's request I am obliged to show how well the scars have healed in the few visible places, mindful of the nine o'clock watershed. I feel more prurient viewers will be disappointed. We then discussed how fit I am – and I move around and oblige with a couple of press-ups and walk down the corridor for them. As he shakes my hand I swear Dr Doctor winks. 'We've done an excellent job, I think. You should be pleased. Lovely, lovely.' He taps my thigh before I'm quick enough to bat his hand away. That was an odd experience. Is that what it feels like to be an object of desire? I feel uncomfortable, and want to avoid him. This is confusing. How could he think I welcomed his comment and action?

On the day of my discharge the team are all standing in a row awaiting the farewell moment. Cameras are rolling, clapper boards clapping, I make a soppy speech about how grateful I am for everything they have done for me, and how I am looking forward to a new life, and I touch elbows with each of the team. There are ways to turn things around, I think.

Suddenly there's a commotion and laughter as Liam leads the way, and The Day Trippers strike up a good old Bee Gees number, their tattoos of *#Fit For Purpose* dominant across bare chests, their voices loud and high; their instruments struggle to keep up as they dance on and smash a cover of 'Stayin' Alive'. Nobody watching can keep still. Ade surprises me most, confidently singing the lead with a strident falsetto, strutting his stuff.

I love these peeps. How can I leave them? Maybe there are ways to see them more regularly. It may be an unexpected consequence of my decision about what to do next. Yes, I've been decisive about my next move.

When we're done, I kiss them all goodbye, with plans and numbers exchanged and promises of visits and keeping in touch. The music is still worming through my head when Graham comes over and tells me why The Day Trippers chose to play 'Stayin' Alive'. While training to do cardiopulmonary resuscitation or CPR, paramedics use this Bee Gees number to practise the correct rhythm to restart the heart.

I'm nearly done in when Graham releases me from his big bear hug and watching tears break free from my eyes, he tells me not to worry, salt is an antiseptic. Paramedic Janice judges exactly the right moment to pipe up, 'Stay away from rivers,' and clean stops the water cascading down my face.

I'm parked up in a small flat in the city centre with a pretty good view. I've just about done enough writing for today, and in a couple of hours' time I have a date with a legal eagle who deals in intellectual property rights; but before that I am going down to the arcade. Once I've sorted the rights out, I'll be able to string the story around the world.

I've done my nails and hair, applied a little light lippy, I'm wearing a snug little dress and heels from a catalogue, and you bet when I step out I'll be turning heads as I trip sassily along the road on a real, 3-D shopping spree in the coolest mall in the district before getting down to serious business.

I am having to remind myself to be a little restrained as my scars are still healing, and unlimited overexertion could be my undoing. I hum to myself in a voice I'm only just beginning to recognise, and really enjoy wearing a dress and high heels, so I'm looking a bit retro as a woman. But still. I haven't braced myself to ring Megan yet, or to visit old friends, but that excitement is in store for the future. I plan to ask Megs to meet up at The Flounder and Lemon, to continue where we left off. I am excited to see if I can make another decision this time. Not to leave without explanation. Not to treat her feelings with such little regard. I'll tell her everything. I hope she's still around and allows me to continue to be a friend.

I'm writing this in a quiet room, looking forward to finishing this manuscript and fantasising about the next exciting step. Somehow all writing suddenly seems irrelevant. Nothing I write can have anything like the value or be as profound as what I plan to do next. But it's good to have had my say. I guess I'll be far too busy in future to be able to tell you anything.

I have enrolled in med school. Yes, in Florence's name, well, mine now. I'm curious to discover if I can help heal people. It'll be tough. I know that. But it seems to me the most worthwhile way to spend the rest of my life.

About the Author

Angela Burdick, born in Kent, holds a BA in Fine Art. Starting her career at JWT Advertising, she later moved to Dublin to open a restaurant and authored three non-fiction books. As an NUJ member, she wrote for publications including *The Irish Times* and *Oxford Times*. Now based in Oxford, she published her novel *A Place of Safety*, worked for the NHS and in the Mental Health sector, and has exhibited installations on medical intervention across major cities.

Acknowledgments

I'd like to say thank you to a few people who've provided encouragement and help in one way or another. I couldn't have completed *Fit for Purpose* without you.

Karima Abdullah, Sofia Altisent, Dominic Burdick, Ericka Kate Burdick for the author photo, Grey Burdick, Clare Carrdus Richmond, Alison Coles, Denise Cullington, Sally Dunn, Lucy Gibson, Gwenaelle, Andy Knapp, Ruth McGrath, Holly Porter, Linda Proud, Ashling Sans, Carolina Santos and Brenda Stones.

My favourite review is from Sally (mother of a doctor). Thanks for telling me you fell off a chair laughing so much.

After the Day Trippers chose to play Stayin' Alive, Gwenaelle, a medical scientist, told me that The British Heart Foundation have a TV advert showing how to learn the rhythm of Hands-Only CPR to Stayin' Alive. It's well worth checking this out.